The Graveyard by the Sea

Reto Koller

The Graveyard by the Sea

A Novel

© 2025 Reto Koller
Publisher: BoD · Books on Demand GmbH,
Überseering 33, 22297 Hamburg, bod@bod.de
Print: Libri Plureos GmbH, Friedensallee 273,
22763 Hamburg
ISBN: 978-3-7693-7613-5

All characters in this book are fictitious and a product of the author's imagination.

Chapter 1

Halvik, northern Norway, 23. August 1993

A light mist hovered over the fjord near Halvik, a sign that summer was coming to an end and making way for a short, but colourful autumn. Winter was near, and the landscape around Halvik would soon be locked in a deep freeze, only to thaw again towards the end of April.

When Linus Pettersen woke up that morning and the last fragments of his dreams faded before his inner eye, he had no idea that today would mark a turning point in his life.

It was the first day of school after the summer holidays, and if it were up to Linus, this day would qualify as a day of mourning on the calendar. He felt as if he had only just stepped out of the classroom yesterday—free, carefree, and full of energy. But now, the time for sleeping in, playing, and fishing was over.

As he made his way to school, he let out a loud sigh, kicked a stone off the pavement, and gazed longingly out at the sea. In his mind, he saw himself on his father's boat, the fishing rod in his hands. He could feel the gentle rocking, hear the soft slapping of the waves against the hull, and smell the salty air. What could be better in life?

The images blurred, and he turned his attention to the peaks of the Lyngen Alps on the opposite shore, slowly bathed in golden light by the rising sun. A few seagulls circled noisily overhead, and he wished he could be as free as they were.

From afar, the voices of children reached his ears, and he reluctantly kept walking. A short time later, the school building came into view. The excited chatter of his classmates grew louder, and he longed to rewind time to the start of summer. Why couldn't he just skip school and go fishing with his dad instead? School was pointless—he didn't need it, just like he didn't need vegetables.

Keeping a safe distance, he observed his classmates running around and wondered how on earth they could be so cheerful. They were all there: Aksel, who was always catching a cold and was blowing his nose even now. Magnus, the overweight boy who was constantly stuffing food into his mouth. Alma, the overachiever who was miles ahead of everyone else. And…! Wait—who was that?

His gaze landed on a girl he had never seen before. She had wavy brown hair, dimples (as far as he could tell from a distance), and was wearing a white, angelic dress with beige sneakers. Even though it wasn't very warm, she stood there without a jacket, seemingly unbothered by the cold. She smiled shyly and, just like him, observed the scene from afar.

Linus found her beautiful at first sight. He couldn't take his eyes off her, as if she were a bright star in an otherwise dark sky. The loud voices and shouts around him faded. He no longer saw his classmates—everything became blurry, indistinct. Everything except her. She was at the center of it all; only she existed.

She reminded him of the graceful mythical creatures from the stories he loved to read. Maybe an elf or a fairy.

She moved her head, glancing around, then took a step forward, hesitated, and seemed unsure. Then she turned away from the commotion and walked in his direction, stopping about five meters in front of him—but she didn't notice him. Instead, she stared out at the fjord, motionless and lost in thought.

Linus followed her gaze, but there was nothing out at sea that could have caught her attention. She was simply staring into the distance, and in her eyes, he thought he saw a hint of sadness.

He grew a little nervous. He didn't know whether to stay where he was or walk away. His feet felt rooted to the ground.

She shifted slightly in his direction, and now he could see the light colour of her eyes. He lost himself in her gaze, a feeling both pleasant and unsettling. This had never happened to him before.

Suddenly, she turned fully toward him, looking directly into his eyes. Then she smiled—the most enchanting smile he had ever seen.

He wanted to smile back, but before he could, she had already turned away and strolled toward the school building.

"Linus, are you dreaming?"

He flinched. His teacher stood in the doorway, motioning for him to come inside.

Linus caught one last glimpse of the elfin girl as she disappeared into the building, then hurried after her.

By the time he entered the classroom, most of the students had already taken their seats. The girl stood uncertainly in front of an empty desk, glancing around shyly before finally sitting down in the second row — farther away from him than he would have liked. Disappointed, he took his own seat and stole a sideways glance at her.

The teacher entered and welcomed everyone to the first day of school. After his opening remarks, he pointed to the new student and introduced her as Jonna Lundberg. She was twelve years old, had recently moved here with her family, and would now be part of their class.

Linus hung on to every word. He didn't want to miss a single detail about Jonna. But unfortunately, the teacher's introduction was brief.

To Linus's delight, however, he then invited Jonna to introduce herself.

Linus watched intently as she rose from her seat and told the class that she had previously lived in Alta and had moved to Halvik because of her father's job. She thought the place was very beautiful but missed her friends from Alta.

The teacher assured her that she would surely make new friends here soon.

Linus listened to Jonna's angelic voice, which sounded as soft as silk. He could have listened to her for hours.

And then there was her shy but enchanting smile—it moved him more than he could explain.

Suddenly, she looked straight at him. Just like before, out in the schoolyard.

One second, two seconds, three sec...; and then she looked back at the teacher. But it had been three seconds— three long seconds.

A sudden jab against the back of his chair made Linus jump. He turned around and found himself staring into the grinning face of his brother, Arne.

"You like her, don't you?" Arne whispered teasingly.

"Shut up!" Linus hissed back.

"What's the matter, Linus?" the teacher asked, looking at him sternly. "Would you like to ask Jonna a question?"

Linus turned as red as a tomato and felt every pair of eyes in the room on him—including Jonna's.

He glanced at her. Her expression was unreadable.

"No, I don't have a question," he replied meekly.

Linus heard the silly giggling of his brother and his friends, Michel and Ole.

Idiots! Linus thought. He would get back at Arne for this.

After the last lesson, the students packed up their books and left the classroom. As his brother Arne passed by, he bent down briefly and whispered, "Go on, get her." He let out a dumb laugh and joined his friends in the hallway. Linus shook his head, slung his backpack over his shoulder, and just caught sight of Jonna leaving the room. He hurried after her and stepped out into the hallway. There she was. She strolled towards the exit, chatting with Ellinor. Linus followed them at a slight distance. Thankfully, Arne had already disappeared. The two girls stepped outside the school building and stopped. Linus paused near the entrance door and looked through a window onto the street.

The sun was low, and the Lyngen Alps glowed in shades of orange. But the magical light show left him cold. He only had eyes for Jonna. Now she pulled a green woolen hat over her head, causing a strand of her hair to fall into her face.

She's so beautiful, Linus thought. He had never seen anything so enchanting in his short life.

"Move it, loser." Linus was shoved aside roughly. Michel shot him a scornful look before leaving the school building with Arne, heading toward the main street. Linus watched them go.

He hated Michel. And Ole too. Why did they always make his life miserable? To make things worse, Arne hung out with those idiots.

He turned his gaze back to Jonna—and froze. She was gone. Wait… no, she wasn't gone. She was moving toward the outskirts of the village, and she was alone. Hesitantly, he watched her go. She was getting farther and farther away from the school building, soon she would be out of sight.

Technically, he was supposed to go straight home after school. That was the rule in his house. But today, he didn't care. He had to find out where Jonna lived. So he hurried after her.

She reappeared in his view on the main street. He followed her as discreetly as possible, passing Café Kystenshuset, the village store, and the church. At one point, she turned around, and Linus instantly froze. Clumsily, he bent down to tie his shoelaces, keeping his head down to avoid suspicion. That's what they did in movies, anyway.

After a moment, he risked a glance forward—and his heart stopped.

She was gone.

Frantically, he looked around in all directions, but he was alone on the street.

Where had she disappeared to so quickly? Had she gone into a house, and he missed it?

He could have ripped his hair out.

Hesitantly, he walked a few more steps along the pavement and stopped in front of a small barn. A narrow footpath led around the barn down to the water. But there was no one down there.

"Why are you following me?"

Startled, he spun around—and found himself staring into the face of an angel. He couldn't get a single word out.

"Why are you following me?" Jonna asked again.

"I-I… uh… I'm not following you."

"Now you're lying too."

He shook his head.

"Then why are you here?"

Linus' thoughts raced. He wanted to say the right thing, do the right thing—but he had no idea what the right thing was. "I-I'm on my way home," he stammered.

"Which house do you live in?"

Damn, now he had trapped himself.

"Up there, on the hill." His eyes wandered up the slope to a row of houses. Jonna followed his gaze.

"I live up there too. The red one with the two fir trees on the left. Which one is yours?"

Uncertain, he glanced between her and the houses. What was he supposed to say now? Crap. He lived at the other end of the village. She'd find out soon enough. Lying wouldn't help.

"You don't live here, do you?"

"No," he admitted quietly. "I live over there, behind the church."

She nodded and looked in the direction he pointed. "What's your name?"

"Linus."

"I've seen you at school."

He nodded.

"The teacher is nice," she said, smiling—this time without shyness.

"Yeah, I think he's okay."

"Were you born here?"

"No. In Tromsø. You, in Alta?"

She nodded.

"Why did you move here?" he asked, even though she had already explained it in school. But he couldn't think of anything better to say, and he wanted to keep the conversation going at all costs.

"My dad got a job in Tromsø. He earns more here."

"What does he do?"

"He's a doctor. He works at the hospital."

Linus' eyes widened. "A doctor? That's exciting!"

She made a face. "Not really. He works a lot, so he's hardly ever home."

Linus nodded.

"What does your dad do?" Jonna asked.

"He's a fisherman."

Her gaze drifted toward the fjord. Linus frantically searched for a way to prolong the conversation. He didn't want to say goodbye to this girl just yet. But nothing clever came to mind.

He saw how she squinted slightly, as if she were in pain. She took a deep breath and let it out slowly. He could tell she was lost in thought. Was she waiting for him to ask something, or was she thinking about something else?

"Do you like sitting on a pier?" she suddenly asked, rescuing Linus from his struggle.

The question surprised him. No one had ever asked him that before. He had never even thought about it. Sure, he had been on a pier many times—he often went fishing with his dad. But did he like it?

"I don't know," he admitted. "I guess so."

"I love piers," she said, smiling dreamily. "It feels like walking out onto the water and leaving the world behind. I love the peace at the end of the pier and the seagulls rocking on the waves. I love the sounds of the water and the wind. It makes you feel one with the sea."

Linus thought about her words. Everything she said was true. But he had never consciously paid attention to those things before.

"There's a pier down there, right?" She pointed towards the water.

Linus nodded.

"Let's go."

"Now?"

"Yeah, why not?"

Several reasons immediately came to his mind: His mother, waiting at home with dinner, the maths homework in his backpack that needed solving. But the most pressing reason was that he was more nervous than he had ever been in his twelve years of life. His stomach felt like it was turning inside out. His legs were on the verge of giving out, and his heart pounded in his chest as if he had just climbed a mountain.

"Alright, I'll come," he heard himself say.

They left the street and climbed down a small slope, pushing through bushes and tall grass. Behind the boathouse, the pier came into view. Linus followed Jonna onto the wooden planks, watching as she sat down at the edge and let her legs dangle. He sat next to her—but not too close.

The sound of the waves lapping against the pier's posts rose up from below. A gust of wind rippled the water's surface, but Linus and Jonna remained silent. Linus, because he had no idea what to talk to her about, and Jonna, because she was probably absorbed in the sounds of their surroundings. At least, that's what Linus thought. He glanced at her from the side. Her face glowed in the evening light, and he wanted nothing more than to kiss her cheeks. He memorized every detail of her face—the fine hairs on her cheek, the dimples, the upward curve of her eyelashes. Her eyes shimmered like emeralds.

"Do you hear it?" she suddenly asked, making him flinch.

"Hear what?"

"What we were talking about earlier …"

What had they been talking about? Ah, right. Water, wind, seagulls.

"Come on, close your eyes," she said, looking at him expectantly. He smiled briefly, turned his head toward the fjord, and closed his eyes.

"Now focus on nature. It's speaking to you."

Linus did as he was told. He hardly dared to breathe, instead concentrating on the sounds around him.

Somewhere in the distance, a generator rattled. A shovel scraped against asphalt. A seagull screeched as it soared overhead. The sound of the water mixed in with the rustling of the wind as it brushed through the reeds by the shore. But all these sounds became background noise—mere distractions. Because above all, he heard Jonna's steady breathing. It was the most beautiful sound of all. Even with his eyes closed, he could see her face before him, hear her voice. And in that moment, he knew that he would never forget her for as long as he lived.

"Did you hear it now?" Jonna asked after a while.

Linus opened his eyes and looked at her. "Yeah, I did."

She opened her eyes too, smiled, and brushed a strand of hair from her face. But suddenly, as if storm clouds had gathered out of nowhere, her expression darkened so quickly that Linus was startled. She turned away and gazed out at the fjord. Her face suddenly looked tired—somehow sad. Linus worried that he had said or done something wrong. He tried to think of what it could be but found nothing. Jonna seemed lost in thought, thoughts he couldn't begin to guess.

Should he ask her if something was wrong?

He left the thought unspoken. And so, they sat there for a long time without saying a word. Linus feared that she now saw him as the most boring boy in all of northern Norway. He thought of his mother, probably watching the clock, waiting for him. His father, maybe already putting on his shoes to go looking for him. Perhaps they had even called the police by now.

He stole a glance at Jonna, whose gaze was still lost in the distance. Something was definitely wrong. Why did she suddenly seem so sad? Did she miss her old home? Her friends?

"I have to go home," Jonna suddenly said, standing up without warning. "Will you walk with me?"

"S-sure," Linus stammered in surprise, scrambling to his feet.

Jonna smiled at him. The melancholy expression on her face had vanished.

They left the pier, climbed up the embankment, and crossed the street. A paved path led between two houses and ended at the old Larsen house. Jonna stopped.

Did she live in the old Larsen house?

Until recently, Aksel Larsen had lived here. He was said to have died of a heart attack. But Linus wasn't so sure about that. To the children of Halvik, old Larsen had been the devil himself. Whenever he saw kids, he would glare at them and chase them away with hissing sounds. And heaven help anyone who got too close to his house. Especially when the kids dared each other to step onto his property. He would storm out the door, furious, waving a stick, and drive them away. The adults had always warned the children to leave the old man alone. He had had a hard life, they said, and wouldn't be around much longer anyway.

"Thanks for walking with me," Jonna said, flashing the most enchanting smile he had ever seen.

"You're welcome," he said, scrambling for something else to say. But Jonna had already turned away and was heading through the garden gate toward the front door. As she climbed the steps to the porch, she turned back to him, held his gaze for a few seconds, and said, "I think you're cute, Linus."

She disappeared into the old Larsen house, leaving Linus standing at the gate, dumbfounded and weak in the knees.

Chapter 2

On his way home, Linus was so lost in thought that he didn't even notice how slowly he was moving forward. The minutes slipped away like sand in an hourglass, and by the time he finally stood in front of his house, his family's dinner had long since ended. He stepped through the door, stripped off his thick clothes, and went into the kitchen, where his abandoned meal was waiting for him on the table.

His mother, who insisted on punctuality, rushed out of the living room, and the expression on her face did not bode well. "Heavens, Linus, where have you been? Why are you coming home so late? Do you have any idea how worried I've been?"

Linus hesitated before answering.

"Well?" his mother pressed.

"I was by the water."

She looked at him, puzzled. "By the water? What were you doing there?"

"I… uh… I wanted to show Jonna the pier."

"Who is Jonna?"

"A new student."

"Linus is in looove, Linus is in looove," sang Arne from the living room, only to be immediately reprimanded by their father.

"I'm not in love!" Linus shouted back into the living room.

"Of course you are," his brother retorted.

"No, you ass!"

"LINUS!" His mother stepped up to him and dragged him out of the kitchen. "Go to your room. No dinner for you tonight."

Linus wanted to protest, but the look on his mother's face said it all. No amount of begging or pleading would change her mind. Fortunately, he still had a tin of biscuits hidden in a safe place. He would have to make do with those.

He yanked himself free, stormed up the stairs, slammed the door behind him, and flopped onto his bed in a sulk.

Let them leave me alone, he thought, throwing a stuffed animal across the room. What did they even know about love? Least of all Arne, that mean jerk. One day, he would get back at him for all his teasing. He was already looking forward to it.

After a while, he closed his eyes and let his thoughts drift back to the pier. He listened to the waves, the gulls, smelled Jonna's floral scent, and saw her sad expression — a look he had never seen on anyone before. Now he wished he had asked her how she was feeling. But it was too late for that. She was in her house, and he was here on his bed. Was she thinking about him too? He hoped so.

When he opened his eyes again, he was under his blanket. His trousers were neatly folded on the chair beside his bed, and he could hear the sound of the coffee machine through the door. His father was saying goodbye to his mother and wishing her a nice day.

Confused, he looked at the clock. It was six-thirty. Had he really slept through the entire night?

He rubbed his eyes and pushed the blanket aside. Fragments of a dream still lingered in his mind—a pier, old Larsen chasing kids off the planks into the water—and he seemed to remember that Jonna had been in the dream too. But no matter how hard he tried, he couldn't recall what role she had played.

He got out of bed and stared out the window. The sun had already risen, and the early morning light poured over the fjord and the sea. The seagulls were cawing as if there were no tomorrow. Two boats chugged southward, and the neighbour was hammering away in his workshop.

Linus watched his father get on his bicycle and ride off toward the harbour. Yawning, he turned away from the window and headed for the bathroom.

An hour later, after devouring twice his usual breakfast portion and being reminded by his mother that he should be home on time today, he stepped outside and set off for school. He thought about the day ahead, about the homework he hadn't done—but today, he didn't care at all, even if it meant extra assignments. He couldn't wait to see

Jonna again. And to mark the occasion, he had even put on his father's aftershave.

When he arrived at school a few minutes later, he couldn't see Jonna anywhere. She wasn't in front of the building, nor inside. He took his seat and waited, but Jonna still hadn't appeared when the teacher entered and began the lesson. Desperately, he glanced at the clock above the door, hoping the teacher had started five minutes early, but the hands of the clock didn't lie. Jonna's chair remained empty. She didn't show up for the second or third period either, nor in the afternoon.

Linus struggled to focus on the teacher's words. More than once, the teacher had to snap him out of a daydream, and eventually, he asked if Linus was feeling alright. Arne answered for him, loudly announcing to the class that Linus must be missing Jonna because he was in love with her. This led to some laughter and a scolding from the teacher.

Linus wanted nothing more than to storm out of the room but thought better of it. He shot a glare at Arne, who was grinning smugly at him.

What an idiot, Linus thought, making a face at him.

The last lesson dragged on unbearably. Linus felt as if the minute hand was moving backward. When the school bell finally rang through the hallway, he packed his books at lightning speed and dashed out the door, startling two classmates in the process. Outside, he turned left onto the main road and headed toward Jonna's house.

He wasn't sure what he planned to do there. Should he ring the doorbell and ask for her? Peek through a window and hope to see her inside? Or would it be more strategic to observe her house from a distance, waiting for her to step outside?

With every step closer to her house, he became more nervous. Two cars passed him, and he turned away so they wouldn't see his face. When Jonna's house came into view, he stopped and looked up and down the street.

No one in sight.

Hesitantly, he turned onto the cobbled path and approached Jonna's house with his head lowered. At the garden gate, he hesitated and glanced back the way he had come. A wave of regret washed over him, and he wished he had just gone straight home.

"Linus?"

He flinched.

Leaning against a garden shelter, not far from the gate, stood Jonna.

"What are you doing here?" she asked.

"I-I... I... You weren't at school."

She lowered her gaze. "I know. I wasn't feeling well. But I'm better now."

She had moved closer—only a meter away now—and he could see that she had been crying.

"You shouldn't be here. You probably have to go home," she said.

She was right, Linus thought. But now that he had seen her red-rimmed eyes, going home was out of the question.

"Are you really okay?" he asked, putting on a concerned expression.

She nodded unconvincingly.

Linus searched for words, but came up with nothing better than, "You didn't miss much. At school, I mean."

She gave him a tired smile and murmured something that sounded like, "That's good."

Linus was about to suggest they go for a walk when she suddenly grabbed his sleeve and pulled him toward a small shelter between her house and the neighbor's property. There, she sat down on a bench and motioned to him to sit beside her.

He gladly accepted.

For a while, they sat in silence, watching the shimmering water of the fjord and the rugged mountains in the distance. Linus knew every peak by name—his father had taught him them when he was little. He especially remembered the nights when he had been allowed to go out on the boat. The water had been smooth like a mirror, the snowy mountains like painted landscapes. Sometimes, the northern lights had added their glow, making everything seem like a scene from a fairy tale.

Their father always reminded them how privileged they were to witness such beauty. Most people in the world would never see nature like this. There were hundreds of thousands who had never even seen the stars because the lights of their cities drowned out all the magic in the sky.

And that, their father always said, was no way to live.

Linus enjoyed listening to his father. He always conveyed his knowledge as if it were a fictional story. He infused every one of his tales with suspense, no matter how dry the subject was. Linus often imagined how he would do the same for his own children one day.

After nearly five minutes of silence, Linus cast a furtive glance at Jonna's house and wondered if her family had gone out, leaving her behind alone.

"Is no one home with you?" he asked.

"Father and Mother are at work in the city," she replied with a shrug. "Uncle Steinar usually looks after me." She hadn't turned to face him but continued staring into the distance.

"And where is your uncle now?"

"Already gone."

Linus wasn't sure whether he should respond to that or keep quiet. After all, it was none of his business. But her expression—so similar to his grandmother's when he left her after visiting the nursing home—troubled him more than anything else.

"Do you like it here?" Jonna suddenly asked.

Did he like it here? What a strange question. He had never thought about it before. "I don't know, I guess so. I don't know anything else," he finally answered.

She nodded absentmindedly, but didn't comment further. So, Linus asked her the same question.

She shrugged indifferently. "It's alright. I always spent my summer holidays here. With Uncle Steinar and Aunt Neja."

"Strange that we never ran into each other before," Linus remarked.

"We weren't in the village much. My uncle usually took me fishing up at Nakkevatnet. Or we went with my aunt to her cabin in the mountains."

"My father is a fisherman too. My brother and I often go out with him. Want to come along sometime?"

A smile formed on her lips, and she nodded. Then they fell silent again for a while.

Linus thought about the scolding he had received from his parents the night before. He glanced at the watch on his wrist. Just past half-past five.

It was high time he went home. He had no desire to be grounded.

"I have to go home," he said reluctantly.

Jonna turned her head and looked at him, aghast. "Can't you stay a little longer?"

Linus looked into her chestnut-brown eyes, and at that moment, he would have promised her the world. What was he supposed to do now? He could have spent the entire evening—no, the entire night—with Jonna. But of course, that was just wishful thinking and not a viable option.

"I… I would love to, but my mum—"

He didn't get any further. She placed her hand in his and squeezed it tightly. "Please. Stay a little longer."

Linus stared at their hands, then at Jonna's hand. He felt her cold fingers entwined with his own. His mind spun. His heart pounded in his chest. No girl had ever held his hand like this before, let alone looked at him this way. The world around him disappeared. He no longer felt his body—only his left hand and Jonna's right hand. At that moment, that was all he needed.

He looked up into Jonna's pleading eyes and nodded.

Later, lying in bed and reflecting on his encounter with Jonna, Linus wouldn't have been able to say how long they had sat there in silence. He only remembered Jonna's cold but incredibly soft hand, the rhythm of her breathing— sometimes faster, sometimes slower—and her gaze fixed on the distance, only occasionally interrupted by a blink.

The entire time, he had been searching for something to say, but every time he thought of a topic, he immediately dismissed it and instead stared out at the fjord. Perhaps Jonna hadn't wanted to talk at all. She seemed content with his silent presence, asking for nothing more than to hold his hand and gaze across the fjord together.

He was glad she wasn't a chatterbox. That would have been unbearable for him. Sometimes silence was enough. Sometimes, you understood each other without words.

At some point—which felt like a thousand years later— she had turned to him, thanked him for sitting with her and holding her hand. Then she stood up, saying she needed to go inside now.

And out of nowhere, she pressed a kiss to his cheek.

Even now, five hours and a grounding sentence later, he could still feel her lips on his skin. But it wasn't just her kiss that he couldn't forget—it was also her empty stare and the long, silent minutes.

He would have given anything to know what she had been thinking at that moment.

Two days later, after a dull evening in front of the TV, Linus crawled into bed at ten o'clock and, to his surprise, fell asleep just minutes later.

Sometime during the night, he woke up to a sound.

He sat up and listened to the silence.

Had he been dreaming?

A loud plop against the window made him jump.

Puzzled, he threw back the blanket and stepped to the window. When he looked down, he saw a dark figure standing in the yard, looking up at him and waving.

It was Jonna.

Linus made sure his bedroom door was shut, then opened the window. "Jonna, what are you doing here?"

"I wanted to visit you. Can you come out?"

"Now?"

"Of course."

"I-I don't know. I'm grounded."

"Your parents are asleep."

Linus glanced toward his door again. If he got caught, he'd probably spend the rest of the year confined to his room.

But Jonna was here… in front of his house.

He had to go out, no matter what.

"Wait, I'm coming down."

He closed the window, put on warm clothes, and tiptoed out of the house.

Jonna was waiting for him with a smile on the porch.

"How did you know which window was mine?" Linus asked as he stood before her.

"I didn't. First, I threw a pebble at that window over there and hid. But no one opened it, so I tried the next one. Got lucky. Your parents didn't hear anything?"

"I don't think so. My dad snores."

"Want to go down to the water?"

Linus hesitated for a moment. "I have a better idea. Come with me."

He led the way, and Jonna followed. He took her behind the house, through the neighbour's garden, and up a steep slope.

They stopped in front of an old, half-ruined house.

"That looks creepy," Jonna said, eyeing the building skeptically.

"Don't worry. I've been playing here for years. It's safe."

He took her hand and guided her inside.

They entered a large rectangular room, with an equally large window on the north side offering an unobstructed view of the village and the fjord.

Linus lit a few candles scattered across the floor with a match. Then he went to the fireplace and started a fire with old newspapers and some logs.

"Come on, let's sit over here," he said, leading her to two wooden chairs by a window.

They sat down, and silence settled over the room.

For a while, they gazed wordlessly at the sleeping village below. Behind them, the fire crackled.

"I'm sorry you got grounded because of me," Jonna said in a sad voice.

Linus shrugged. "Oh, forget it. It's not your fault."

"I still feel responsible."

"Don't worry about it. It's no big deal."

Jonna smiled and looked back out the window.

Linus watched her from the side. He wanted to kiss her so badly.

But he had never kissed a girl before. Did he even know how? He had seen it in movies countless times, always wondering what it felt like.

Now, here he was, with the perfect chance to find out.

But mustering the courage... that was another thing entirely.

When they returned, Jonna stood in front of his house, her eyes meeting his.

His pulse pounded so hard he feared she could see it in his throat.

Then she leaned forward and kissed him.

Linus didn't know what was happening.

How long had it lasted? A second? Maybe three? Or ten minutes?

She turned and slipped away.

"Jonna, wait!" Linus called after her.

She stopped and smiled at him.

"I... I wanted to ask you something," he stammered.

"Yes?"

"I feel like something is bothering you."

She frowned briefly, then smoothed her expression and placed a hand on his arm.

"Everything's fine, Linus. Don't worry. I'm okay."

Then she smiled, kissed him again, and disappeared into the twilight of the late summer night.

Chapter 3

Christmas and New Year had passed. Several weeks had gone by since the kiss in front of Linus' house, and he was happier than ever. He and Jonna had become a couple, which was entirely new territory for Linus. He had never had a girlfriend before, and he was convinced that there was nothing more wonderful in the world. He wanted to spend every free minute with her, and he was glad that Jonna felt the same way. Their hideaway in the old house on the mountain had become their favorite retreat. They spent many evenings and nights there, sharing their wishes and dreams with each other.

However, during this time, Linus increasingly noticed how much Jonna suffered from the lack of parental care. Her father worked almost day and night, and although her mother didn't financially need to work five days a week, she wouldn't give it up. As a result, Jonna spent a great deal of time at Linus' house.

One evening, Linus overheard a conversation between his father and mother. They were talking about how sorry they felt for Jonna and how they had come to see her almost like their own daughter. They debated whether they should talk to Jonna's parents about it but ultimately decided against it, as they felt it wasn't their place to interfere in her family matters.

In the months that followed, not much changed in the situation—until the day Jonna's father suffered a stroke and passed away. It happened completely unexpectedly, right at home in the driveway. He had stepped out of his car, collapsed, and never regained consciousness. A rescue helicopter was called in, but the doctor could do nothing for Jonna's father.

When Linus heard the news, he dropped everything and rushed to Jonna's house. Her mother stood in the doorway, looking like a broken woman, weeping bitter tears. Linus found Jonna sitting a bit further away, on a bench near the arbour. They hugged for what felt like an eternity, until Jonna finally asked if he would take a walk with her.

Linus knew that a difficult time lay ahead for Jonna, and he tried to encourage her. She didn't speak much, mostly listening to his words, and after a while, she simply said that she now felt even lonelier.

That statement hit Linus right in the heart, even though he knew she hadn't meant it that way. She wasn't referring to him but rather to the already difficult dynamics within her family.

However, her worries didn't turn out to be true, as became clear a few weeks later when her mother quit her job and was suddenly at home almost all the time. For

Jonna, this was an entirely new situation, and Linus hoped that it would bring positive changes within her family.

But soon he realized that Jonna was struggling with the sudden changes. She didn't exactly ignore her mother, but she also didn't give her a real chance to repair their strained relationship.

When Linus brought it up, she only said, "I can't just pretend everything is fine now, as if we've always had this great mother-daughter relationship. Too much has happened, my feelings have been hurt too many times. Besides, you are my family now."

And Linus knew she truly meant it.

Throughout the time they spent together, Linus always had the feeling that something dark was weighing on Jonna. He saw it in her eyes, which often seemed distant and sad. Even during their very first meeting—which now felt like a lifetime ago—he had sensed that she was carrying a heavy burden.

He had asked her about it a few times, but she always assured him that everything was fine and that he didn't need to worry. She was simply a bit melancholic sometimes, but it had nothing to do with him; it was just part of her nature.

At first, he had believed her, but as time went on—and as he grew older and more mature—he realized that there was more to it than met the eye.

That didn't change in the years that followed. The only difference was that their lives had become busier, and school had grown more demanding.

After finishing secondary school, Linus secured an apprenticeship as a carpenter at Gunnar's workshop in Halvik. Jonna went to college and later university to study medicine. From that point on, they didn't see each other as often as they had before.

Jonna spent most of her time attending lectures, burying herself in books at the library, and when she wasn't studying, she was too exhausted to do much.

Often, they would simply lie together, talking about the past, the future, their lives, their families.

They talked about getting married, about having children; they imagined sitting at home by the fireplace — Jonna knitting, Linus reading the newspaper, and their children playing on the floor with Lego bricks.

That thought always made them laugh. But this was how they envisioned their future—or rather, how they wished their future would be.

When Linus completed his apprenticeship, Gunnar offered him a permanent position. Linus loved working as a carpenter, and in a country where almost all the houses were made of wood, carpenters were always in demand.

Jonna was immensely proud of Linus and happy that he had found his calling. She, on the other hand, still had two more years of study ahead of her before she could even start looking for a job.

Since Linus was already earning good money, they rented a small apartment just outside Halvik, with a view of the fjord.

Some time after moving in, Linus noticed a slight change in Jonna's demeanor. She was happier, lighter than she had been in previous years.

The separation from her old home seemed to do her good. The distant, empty look in her eyes had almost completely disappeared.

When Jonna finally received her doctorate at the end of her studies, she and Linus both felt the urge to get away for a while, to have some time just for themselves.

Linus quickly converted an old delivery van into a cozy camper, and on a grey Sunday morning in July 2003, they left Halvik behind and drove south.

They had no plans to leave Scandinavia. They wanted to stay in the northern regions, where the temperatures were more pleasant and where there were fewer people.

They sought solitude, and they could only find it here in the north.

For the first time, they were truly on their own, away from home, and they relished every moment.

They camped by rivers and lakes, on small hills in the otherwise flat landscapes of Lapland. They fished and hiked as much as they could.

At the beginning of their journey, the midnight sun still shone overhead. By late August, the first northern lights had already begun to appear in the sky.

It was on one of those colourful nights that Linus knelt before Jonna and asked for her hand in marriage.

Chapter 4

In early summer 2004, Jonna and Linus got married in the church of Halvik. Almost the entire community was invited, and the two were showered with gifts. The greatest gift came from Linus' grandfather, who let them rent his house, as the time had come for him to move into a retirement home. A few months after they moved into their new home, Linus' brother Arne took up residence in the basement apartment of the house.

On a stormy evening in July 2004, Jonna told Linus that she was pregnant. Linus could hardly believe his luck and was overjoyed. The very next day, he began planning the nursery, crafting a crib in his workshop, building a dresser, and carving countless wooden toy animals. Linus' father was bursting with pride and even bought a fishing rod for his future grandchild.

Three months passed when, one evening, Jonna suddenly began suffering from excruciating abdominal pain. Linus immediately called the village doctor, Olsen, who arrived just a few minutes later. By then, Jonna had already lost a significant amount of blood. Linus could see what that meant from the doctor's expression.

The days and weeks following the miscarriage were, as expected, incredibly difficult. Jonna withdrew into herself, while Linus threw himself into his work. Despite everything, they often talked to each other during this time, sharing their feelings and thoughts, helping one another process what had happened.

It was precisely during this time that Jonna opened her heart and entrusted Linus with her darkest secret—a secret she had carried for far too long, a secret that had cast her soul into darkness.

For Linus, her story was the worst thing he had ever heard in his life. Now he knew that his instincts had never deceived him. Now, everything was out in the open. And he swore to himself that someone would pay for his wife's suffering.

The thought consumed him, day and night. It gave him no peace. He became sullen, withdrawn, and sad. Jonna soon regretted ever confiding in him. But it was too late. She had made her decision, and now she had to live with it.

Sometimes, however, when life is overshadowed by dark clouds, a ray of light appears, breaking through the darkness.

Because Jonna was pregnant again.

What the couple didn't know at the time, though, was that their baby would never get to meet its father.

Chapter 5

Tromsø, February 2018

Harald Strøm stepped out of the building of his editorial office, took a deep breath, and closed his eyes for a brief moment. He felt a slight sting in his lungs as he inhaled the icy Arctic air. The north wind carried freezing temperatures from the High Arctic, turning the area into a deep freezer.

Harald observed the bustling activity in the pedestrian zone and was amused by the heavily bundled-up tourists. The Nordic winter had attracted many visitors to the city, and accordingly, there was a steady flow of people strolling past the shops and restaurants.

Harald decided to treat himself to a tobacco pipe. He reached into his jacket pocket, pulled out his pipe and tobacco pouch, routinely packed the tobacco into the pipe, and lit it. A sweet scent spread through the air, and he felt the tension gradually leaving him.

He thought about the morning, which had dragged on endlessly. He had spent hours trying to make the editor-in-chief interested in his story about money laundering in a local industrial company. Unfortunately, the editor had no interest in the sensational story, which was, on the one hand, incomprehensible to Harald and, on the other hand, very frustrating.

He had thrown all the evidence he had gathered over three months right onto his boss's desk, only for his boss to dismiss it as nonsense.

What an arrogant fool, thought Harald. He had no idea. He thought he knew everything just because he had once worked for a big newspaper in Oslo. His previous boss would have jumped at such a story.

What puzzled him the most, however, was that his boss did not even remotely consider the almost irrefutable evidence to be explosive. It almost seemed as if he lacked the courage to publish such an incendiary report in the local newspaper. That the report would cause massive waves was undisputed.

But that was exactly what made this job so thrilling. And his boss should understand that too.

In his 51 years of life, with nearly 30 of them spent in journalism, Harald had never encountered such a stubborn superior. It was not the first time he had considered turning his back on the job and spending the last ten or so years of his career doing something entirely different.

But every time he asked himself what that should be, he got stuck.

Annoyed, he kicked away a chunk of ice, nearly hitting a passerby. The man flipped him off. Harald raised his hand in apology, pulled up the collar of his jacket, and fished his phone out of his pocket.

For a moment, he stared at the display without selecting anything. After a minute, he opened his text messages and wrote to his wife, Runi, telling her that he was heading to Halvik and would therefore be home a little later.

Then he put the phone away again and looked at the display window of a lamp shop. Despite the light-giving merchandise, the store looked gloomy inside. No one was there, and Harald saw his own reflection in the window.

Grey stubble had sprouted on his face, reminding him that he had planned to shave that morning, but had skipped it out of laziness.

Did he have dark circles under his eyes?

He stepped closer and confirmed his suspicion. He needed more sleep.

In recent days, he had been thinking too much, which had cost him several hours of precious rest.

Sighing, he tapped the remaining tobacco out of his pipe, went into the underground garage, and retrieved his car.

Five minutes later, he was driving over Tromsø Bridge, leaving the city behind and heading toward Halvik. From the bridge, he could see the city cemetery on the left-hand side. He briefly considered stopping by but decided against it.

Instead, he thought about the whistleblower for his money- laundering story.

He wanted to speak to him again in person to investigate a few things. He had already learnt a lot from him, but another visit could not hurt.

Who knew, maybe he still had something up his sleeve that he had not revealed yet.

On his way out of the city, he received a message on his phone from his father.

That was just what he needed.

He threw the phone into the center console without reading the message. He already knew what it said: nothing but accusations and complaints because he had put him in a retirement home, as he could no longer take care of himself. And the stubborn old man simply refused to accept that.

Yet the home was practically a five-star hotel.

Harald sighed and hoped that his father would soon get used to his new circumstances. Otherwise, the next weeks, months, or even years would be quite exhausting. As an only child, Harald was unfortunately the sole recipient of these outbursts, and slowly but surely, he had had enough.

Life with his father had always been difficult since childhood.

He could not remember a single time his father had praised or encouraged him.

No matter what he did, he never received a kind word from him, let alone love.

He was an emotionally cold man who showed no interest in others—not even his own family.

He recalled a moment when he had been sitting by the fjord with his father, fishing. They had not spoken for nearly half an hour, which was not unusual, but then, suddenly, his father had said:

"Son, the world is a hard place. You will find that out soon enough. Right now, you are still too young to understand. But one thing I have learned in my old age: no one has any significance in this world. Not me, not your mother, and not you. You will never be of any importance. Life doesn't give a damn about you."

What was he supposed to do with such a statement as a child?

Nothing.

At the time, Harald had not been able to grasp his father's words. But since he had heard them repeatedly over the years, he had never forgotten them.

And they had shaped him.

For a long time, he had struggled with a barely existent sense of self-worth, which had especially hindered his academic performance. Fortunately, he had managed to turn things around in high school and brought home better grades.

But by then, his father had already stopped caring. Alcohol had taken over.

After fifty minutes of driving, Harald parked his car in front of a house near Halvik. Dark clouds had gathered, signaling an impending snowfall. As he approached the front of the house, he noticed that there were neither footprints nor tire tracks visible.

No one had entered or exited this place in a while.

With little hope, he rang the doorbell, waited, rang a second time, but no one answered.

Damn.

He glanced through the living room window but saw no one inside.

"Can I help you?"

Harald flinched and turned around.

A man in his seventies, with grey, shoulder-length hair and glasses, stood just a few meters behind him.

"Jeez, you really startled me."

"Sorry about that. Are you looking for the Haugens?"

"Yes."

"They're on vacation. Won't be back for another three weeks."

"That's unfortunate. Oh well, nothing to be done. Thanks for the info."

"I have their number. Want me to pass on a message?"

"No, that's alright. I have it myself."

"As you wish." The man waved and shuffled off.

Harald got back into his car and started the engine. As he did, he noticed the old man hiding behind a plant in his living room, watching him.

Smirking, Harald backed out of the driveway and was about to head toward Tromsø when he remembered the Kystenshuset Café in Halvik.

He would kill for a coffee.

So he turned right and drove toward Halvik. On the way, it began to snow, and the landscape disappeared behind a curtain of white. The road to Halvik led between two towering mountain slopes, gently descending toward the sea. Now and then, a house appeared, but there was no sign of life anywhere.

On a clear day, it must be wonderful to live out here, Harald thought. But now, when visibility was barely fifty meters and the snow cut him off from the rest of the world, it was the last place he would want to be.

He drove around a long bend, and then the village appeared before him. It lay at the foot of a towering mountain, stretching about a kilometer southward. It looked quite idyllic, with many small and larger houses, a church (which, as always, had claimed the best spot), a harbour, and a large warehouse right beside it.

After a few hundred meters, he spotted the neon sign of the café, which also doubled as a small guesthouse.

Harald pulled into the carpark and turned off the engine. As he stepped out, he took in the house's appearance. It had two stories, white wooden paneling, and blood-red window frames. On the right side of the house, a small, square tower with a gabled roof extended one floor higher. On three sides, there were floor-to-ceiling windows, and inside, Harald could make out a sofa, a side table, and a telescope pointed toward the sea.

When he entered the café, he found only a few guests inside. He sat by the window and ordered a coffee and a piece of streusel cake from the waitress—an older woman with short hair and a voice that could have belonged to a man.

He had not been to Halvik often, but he liked the place. It was quiet, remote, and offered a magnificent view of the Lyngen Alps. No road extended beyond the village. From here, one could only continue the journey on foot or by boat.

The waitress brought the cake, and Harald hungrily took a bite.

With each mouthful, his anger over the work situation and the endless negotiations with his father faded a little more.

And after he had washed down the last piece of cake with a sip of coffee, he felt that he had been angry long enough.

Something had to change.

With the story about money laundering, he could have landed a front-page headline.

But he could forget about that now.

So what options did he have?

The answer was relatively simple: The rival newspaper had already offered him a job twice, which he had always declined.

Why, he didn't really know.

Probably out of habit or out of fear of change, of something new. Hard to say.

Maybe a bit of everything.

But now he had reached a point where he needed to leave his comfort zone and set sail for new horizons.

His wife had been telling him this for years. He shouldn't make himself dependent on this newspaper.

There were others who would appreciate his stories more than his current employer.

And she had been right—he was well aware of that.

Only, he had never dared to take that one last step.

It was always that final step that was the hardest.

But without it, he would never bring about change.

Maybe he should just take the step, if only for his wife's sake.

She had been right about so many things—that was something he had always admired about her.

She had been right in most cases, always made the right decisions, whether it affected just her or both of them.

Often, they had even placed bets for fun, and he could hardly remember a time when he had won.

Smiling, he took one last sip of coffee, paid the bill, and left the café.

When he stepped outside, he did not immediately return to his car. Instead, he wandered down to the water and walked along the shore, heading south.

The snow clouds had cleared, and the sun barely managed to rise above the high mountain behind the village, making the fjord's water glisten.

A single boat chugged toward the harbour, not far from the shore, accompanied by a flock of screeching seagulls.

The gentle lapping of the waves was audible, and if one listened closely, the distant ringing of a buoy could be heard.

After a while, Harald reached a church with an adjacent cemetery. Most of the gravestones were covered in snow.

He left the path, climbed a small embankment, and reached the first headstones.

A few had been freed from the snowdrifts, making their inscriptions legible.

From a distance, he noticed three gravestones that were larger than the others.

Additionally, all three stood close together, and right next to them, a man-high boulder rose, with some engraved letters faintly visible on its surface.

Curious, he stepped closer to the rock and brushed off the remaining snow, revealing the entire inscription.

The brothers Arne and Linus Pettersen went out into the fjord on February 3, 2005, together with their friend, Steinar Lundberg, to bring their nets to safety before the approaching storm. Unfortunately, the storm was stronger and carried away three of our beloved villagers forever. May they rest in peace, whether in storm or gentle breeze.

Harald read the inscription a second time. Then his gaze wandered to the gravestones of the fishermen who had perished.

Linus Pettersen	Arne Pettersen	Steinar Lundberg
15.06.1981	08.02.1979	13.04.1952
03.02.2005	03.02.2005	03.02.2005

What a tragedy, thought Harald. What kind of storm must that have been?

The story of the three fishermen didn't ring a bell, which surprised him because the newspapers had certainly reported on the event. Or maybe he had simply forgotten about it. After all, the incident had happened thirteen years ago.

A car pulled into the church carpark and came to a stop. An older man got out. With a bouquet of flowers in his hands, he trudged somewhat awkwardly through the deep snow toward the cemetery. He stopped in front of a gravestone, brushed off the snow, and touched the engraved name with his fingertips. Then he placed the bouquet on the grave.

For a moment, the man stood motionless by the grave, his head bowed, his eyes closed.

Harald turned away and left the man to his grief. Once more, he read the inscription on the monument and wondered what could have gone wrong for these three fishermen that day. Shipwrecks happened now and then in the area, but for three people to lose their lives at once was highly unusual.

He had spent enough time out at sea with his father to understand the dangers. His father had always pointed out the risks to him and taught him how to handle them. At least that was one thing he had learned from him.

His father had always added, "This here is the real school of life, my boy. Not those books you're always reading."

Harald's love for books was something his father had never understood.

Reading was a waste of time and money, he had always said, and Harald should focus on the important things in life—like fishing.

Harald could still hear those words in his ears as if he had just heard them yesterday.

His mother had usually defended him when she overheard these remarks, but his father didn't care.

Back then, Harald had sworn to himself that he would encourage his own children to read, take them to the library, and read stories to them—all the things he had wished his own father had done.

His father hadn't even given him money for books.

He remembered a rainy afternoon in late April. He had just turned fourteen when the librarian approached him and asked if he wouldn't prefer to borrow the books instead.

With an embarrassed look, he admitted that he didn't have the money to do so.

She looked at him sympathetically for a moment and then told him to come back the next afternoon—she had something for him.

The following day, Harald arrived at the library full of anticipation, and when Liz—the librarian—saw him, she disappeared into her office and returned shortly with a cardboard box.

She placed it in front of him on the floor and said, "These are all books my children collected over the years. They're grown now and have no use for them anymore. I want you to have them. I have three more boxes at home.

When you finish these, let me know, and I'll bring you more."

From then on, Harald read all the books in his room at home—without his father ever noticing.

"Good afternoon!"

Harald flinched. The old man who had stepped out of the car earlier was looking in his direction and had raised his hand in greeting.

"Hello!" Harald called back.

The man began walking toward him with a slightly hunched posture.

When he finally stopped in front of him, Harald saw just how old the man really must be.

His face was a map of wrinkles, his lips dry, his eyebrows bushy, his eyes weary and marked by a long life.

He wore a grey cap that had seen better days, a black coat with the collar turned up, and a woolen scarf that was probably even older than the cap.

"Do you have a family member buried here?" the man asked in a hoarse voice.

"No, I'm just passing through the village and wanted to stretch my legs a bit. I happened to come across this cemetery."

The man nodded. "A beautiful location, isn't it?"

"You could say that."

"I come here every week—fourteen years now. My wife is buried here. I always bring her a bouquet. I did that for all 52 years of our marriage."

"52 years?"

The man nodded. "Yes, 52."

"My respect."

The man laughed. "Thank you. But it wasn't always easy. We had our ups and downs, just like everyone else."

Harald nodded in agreement and thought of Runi.

"My name is Rasmus."

"Harald Strøm." He extended his hand.

"Did you know the three fishermen here?" Rasmus asked, pointing to their gravestones.

"No. This tragedy is something I'm only learning about today," Harald replied.

"I remember well the night that terrible storm raged. It even took down a tree in my yard."

"Did you know the fishermen?"

"Of course. In a small village like ours, everyone knows each other."

"This must have been a terrible blow to the community," Harald speculated.

"It certainly was. The Pettersen brothers were well-liked by everyone. Steinar, a bit of an oddball and a real character, was particularly well-known."

Harald shook his head in sorrow. "A tragic accident."

Rasmus' gaze briefly swept over the graves. "If it really was an accident..."

Harald looked at him in surprise. "What do you mean by that?"

Rasmus shrugged. "Well... you know how it is in small villages—stories spread quickly when something terrible happens. I probably shouldn't have said anything."

"You think it wasn't an accident?"

"It doesn't matter what I think. I just know that back then, there were rumors going around that something about the whole situation wasn't right."

"And what made people believe it was something other than an accident?"

"Well, like I said, it was all just rumours. No one had any proof to back up their claims. But it was common knowledge that Steinar was jealous of the Pettersen family because they were making a lot of money with their fishing business, while he was barely scraping by and, on top of that, had to rely on working for the Pettersens to make a living. It was also known that he frequently argued with the brothers. What those arguments were about, I don't know. I only know that all three of them were highly experienced fishermen and should have been able to handle such a severe storm."

"So, you mean to say that maybe someone had a hand in it?"

Rasmus shrugged again. "It's possible. But we'll probably never find out. And that doesn't really matter. It wouldn't bring them back to life."

He smiled, revealing his yellowed teeth.

"What did the police say about it?"

"I don't know. I never spoke to an officer. You'd have to ask one of the family members who were involved."

Harald nodded.

"Forget what I just told you," Rasmus said, patting Harald on the shoulder. "It was—and still is—a sad thing, no matter what. Let the dead rest in peace."

With these words, he turned and shuffled away.

Harald watched him go.

Rasmus passed by his wife's grave once more, ran his hand over the gravestone, and then made his way to his car.

A moment later, he turned onto the main road and disappeared from Harald's view.

What a story, Harald thought.

He turned back toward the resting places of the fishermen and let Rasmus' words sink in.

Back then, this could have been a fantastic investigative story for him as a journalist.

Who knows what he might have uncovered?

He wondered whether—and what—his newspaper had reported about the incident at the time.

For the last time, he read the inscription on the monument. Then he left the cemetery the same way he had come.

Chapter 6

Halvik, 2005

Karl Godal gripped the rudder tightly, trying to keep his small fishing boat on course. He had known that a storm was coming—the meteorological service had warned about it. But the meteorologists had been off by two hours in their timing.

He took a swig from his flask and enjoyed the warm sensation spreading through his body from the inside. He had actually planned to stop drinking, but the bottle had just looked too tempting. The problem was, it was always empty far too quickly.

Today was no exception, and that annoyed him.

I need a bigger flask, he thought.

According to the GPS, the harbour was still about two nautical miles away. He wanted to be back in port as quickly as possible. He was worried about his boat. It was all he had left.

A loud bang startled him. Confused, he looked around the cabin.

What the hell was that?

Boom!

Again.

He stood up and walked to the cabin door.

Boom!

There—now he saw it. A rope was hanging loosely from the roof of the wheelhouse, slamming against the windshield. He switched on the autopilot, stepped out into the storm, and tried to grab the flailing rope. Not an easy task in this wind.

After several failed attempts, he finally managed to catch it and tie it back down securely.

As he was about to return to the cabin, he heard a scream.

A long, drawn-out, blood-curdling scream.

Startled, he looked out into the raging sea but could barely see ten meters ahead.

Could another boat be nearby?

"HELLOOO!" he shouted as loudly as he could.

No response.

He shouted again, with the same result.

"Damn it!" He slammed the door shut and circled the wheelhouse, holding onto whatever he could grasp, trying to pierce through the storm with his tired eyes.

It was useless. He could barely see the bow of his own boat.

Cursing, he went back inside and reached for the radio.

"This is the Røron. Can anyone hear me?"

Static.

"This is the Røron. Is anyone in the Halvik Bay?"

Again, only static.

Now he wished he hadn't emptied the flask. His head started spinning, and he took a deep breath to steady himself. Then he sent out another radio call, but again, no response.

Maybe someone was drifting in the water.

What should he do now? Head to shore and pretend he hadn't heard anything?

What if someone really was in distress?

He glanced at his GPS.

A little more than one nautical mile to the harbour.

His boat didn't have AIS, a position-tracking system, or else he might have seen another boat on the screen — provided that boat had one too.

He rummaged for his phone and called Øyvind Johansen. He was something like the harbor master, although the title was a bit of an exaggeration for the handful of boats docked in Halvik. But Øyvind usually knew who was out at sea.

After what felt like an eternity, a drowsy voice finally answered.

"Yeah?"

"It's Karl. Are you already in bed?"

Silence.

"Øyvind, are you there?"

"Yeah, I'm here. It's... damn it, Karl, it's one in the morning!"

"I'm out in the fjord," Karl continued, ignoring Øyvind's complaint. "I think I just heard a scream."

A long sigh came from the other end.

"A scream?"

"Yeah. I was just outside the cabin when I heard it. A high-pitched, piercing scream. Could have been a woman."

Karl noticed that his tired tongue was struggling to keep up as he spoke.

"Karl, there's a storm raging out there. What the hell are you doing in the fjord?"

"I miscalculated, I'm on my way back."

"Have you been drinking?"

"Oh, shut up, you idiot. I think someone out here is in trouble."

There was silence for a moment.

"Head to the harbour, Karl. You're the only one out there. No one else is crazy enough to go out in this weather."

Karl grew angry.

"I'm out here, aren't I? The weather service said the storm would come later. It's possible someone else got caught in it too."

"Fine. If you hear anything again, call me. In the meantime, I'm going back to sleep. I have to be up at five."

"But—"

The line went dead.

Karl angrily stuffed his phone away and stared out into the storm through the wet window.

What a damn stubborn fool!

From his seat, he opened the cabin door, shouted one last time into the storm, waited a few seconds, but received no response.

Then he shut the door, checked his GPS device, and chugged back toward the home port.

Chapter 7

Tromsø, February 2018

When Harald returned to the editorial office the next day, the first thing he did was search the newspaper's digital archive for any reports on the tragic accident involving the fishermen. It didn't take long before he came across a story by his colleague, Terje, who had published an initial report on February 5, 2005.

As announced by the local police in a press release, an unmanned fishing boat was discovered ashore in Halvik the day before yesterday morning. According to official statements, the boat belongs to a local fisherman, whose name cannot be disclosed for privacy reasons. However, the boat's owner was not the one at sea—rather, it was the fisherman's sons, as the police further stated. As of now, there is no trace of the two men. Additionally, the police have confirmed that a third person has also been reported missing. Whether this person was on board the boat at the time is still under investigation.

A violent storm had raged through the area the night before. Authorities assume that the crew encountered distress at sea and was swept overboard. A large-scale search operation is currently underway. However, hopes of finding the three fishermen alive are dwindling by the hour.

Anyone with relevant information about the incident is urged to contact the Tromsø police at the following number: 077 80 61 00.

Harald read through the text a second time.

It seemed that, at the time, his colleague hadn't had access to much information. However, another article had been published on February 7, 2005.

Two days ago, we reported on the search for three missing fishermen in the Ullsfjord and Sørfjord. According to an update from the police today, the search is still ongoing.

Authorities have now confirmed that the third missing person was also on board the boat. However, the investigation of the vessel has provided no insight into what may have happened on board.

At this time, police do not suspect foul play. However, the investigation remains open, and authorities will provide further updates as soon as additional details can be released.

Harald couldn't recall the story. Why hadn't he heard about it back then?

After further searching, he found another article that had been published the following day.

The search for the three missing fishermen from Halvik took a dramatic turn today. Yesterday evening, around 7 PM, a passerby discovered a bloated corpse on a beach near Halvik. The formal identification of the body has not yet been completed. However, the newspaper has received unconfirmed reports suggesting that it may be one of the fishermen who had been aboard the ill-fated boat. The other two remain missing. The chances of finding them decrease with each passing day.

The currents in this region can be extremely strong, raising the possibility that the two missing men may have been carried out to the open sea. The search operation—led by the coast guard, police, and fire department—is still ongoing.

Another report followed on February 15, 2005.

Last night, a fisherman spotted a body floating in the water south of Halvik. The police were immediately dispatched and recovered the body. As the authorities announced this morning, the deceased person was one of the fishermen who had disappeared during the night of February 3rd to 4th. The search for the third missing person continues.

On February 20th, the final report on this tragic event was published.

As the police announced last night, the search for the last missing fisherman has been officially called off. The police have also released the names of the three deceased fishermen: Arne and Linus Pettersen (brothers) and Steinar Lundberg. The bodies found after the accident belonged to the two brothers. The body of Steinar Lundberg was never recovered.

Authorities assume that he either sank or was carried out to the open sea.

The memorial service for the three fishermen will take place on February 26th at Ullsfjord Church in Halvik.

Harald leaned back and sank into thought.

In his mind, he saw the boat being tossed around by the storm. He saw the three fishermen struggling with all their might to avoid being swept overboard.

He could hear the wind, the men's screams, the crashing waves pouring over the deck.

He himself had once been caught in a storm with his father.

However, at that time, they had only been about one nautical mile from the safety of the harbour and had managed to return unharmed.

Still, it had been a defining experience for him.

He had been terrified, but the only thing his father had shouted to him in the storm was:

"Pull yourself together! We are men—we don't get scared!"

What had gone wrong with the three fishermen from Halvik?

And what was behind the rumours Rasmus mentioned?

Could they really be trusted?

Harald stared out of the window and watched a boat making its way out into the sound.

Next to the wheelhouse, a man in a yellow raincoat stood, wearing a life jacket over it.

Had the Pettersen brothers and Steinar Lundberg also worn life jackets?

The newspaper reports hadn't mentioned life jackets.

But that didn't necessarily mean they hadn't worn them.

Arne's and Linus's bodies had been recovered, which could indicate that they had been wearing life jackets.

Harald saved the newspaper articles to his desktop, went to the break room to get a coffee, and sat down at a table near a window.

Magnus, a colleague, entered the room and helped himself to a coffee as well.

After taking a first sip, he asked Harald about his progress on the money laundering case.

Harald had no desire to talk about it and simply replied that he was still waiting for a response before he could write the article.

Magnus nodded, sat down at a table, and began flipping through the day's newspaper.

As a journalist, Harald had seen a lot over the years — families murdering each other over money, corrupt officials, drug addicts stabbing their own friends for a fix — the whole spectrum.

At first glance, the story of three lost fishermen didn't seem particularly sensational, and he feared that his boss would see it the same way.

Still, his journalistic instincts told him that there was more to this story than met the eye.

Maybe Rasmus was right about his suspicions.

Although, it wasn't really a suspicion—more of a gut feeling.

But it was precisely this kind of feeling that had rarely failed him in the past.

He had felt the same way about the money laundering case—and in the end, he had been right.

So why not here as well?

The question now was: how should he proceed?

First, he would have to convince his stubborn boss to greenlight the story—something that wouldn't be easy.

Before that, however, he needed to gather more information to make sure his gut feeling wasn't misleading him.

With the limited knowledge he currently had about the case, his boss wouldn't approve the article anyway.

The first step would be to speak with the police—specifically, the investigator who had worked the case at the time.

Then, he would head to Halvik to find out who in the village might know more about what had happened.

The best sources would likely be the victims' family members—assuming they were willing to revisit the dark past.

Around noon, Harald left the editorial office and picked up a small pizza from the Italian restaurant.

With the cardboard box in hand, he strolled a few meters further and sat down on a bench by the harbor.

It was bitterly cold, and the pizza would lose its warmth in no time—but he didn't care.

He didn't want to sit indoors.

He needed fresh air and the sound of the water.

The sun shone through a few clouds, gently caressing the surface of the sound's water. It was almost windless, and the sea looked as if one could walk across it. A fishing boat entered the harbour, accompanied by a flock of screeching seagulls. Further in the distance, a tourist boat was preparing to set off to Skjervøy to observe orcas. However, since most orcas had already moved on by February, he doubted that the seasick tourists would see anything other than the inside of their sick- bags. Far out at sea, it was usually not as calm as it was here in the sound.

He pulled out his phone and scrolled through the messages from his wife. For a moment, he read through her old messages, considered what he should write to her, and then decided on: *No need to wait for me, having a pizza at the harbour. Love you!* Before sending the message, he glanced across the water, over to the Arctic Cathedral and the city cemetery, watched a boat manoeuvering under the bridge, and then sent the text. Afterward, he put his phone away again and thought about the fishermen from Halvik who had perished. He wondered whether their relatives still lived in the area or had perhaps moved far away. If he couldn't track them down, he might as well forget about his story. Without inside knowledge from the victims' families, he was unlikely to get any useful leads.

Twenty minutes later, he was back in his office, sifting through all his notes on the money-laundering case for almost two hours, hoping to find something he had not yet considered in his previous report. In the end, he had to admit that, first, he wasn't fully focused, and second, he had found nothing that he hadn't already used.

Frustrated, he tossed the notes onto his desk and ran his hands over his face. There was no point in continuing here. At least not in the next few days. As long as his key witness was on vacation, he wouldn't make any progress anyway. So, he might as well focus on the fishermen's story. He needed to get in touch with the police. Fortunately, he had an old school friend, Jørgen Mikal, at the department, who had helped him with previous investigations.

Harald grabbed his phone and called Jørgen. "When I hear your voice, it must be about a new story," the policeman answered.

"Can't deny that," Harald replied.

"Well then, let's hear it."

Harald briefly explained how he had come across the graves of the three fishermen in Halvik and what Rasmus had told him about the story.

"Hmm… That story sounds familiar," Jørgen said. "But I wasn't involved in the investigation back then."

"And who led the investigation?"

"Good question. I don't know off the top of my head. But I can find out for you if you want."

"That would be great."

"Do you really think there's something to it?"

"It's my job to find out. It wouldn't be the first time I uncovered something, would it?"

"True enough. Alright, I'll check our records and get back to you."

"When can I expect your call?"

"In three weeks."

"What?"

Jørgen laughed. "Just kidding. Give me a few hours. You'll have my answer by tomorrow at the latest."

Harald thanked him and hung up. That was a start, he thought. Whether the investigator would actually be willing to talk to him was another matter.

He shut down his computer, retrieved his car from the underground garage, and headed home. He planned to continue working there; it was more comfortable.

Blazing light illuminated the Tromsø Sound Bridge. The sun was low on the horizon, as was normal in February. He drove past the Arctic Cathedral toward Gammelgården. There was little traffic, so ten minutes later, he was already stepping out of his car in front of his house. As he approached the house, he paused for a moment, looking at the facade and thinking that a new coat of paint wouldn't hurt. He had bought the building eleven years ago and had never renovated it since. Now it was definitely time. Maybe he would choose a different color—dark green instead of red. Or maybe a dark gray? The house would have a completely different look, as if moving into a new home. A new chapter, another phase of life. But did he want that? There was something comforting about the familiar. You knew everything, were accustomed to it, felt at home. And yet, something new would fit into his life. Even if it was "just" a new boss—or even a new job.

A few minutes later, he was sitting at his computer and opened the browser. He was curious to see if anything could be found about the incident in Halvik. However, he didn't have high hopes.

The first thing he came across were the newspaper articles he already knew. So, he typed the name Linus Pettersen into the search engine. There were several results, but the first three could immediately be ruled out. One was a dermatologist from Trondheim, the second a painter from Kirkenes, and the third a bank robber who had been caught in a suburb of Oslo four months ago.

The fourth entry couldn't be opened, and when he clicked on the fifth result, a small report appeared on the website of a local clothing boutique. The report had been written in 2004, so quite a while ago. It was about the renovation of the boutique, which had been carried out by a carpenter named Linus Pettersen. Below the report was a photo showing a young man posing inside the clothing store with a saw and a hammer. The walls were clad in dark green wooden paneling in an American style. There were wooden shelves everywhere in white and light brown colors, and the floor was covered in golden-brown parquet.

Harald examined the man in the photo more closely. He had slightly longer hair peeking out from under a green cap. He wore a three-day beard, had a well-built upper body, and strong hands. He smiled contentedly at the camera, seemingly proud of the work he had done.

Was this Linus Pettersen from Halvik?

Harald searched for his brother Arne. There was only one entry—the one from the well-known newspaper report.

Next, he searched for Steinar Lundberg. Again, the first mention was in his newspaper's article. But beyond that, there was nothing. The internet wasn't going to provide him with any further information.

Sighing, he glanced at his phone. No message from Jørgen.

What should he do now?

He could drive to Halvik to speak with Rasmus again. Rasmus certainly knew more than he had shared in front of the church. The problem was that Harald didn't even know his last name, let alone where he lived. He might be able to find his name on the gravestone—assuming he could even locate it among all the others. His best bet might be to ask around at Café Kystenshuset to find out more about him.

Harald checked the time. It was 4:45 PM. The drive would take an hour, and if the restaurant was closed, he would have to turn back empty-handed. Two hours of driving for nothing. He searched online for the restaurant's opening hours but found no listing.

Damn it!

He looked at his phone again, but still, no message from Jørgen had arrived. Grumbling, he stood up, walked to the window, and gazed outside. The sun had disappeared behind the mountains, casting the land in blue light. The snow on the mountain slopes had taken on the colour of pale ink, and the first stars were beginning to glow in the sky.

His thoughts drifted to Halvik, and he imagined what it must be like to live there—so remote, surrounded by towering mountains, fjords, and lakes. As beautiful as it was, he also imagined it to be incredibly lonely. Living like that wasn't for everyone. The village community could be a blessing or a curse. Normally, the residents of such small communities stuck together. But the opposite could also be true. A tragic event, like the boat accident, could put a small village and its residents to the test. The community suffers, familiarity fades, skepticism and distrust take hold, and the rumour mill begins to churn. Perhaps it had been no different thirteen years ago.

As a journalist, he could now expect two possible scenarios: either the villagers would welcome him openly and be willing to talk to him, or—what seemed more likely to him—they would be reserved and tell him to go to hell.

Either way, he was curious to see what the coming days or weeks would bring.

Chapter 8

The next day, at half past three in the afternoon, Harald finally received the long-awaited call from Jørgen. He informed him that Tobias Grønvoll had been the investigator at the time. However, he had been retired for three years. Harald got Jørgen to give him the address and phone number, thanked him, and hung up.

For a moment, he stared at the address, wondering whether he should show up unannounced at the retired policeman's house or call him first. He decided to go directly. From experience, he knew that people were less likely to refuse someone in person than over the phone.

A few minutes later, he was crossing Sandnessund Bridge towards Kvaløya. Snowfall had begun, along with the wind. On the bridge, the snowflakes blew horizontally over his car, and he had to grip the steering wheel tightly. The weather station at the start of the bridge showed a wind speed of eighteen meters per second. At twenty-five meters per second, the bridge would be closed. If that happened, he wouldn't be able to return easily unless he took a three- to four-hour detour.

He looked south, where the snowfall had not yet started, and the last daylight stroked the mountain peaks. The sea was rough, waves crashed against the shore, and the seabirds had retreated onto driftwood, turning their backs to the icy wind.

After crossing the bridge, he turned right and followed the road until the voice from his navigation system instructed him to take the next turn to the right. He followed the directions and steered his car into the driveway of a generously built house that bordered directly on the sound, offering a view of Tromsøya. A red pickup truck was parked in front of a garage, its frame still decorated with Christmas lights that were still switched on.

Harald stopped his Volvo behind the pickup and looked toward the house. A few lights were on behind the windows, but otherwise, everything seemed quiet. As he got out, a man emerged from behind the garage, dressed in a yellow-lit thermal suit. He held a shovel in his hands.

Harald got out and approached the man. He was unusually tall—easily two meters—broad as an American refrigerator, and he had a full beard. His nose was as red as a clown's. Either he was suffering from the cold, or he had a cold.

A little uncertainly, Harald approached the imposing figure.

"Tobias Grønvoll?" he asked, extending his hand.

"That's me," the man replied, his voice nasal.

"I'm Harald Strøm—from *iNord*."

Tobias shook his hand and looked at him questioningly.

"I got your address from Jørgen Mikal," Harald said. "He's an old school friend of mine and my contact at the police whenever I have questions about ongoing investigations."

Tobias nodded and placed his hands on his hips.

"I had a conversation with Jørgen yesterday about an incident that took place thirteen years ago in Halvik."

Tobias's expression changed almost imperceptibly. Still, Harald was convinced that Tobias knew exactly what he was talking about. The retired officer furrowed his brow and studied Harald for a moment.

"You mean the boat accident?" he asked.

"That's right. I'd like to learn more about the incident."

More wrinkles formed on Tobias's forehead. "And why?"

"Let's put it this way: I want to take a closer look at the circumstances of the accident. I recently heard that there was some speculation in the village at the time that questioned how the accident actually happened. I want to find out why these rumours started. And that's where you come in. Maybe you could provide me with some information that could help my research."

Tobias looked at him thoughtfully for a while. "That's information I can't just hand over to the press or anyone else."

"I'm well aware of that. But I had hoped you could share your personal opinion on the matter. What was unusual about the case? Which witnesses did you deal with? Were there any inconsistencies, any unanswered questions?"

Again, Tobias studied him for a long moment before answering. "Coffee?"

A short while later, Harald was sitting in a comfortable armchair with a view of the sound. Tobias was busy in the kitchen, and Harald took the opportunity to look around the living room. There was an unusual amount of furniture, making the space feel completely cluttered. A huge sofa stood in the far corner. The television was the size of a movie screen. There was a dining table with eight chairs, and next to it stood a wooden cabinet that looked like it had been around since his great-grandfather's time.

On a sideboard, there was a photo of Tobias with his family—a woman and two girls. Next to it were more pictures of the children in their younger years.

He heard Tobias sneeze, followed by a curse, and Harald hoped that Tobias hadn't just sneezed into his coffee.

A minute later, he reappeared in the living room. He held two steaming cups in his hands, placed both on the side table, and sat down on a chair opposite Harald. "Sorry, I had to sneeze and spilled half the cup in the process. This wretched cold has been dragging on for two weeks now. It's driving me half-mad."

"I know that feeling."

Tobias blew his nose loudly, took a sip of coffee, and leaned back in his chair.

Harald set his cup back on the table and crossed his legs. "Here's the thing: I was in Halvik recently because of a story I've been working on for a while. It's about money laundering in a major local company."

Tobias raised his eyebrows. "Money laundering?"

Harald nodded.

"Which company?"

"Paulsen Builders AS."

Tobias stared at him in disbelief. "What? Are you crazy? The biggest construction company in town?"

"I've found some very incriminating evidence that can be easily proven with witness testimonies."

Tobias looked at him silently for a while. "But...?"

"But—the witnesses are afraid of the consequences."

Tobias pursed his lips. "You're walking on thin ice, my friend. That Paulsen practically owns half the city. You'd be making a very powerful enemy."

Harald shrugged. "If I could prove it, he'd end up behind bars anyway. But that's not why I'm here. While researching the money laundering story, I accidentally discovered the graves of the three dead fishermen. You probably know their names."

Tobias nodded.

"Until that day, I had never heard or read anything about this accident. Which is odd, on the one hand, because I was already working for the newspaper back then. But on the other hand, it makes sense, since I was living and working in Harstad at the time of the incident. I searched our archives for newspaper reports from back then and found five articles about the event. We had written five reports. Unfortunately, they weren't very detailed—just dry facts, no background information. And it's precisely this background that interests me. And I'm sure you could help me with that."

After a few seconds of silence, Tobias asked, "Why do you want to reopen this old case?"

"Call it journalistic curiosity," Harald replied. "The story intrigues me. Especially because, until yesterday, I had never heard of it before. And the sight of those three graves moved me—not least because I used to go fishing with my father all the time." He leaned forward in his chair. "I've been working as a journalist for years. In this job, you develop a certain instinct for uncovering hidden truths. As a former investigator, I don't have to explain that sense to you."

Tobias studied him silently for a while, chewing on his lower lip and furrowing his brow deeply. "I understand that, as a journalist, you probably ask yourself more questions about certain things than others might. I did the same as an investigator. And yet, I still don't quite understand why you want to dig up this tragedy again." Now Tobias leaned forward as well. "So, what are you not telling me?"

Harald stared at him like a schoolboy caught in a lie. "Well, I... fine. Two days ago, when I was standing by the graves, an old man approached me, and we got to talking. After a while, he told me about the accident and how well he had known the three fishermen. It had been a heavy blow for the village community—back then. And at the end, he added that the supposed accident might have been something else entirely. At first, I didn't understand what he meant, so I pressed him for details. And then he said that there had been disputes among the three fishermen before, and that this Steinar Lundberg was a loner and had been jealous of the Pettersen family."

Tobias looked at Harald with raised eyebrows, his hands forming a fan in front of his mouth. For a few seconds, he said nothing. Harald watched him and had a faint fear that Tobias was about to laugh in his face. But he didn't. Instead, he leaned back with a deep sigh and rubbed his face as if he were tired.

"Well, that's an interesting story," he said, pulling the left corner of his mouth back. He turned his gaze away and looked out the window. Harald waited for Tobias to say something. But he seemed lost in thought, and Harald didn't want to interrupt him.

After almost a minute, Tobias turned back to him. "To be honest, I found the whole thing a bit strange back then myself."

Harald hesitated. "Strange? In what way?"

"Well, not so much the accident itself. But the investigation turned out to be somewhat—how should I put it—complicated."

"What do you mean by that?"

"Interviewing the relatives and witnesses was no easy task."

"And why not?"

"I shouldn't even be telling you this. This is confidential information from the investigation."

"But the case has been closed for quite some time now, hasn't it?"

Tobias gave a faint smile, stood up, and walked to the window. With his arms crossed over his chest, he stood there, looking out at the sound once more. "The conclusion of the investigation was never satisfying to me."

"And why not?"

"Hard to say. You know that gut feeling. You just sense that something isn't right, but you don't know what, and you can't prove it. It wasn't the first time I experienced that in my career. But during the investigation in Halvik, my concerns were particularly strong."

"What made you feel that way?"

He shrugged slightly. "During the questioning of witnesses and the people who had close contact with the deceased, I often had the impression that there was more to it than they were willing to admit. And yet, I never found any concrete evidence to justify my suspicions. It was quite frustrating."

"How did you first hear about the accident? How did it all begin?"

"We received a call early in the morning from a local resident. He reported an abandoned boat that had washed ashore. He knew the owner and couldn't reach him. We informed the coast guard and drove to Halvik. Once we arrived, we immediately started searching for clues. At first glance, there was nothing to suggest a crime. There were no bloodstains on board, no signs of a struggle. Plus, we knew that a violent storm had raged the night before.

Strangely enough, we found four life jackets in the cabin, which surprised us. Why hadn't the crew worn them? Or were there others that we didn't know about? The owner confirmed that his boat was only equipped with four life jackets. So, we had to assume that the fishermen weren't wearing any—at least none belonging to the *Malini.* That was the name of the boat. I remember that clearly."

"And who owned the boat?"

"The Pettersen brothers' father, John Pettersen."

"Did John Pettersen know that his sons had taken the boat out?"

"Yes. He had actually asked them to retrieve the nets before the storm hit."

Harald nodded, pulled out a notepad, and scribbled down a few key points. "What happened next?"

"We started interviewing the witnesses—or rather, the so-called witnesses. The accident happened late at night during a storm. There were no real witnesses."

"Who did you interview then?"

"The parents of the two brothers, of course. But they couldn't tell us much. They only knew that Arne and Linus had set out around eight o'clock in the evening or so and never came home."

"Were the brothers still living at home at the time?"

"No, they weren't. If I remember correctly, John Pettersen mentioned that Linus or Arne would usually call him after work to give him an update. That night, however, he waited for the call in vain."

"Who reported them missing?"

"That was Ronald Thoresen."

Harald jotted down the information.

Tobias turned to him. "What would you do if you found out the details of the investigation?"

Harald had to think about Tobias's question for a moment. The answer was actually simple. He would use them for his story. The problem was that he probably wouldn't be allowed to. "Well," he said after careful consideration, "if there's something worth writing about, I'll publish a report in the newspaper. It all depends on what I find out and whether it can be made public."

Tobias nodded and sat back down in his chair. He stared at Harald for a moment, then said, "Alright. I'll tell you what happened back then. But you have to promise me something..."

Harald looked at him questioningly.

"Before you publish anything, you have to show me your report."

"That can be arranged."

Tobias nodded, took a sip of coffee, and leaned back. "At the beginning of the investigation, I naturally assumed it was an accident. Everything pointed to that. Only weeks later, after interviewing a lot of people, did I start to feel that something was off. Take John Pettersen, for example. He simply couldn't understand how this accident could have happened. His sons had been going to sea with him since early childhood; they knew the waters around Halvik like the backs of their hands. They had been out in storms countless times before, and nothing even remotely dangerous had ever happened. He knew how his sons worked, how conscientious they were, and how skilled they were—better than most their age. And yet, they never came back. He never explicitly said that he believed anything other than a tragic accident had happened, but his statement that he couldn't explain the accident only reinforced my intuition."

Harald cleared his throat. "But John must have understood that even professionals can have things go wrong. Especially in a heavy storm."

"Of course. He was aware of that. But he wasn't the only one who thought this way. Even the harbor master found the accident puzzling. The only person who wasn't surprised was Steinar Lundberg's wife."

"Oh really?"

Tobias nodded. "She said that the Pettersens would do anything for money, even take their catch in the face of great danger. She blamed Linus and Arne for her husband's death. She said they were a greedy family who would stop at nothing."

"Pretty harsh."

"You could say that."

"Were you able to verify her statement?"

"What do you mean?"

"That the Pettersens would do anything for money."

Tobias shook his head. "No, I don't believe that. John never gave the impression that he would go to extreme lengths for a catch. As far as I know, he was—and still is—well-liked in the community. During my investigation, only Neja Lundberg spoke disparagingly about the Pettersens."

"I see. Did Steinar Lundberg's widow suspect foul play?"

"No, she didn't. But I distrusted her from the start. Something about her demeanor bothered me. One moment she was devastated, the next she was as composed as a professor giving a lecture. I couldn't figure her out, nor her accusations against the Pettersens.

After speaking with Neja Lundberg, I tried to learn more about the relationship between the Lundbergs and the Pettersens in the village, but I wasn't very successful. In a small town where everyone knows everyone, no one wanted to speak ill of anyone else."

He shook his head. "The case files are in the police archives. You won't be able to get your hands on them."

"Too bad..." Harald said, disappointed, although he had expected this answer.

"I can offer you a deal," Tobias said with a serious expression.

"A deal?"

"I'll give you the names of the witnesses I interviewed back then. I don't need to remind you that my name stays out of your newspaper report."

"Of course."

Tobias walked over to a sideboard and returned with a notepad and a pen. After sitting back down, he scribbled a few names onto the paper. From a distance, Harald couldn't make them out. Tobias tore off the sheet and held it up in front of Harald's face. But before Harald could take it, Tobias pulled it back again and gave him a sharp look.

"I want to read the report first!"

Harald nodded. "Don't worry, you can count on me."

Chapter 9

Half an hour later, Harald parked his car near the Hurtigruten terminal and strolled along the waterfront toward the city center. He was hungry and needed to eat something. Runi wasn't home, so it didn't matter if he didn't go straight back. Still, he sent her a quick message to let her know that he was staying in town for a bite to eat.

Near the harbour, he entered a small Italian restaurant, sat by the window, and ordered a pizza with salami and mushrooms, along with a lemonade. Then he pulled out Tobias' note. Five names were written on it:

> Ronald Thoresen (passerby who found the boat)
> John and Anne Pettersen
> Øyvind Johansen (harbor master)
> Neja Lundberg (widow of Steinar Lundberg)
> Jonna Olsen (widow of Linus Pettersen)

That wasn't a lot, Harald thought. There were probably plenty of other people in the village who also had something to say about the incident. But since the investigators had quickly concluded it was an accident, there had likely been no reason for further questioning.

Today, however, the situation was different from thirteen years ago. For most, the incident had likely faded into the background. Maybe, after all these years, they were more willing to talk, ready to share something they hadn't dared to say back then. Harald had enough experience to know how a story could suddenly take an entirely different turn years later.

The question was whether the people Tobias had mentioned still lived in the area. It was entirely possible that some had moved away or even passed away. And if, against all odds, he managed to find them all, there was no guarantee they would want to talk to him about the accident.

There were still many unknowns in this equation.

He gazed out the window, watching the passing pedestrians. A man, accompanied by a teenage boy, entered the bookstore across the street, and Harald immediately thought of his own father. As a child, he had wished his father would take him to a bookstore. But his father had never made time for that. He had always preferred to stand alone by the water, fishing rod in one hand and a beer in the other, leaving all parenting and family matters to his wife.

And now, decades later, his wife was gone, and he himself was in a nursing home, longing for a family that would take care of him. The irony of fate. Now his father knew what it meant to be alone, to have all the time in the world to reflect on his life and mourn the past. But now it was too late. He had his chance and never took it.

Harald didn't feel any sense of pleasure about it. No, it made him sad. The fact that he had no desire to visit his own father said it all. But spending time with him was about as enjoyable as sitting in the dentist's chair, gripping his thighs in pain as the drill went to work.

But that was just how it was, and there was no point in dwelling on it too much.

Twenty minutes later, Harald left the restaurant and headed home.

At home, he sat down at his computer and checked the time. It was seven in the evening. Runi wasn't home yet, so he used the time to search the internet for the names on Tobias' list. His first search was a success: Ronald Thoresen, the man who had found the boat, lived at Solstrandvegen 3 in Halvik.

Next, he looked up John and Anne Pettersen, the parents of Linus and Arne. He found them as well. They lived at Skifervegen 26, also in Halvik.

Øyvind Johansen, Neja Lundberg, and Jonna Pettersen, however, he couldn't find. That meant he would have to track down their addresses in person.

He shut down the computer, made himself a coffee in the kitchen, and sat down in the living room.

Runi's knitting lay beside him, and at that moment, he missed his wife. He glanced at his phone but saw no message from her. Sighing, he turned on the TV and watched the evening news.

Chapter 10

Harald drove past *EISCAT*, the research station for the northern lights, and thought about the day ahead. He had woken up early, had breakfast, then watched the news on TV, and an hour later, showed up at the office. He had to attend an editorial meeting so dull that he had nearly fallen off his chair from sheer boredom.

Now, he steered his car through Breivikeidet Valley toward Halvik. There weren't many houses in the valley. Now and then, a small settlement would appear, or a single house stood isolated among the masses of snow. The trees were freshly dusted with frost, the road was white as a bedsheet, and the air was bitterly cold. The car's display showed minus 22 degrees. The landscape was frozen, motionless, and silent.

After about thirty minutes, Harald turned off the main road toward Nakkevatnet. He drove up the long, winding curves to the lake at an excessive speed, then finally pulled into a roadside bay and came to a stop. Stepping out of the car, he leaned against the door and took in the view of the lake and the small plain to his left, which stretched out to a steeply rising mountain range. The lake was frozen over, and smoke was rising from a fishing cabin on the opposite side. The sun illuminated the surrounding mountain peaks, their slopes streaked with dark rock formations that made them appear even more imposing.

After the long winter darkness, the sunlight was a blessing, and despite the prevailing silence, he could almost feel how the landscape was soaking up the rays.

Harald thought of the days and nights he had spent with his father in their cabin at Laksvatn. As a child, he had enjoyed those trips—at least in the beginning. But soon, his father changed. He became grim and withdrawn, always finding something to criticize. The worst part, though, was the drinking. The trips gradually turned into drinking binges, with fishing becoming just an afterthought.

He remembered one evening when he was about eleven years old. They were in their cabin, had just finished dinner, and his father was downing his ninth bottle of beer. Drunk as he was, he got up, muttered something about going fishing, and staggered out.

It was mid-April, and only a few spots on the lake still had ice thick enough to walk on safely. But his father didn't care, and so, inevitably, the ice gave way beneath him, and he plunged into the water.

Harald, who had followed him unnoticed, watched as his father resurfaced, gasping, desperately trying to claw onto the edge of the ice, but barely managing. Again and again, he slipped back into the freezing water, only to try once more a few seconds later.

For a long moment, Harald stood motionless, paralyzed by a dizzying storm of emotions. He wanted to run forward, to save his father from certain death. Then again, he wanted to stay behind the tree and watch him drown.

It was a horrific moment of indecision. He felt as if he were fighting against a wall. A magnet pulled him onto the ice; a rope held him back.

After what felt like agonizing seconds—or minutes, he couldn't tell—pity won out, and he rushed forward to help his father.

Now, three decades later, he wasn't sure if he would do the same again.

Should he be ashamed of that thought?

Maybe. But it was his thought alone. No one could judge him for it.

Twenty minutes later, Harald drove into the village of Halvik. He glanced at his navigation system. Ronald Thoresen lived at Solstrandvegen 3. That was the next street on the right.

He turned in and pulled up in front of a yellow, rather run-down house. The paint was peeling everywhere—on the facade, the window frames, it didn't matter. A few roof shingles were missing, and the garden shed had no roof left at all. An old Hyundai stood in front of the garage, long past its prime.

Harald parked right behind it and got out.

On the drive here, he had prepared several questions, but he dreaded his interview partner's reaction.

Maybe Ronald wanted nothing to do with the story anymore and would chase him off the property.

Harald stepped up to the door and rang the bell. It took almost a minute before the door hesitantly opened, revealing a somewhat stocky man in his seventies, with thinning gray hair, old-looking clothes, and a tomato-red face. His face was covered in stubble that was clearly older than three days, a few nose hairs blended in with the whiskers on his upper lip, and his eyebrows grew wildly in all directions.

"Yes?" he asked.

"Good day. My name is Harald Strøm. I'm a journalist with *iNord* newspaper. Do you know it?"

He nodded. "Of course."

"I'm investigating a story that took place here in 2005 when…" He didn't get any further.

"I know already. The boat accident," Ronald Thoresen interrupted.

"Exactly. I'm aware that the incident happened quite some time ago. Back then, I wasn't living in the area for a while, so I don't know the details of the accident—only what was mentioned in the newspaper reports. I'd like to revisit the story and provide a more detailed account of the events. For that, I rely on witness statements."

Ronald looked at him with his tired eyes, scrutinizing him. "And what makes you think I know anything about it?"

"You were the one who found the fishermen's boat, weren't you?"

He was silent for a moment. "That's right. How do you know that?"

"I had access to the police records."

Ronald nodded hesitantly, his expression slightly relaxing. "Do you want to come in? Otherwise, I'll freeze out here."

Harald was led into the kitchen, where he was offered a seat at the table. The house smelled of old furniture and stale air. Rugs were scattered everywhere, even in the kitchen. They were worn and threadbare, their colours faded over the years. A cat wandered around the room, and the area around its food bowl looked like a litter bin.

"Want some coffee?" Ronald asked, reaching for a pot.

"That would be nice, thanks."

While Ronald boiled water and scooped instant coffee into the cups, Harald pulled out his notebook. He flipped through the pages briefly, and when he came across his notes on the money laundering case, a queasy feeling crept into his stomach.

"Who have you talked to so far?" Ronald asked.

"You're the first," Harald replied.

"So, you don't know much about the story yet?"

"Not much. As I said, only what was published in our paper at the time."

Ronald peered at him over the rim of his glasses. "Didn't you just say you had access to the police records?"

Harald hesitated for a moment but quickly recovered. "That's true. But I wasn't allowed to read everything—data protection laws, you understand?"

Ronald seemed to think about this for a moment but didn't respond. Instead, he placed two cups of coffee on the table and sat down.

Harald reached for his cup and took a sip. The moment the coffee hit his tongue, he had the urge to spit it right back out. It tasted like... well, like nothing. Or like dishwater.

"So..." Ronald said, taking a sip himself and clearly enjoying the coffee. "How can I help you?"

"My first question is about the boat you found. Did you notice anything unusual about it?"

Ronald looked out the window for a moment, then shook his head. "No. I don't remember anything in particular. Except, of course, that boats don't usually land on that pebble beach—they tie up at the harbour. And the boat was empty, with no crew on board. That struck me as odd right away. I recognized the boat immediately. It belonged to John Pettersen."

"What was the boat's name?"

"*Malini.*"

"Unconventional name..." Harald remarked, jotting down the boat's name.

"If I'm not mistaken, the name comes from India."

"Did the Pettersens have any connection to India?"

Ronald shrugged. "I think John worked on a fishing boat in India when he was young. But I'm not sure."

Harald noted: *India.*

"What did you do after you found the boat?" Harald wanted to know.

"I climbed into the boat and searched for the crew. But I didn't find anyone."

"Was there anything lying on deck that caught your eye?"

Ronald thought again, furrowing his brow. "No. But to be honest, I wasn't really focusing on objects."

Harald nodded. "And then you called the police?"

"No, not right away. I went straight to the Pettersens' house and rang the doorbell, but no one answered."

"What time was that?"

"You're asking a lot of specifics. I don't remember exactly. A little after six in the morning, if I recall correctly."

"A bit strange that no one was home at that hour, isn't it?"

"Not necessarily. John often went out on the boat at four in the morning, and his wife occasionally helped out at a nursing home."

Harald gave him a questioning look. "But his boat was empty… so he couldn't have gone out fishing."

"He doesn't only own the *Malini*. He has two others— one in Tromsø and another down at the harbour."

"I see," Harald said, making a note of that. "And what happened next?"

"I first thought about driving over to Arne and Linus' place, but then I decided to call the police. So, I went home and dialled emergency services."

"Did you return to the boat afterward?"

"Of course. The police asked me to wait there for them."

"Did it take long for them to arrive?"

"About an hour."

"And in that time, you didn't see anyone near the boat?"

"I did, actually. After a while, John, Anne, and Linus' wife showed up."

"Did the police inform them?"

"I believe so."

Harald nodded and stared at his coffee cup. He wondered if it would be rude to leave it completely untouched. The brew was undrinkable.

He glanced at his notes. So far, Ronald hadn't been able to tell him anything particularly useful. But then again, that wasn't surprising—after all, he had only found the boat and reported it to the police.

"Did you know the Pettersen family well?" he asked.

Ronald shrugged again. "'Well' would be an exaggeration. In a small village like this, everyone knows everyone. They were a nice family. But it's not like we visited each other's homes. At least not before the accident."

"Afterward?"

"Only once. I wanted to offer my condolences."

Harald nodded. "Did the Pettersens ever tell you how the accident happened?"

"No. But no one really knows to this day. There was a terrible storm that night. One of the worst I've ever seen here. The obvious assumption is that the three of them fell victim to the storm. Something must have gone terribly wrong on board."

"Is it common to go out in such weather?"

Ronald leaned back in his chair. "No idea. I'm not a fisherman. You'd have to ask John."

"Do you know if his sons got along well?"

"I think so. I never heard or saw anything to suggest otherwise. They grew up here in the village, and I've known them since they were little rascals, but they weren't the only kids in town." He took a sip of his coffee and let out a quiet burp. "That's about all I can tell you about the family."

"How well did you know Steinar Lundberg?"

Ronald flinched slightly, and Harald couldn't tell whether it was because of the question or the coffee he had just brought to his lips. But by now, it surely wasn't hot anymore.

"I knew him, yes."

Harald waited for him to say more, but Ronald just stared at him blankly. "And what was he like?"

"What do you mean?"

"What kind of person was he? Was he nice, mean, arrogant, or helpful?"

Ronald looked out the window. "Hard to say. Steinar had many faces. He could be hot-tempered, but also gentle as a lamb. With him, you never knew where you stood."

"What was your relationship with him? Was he a friend?"

"God forbid! No, he certainly wasn't a friend. We ran into each other at the café, at village meetings, or occasionally while out for a walk."

"You just said he could be hot-tempered. When or where did that show?"

"Well, I remember one incident at Café Kystenshuset. I was sitting not far from Steinar and another guy—I didn't know him—and I followed their conversation. They were talking about buying a boat. At first, they spoke as if they were old friends. But when the stranger named a price for the boat, Steinar shot up from his chair and slammed his fist on the table so hard that the drinks spilled. He started shouting at the man, calling him a greedy bastard and telling him to go to hell, or else he'd lose his temper. The stranger, who was smaller and weaker than Steinar, got up and fled through the entrance. Steinar then paid for the drinks and left the café as well."

Ronald took a breath. "And that reminds me of another incident, though I wasn't there myself—I only heard about it. Apparently, he once had a heated argument with his neighbour, Trond. Trond had blown snow onto Steinar's property with a snow blower. Whether it was intentional or not, I can't say. But apparently, Steinar lost his mind and went after his neighbour. Neja, his wife, managed to stop him at the last second, probably preventing something worse."

"Did he treat his wife the same way?"

"Not that I know of. But what happened behind closed doors, I can't tell you."

"Does Neja still live in the village?"

"Sure. Right at the village entrance. When you come down the hill, you'll see her olive-green house."

Harald noted the location of the house. "Is there anything else you can tell me?"

Ronald thought for a moment. "No, I don't think so."

Harald closed his notebook. "Thank you very much for taking the time to talk to me."

"My pleasure." Ronald crossed his arms over his chest. "But tell me, wasn't there already enough coverage of the tragedy back then?"

"There was coverage, that's true. But what was reported wasn't very satisfying to me. I just want to gather more background on the accident and form my own picture of what happened."

Ronald peered at him over the rim of his glasses. "Do you think something fishy was going on?"

"No idea. Maybe. I just have a fascination with old stories that have an unusual ending."

Ronald threw up his hands. "There was nothing unusual about it, I'm sure. The storm was so violent that it could have taken the lives of even three experienced men. Tragic, but these things happen. It wasn't the first time."

"I understand that."

Harald glanced out the window briefly, searching for a final question, but nothing came to mind. So, he tucked his notebook into his jacket pocket and thanked Ronald for talking to him about the accident—and for the excellent coffee.

"You barely touched it," Ronald said, pointing at Harald's cup.

"I know, I'm sorry. I already had too much coffee today."

"I get that," Ronald replied and walked Harald to the door. They said their goodbyes, and Harald got into his car and drove off.

However, only a few hundred meters down the road, he pulled into a parking space near the water, got out, and leaned against the passenger door.

A fishing boat with two fishermen in yellow gear chugged away from the shore and headed toward the open sea. On the pebble beach, two seagulls squabbled noisily over the remains of a crab.

Harald reflected on his conversation with Ronald. He hadn't learned much. But he hoped for more from his upcoming interviews. The Pettersens or Neja Lundberg probably had far more to say about the case than Ronald did. Then again, they might not want to talk to him at all. The memories of those events were surely painful, and who liked talking to strangers about their deceased family members?

He checked his watch. It was half past two in the afternoon.

Who should he visit first? The Pettersens or Neja Lundberg?

After everything he had heard about Steinar, he was more intrigued by the conversation with Neja. Her husband seemed to have been quite a character. Even Rasmus had called Steinar "an original," whatever he had meant by that. If Steinar had truly been so hot-tempered, that could be significant for his investigation.

He took one last look at the fjord, got back into the car, and drove to the Lundbergs' house.

Chapter 11

As Ronald had described, Harald quickly found the olive-green house at the edge of the village. It stood slightly apart from the road, alone on a small hill, surrounded by several snow-laden fir trees. Their branches looked as if they were covered in oversized popcorn.

An older model grey Mercedes was parked in the driveway. Leaning against the garage were touring skis, and in a kennel nearby, a husky began barking loudly as Harald stepped out of his car. From a distance, he examined the enclosure, just to make sure no door was left open.

He had barely taken five steps away from his car when the front door burst open, and a tall, lanky woman appeared in the doorway, eyeing him warily. She had short brown hair with a hint of grey at the roots. She wore tight jogging tights and a hooded sweatshirt.

"Rako, be quiet!" she shouted toward the kennel, following up with a piercing whistle. The husky immediately sat down, fixing its gaze on its mistress, tongue hanging out.

"Can I help you?" the woman asked, directing her words at Harald, her brow deeply furrowed.

Her voice was somewhat hoarse, though Harald couldn't tell if it was from smoking or a cold. She looked a little worn, with dark circles under her eyes and sunken cheeks.

"My name is Harald Strøm," he introduced himself as he stepped closer. "I'm a journalist with *iNord*. A few days ago, I happened to come across the graves of the Pettersen brothers—and that of your husband."

He waited for a reaction, but there was none. Her expression remained blank. He noticed the nameplate beside the doorbell. In addition to *Neja Lundberg,* another name was listed: *Lina Trygg.*

Neja looked at him with a hint of impatience, so Harald continued his explanation. In a few short sentences, he outlined his intentions and what he had uncovered so far. The wrinkles on Neja's forehead deepened, and her gaze grew even more distrustful. She crossed her arms over her chest—whether because of the cold or because of Harald, he couldn't tell.

But he wasn't deterred. "After reading our newspaper's reports, I felt that the deceased didn't receive the attention they deserved. Brave men like your late husband and the Pettersen brothers deserve more than a few dry words."

Neja took a few seconds before responding. "I… I don't quite understand what you mean."

"Well—I'd like to learn more about the accident. The newspaper articles back then were just factual reports. But

I want to tell the stories of the men who died that day. I want to write about their lives—who they were, what they did, what dreams they had, and how their loved ones experienced the tragedy."

Neja pursed her lips, glanced briefly at her dog, which had now lain back down, then turned her attention back to Harald.

Her expression had changed slightly. Where there had been hardness before, there was now something resembling sadness. The tall woman suddenly seemed deflated, as if all the tension had drained from her body.

Harald felt uneasy, already picturing himself walking away empty-handed.

"To be honest, I have no interest in reliving that tragedy," Neja Lundberg finally said, looking at him defiantly.

"I completely understand," Harald replied sympathetically. "And I don't want to reopen old wounds. I had just hoped that, with one final, more in-depth report, I could give the deceased the respect they deserve."

"I don't think anyone cares about that anymore."

"I wouldn't be so sure. Old stories have fascinated people for ages. And since this tragedy happened in our region, people are all the more interested. It was also somewhat mysterious, if I may say so. To this day, no one knows what really happened."

Neja looked at him as if he had just said something foolish. "I don't see it that way," she said stubbornly. "My husband and the Pettersen brothers went out to sea during one of the worst storms in decades, got caught in distress, and went overboard. That's what happened. These things happen. It wasn't the first time, and it won't be the last."

The indifference in her voice unsettled Harald. He wasn't sure if it was because of his questions or if she simply had no desire to talk about the incident.

"I know," he said through clenched teeth. "Still, I'd like to ask you a few questions. It would really help me."

Neja raised an eyebrow and shook her head thoughtfully. Her gaze drifted into the distance for a moment before she turned back to Harald. "Why don't you ask Linus and Arne's parents? Or better yet, the police? I have absolutely no interest in revisiting the past."

Harald nodded. "Linus and Arne's parents are on my list as well. But to get the full picture, it would be helpful to speak with everyone involved. Your name wouldn't be mentioned in my story, of course—if that's what you're worried about."

She shook her head. "That's not the issue. I just don't see the point in all of this."

Harald searched for a suitable response. In his line of work, he constantly faced resistance. Most of the time, however, he got what he wanted. But there were also the tough cases—people who simply wouldn't budge.

"Wouldn't it be nice if your late husband had a tribute in the newspaper? Something more than just a dry factual report?"

Neja gave him an intense look, and he had the feeling she wanted to respond. But instead, she just cleared her throat twice and gazed past him toward the fjord. Harald considered whether he should try another argument, but he realized he had none left.

This was probably the end of the road with Neja Lundberg.

Just as he was about to give up, she suddenly said, "Alright. I'll answer a few questions. But not here, not now. I don't have time. We can meet the day after tomorrow at ten o'clock at Café Kystenshuset. Does that suit you?"

"I'll be there."

Neja forced a strained smile, gave him a brief nod, and left him standing at the door.

Harald walked back to his car, inwardly jubilant, completely ignoring the deafening barking of the husky.

Chapter 12

Jonna Olsen sat at the kitchen table, drinking her usual evening cup of decaffeinated coffee. She felt exhausted and drained. It had been a long and tiring day, undoubtedly worsened by the headache that had started during the night.

Her day had begun early; she had prepared breakfast for the children and packed lunch for her husband. Then she had driven to Tromsø to start her early shift at the hospital. As always, there was plenty to do. The pediatric emergency ward had been flooded with one sick child after another—some with high fever, others completely exhausted and dehydrated. One child had broken an arm, another had a fractured nose. There was a little bit of everything, and by the time she left the hospital nine hours later, she could hardly wait to take a warm bath at home and have a cup of coffee.

Kristoffer and Karoline were in bed, and her husband was outside clearing the snow.

She took a sip of coffee and debated whether to go to bed right away or watch some TV. What she really longed for was the warmth of her quilt and the softness of her pillow. She wanted to close her eyes and just sleep. The only thing standing in the way of that wish now was Eirik's desire for intimacy. And his idea of intimacy was entirely different from hers.

"Do you want to have sex?" he would ask, and she would reply, "If you want."

That seemed to be enough for him, and five minutes later, it was usually over. He would fall asleep, and she would slip into the bathroom.

No, that was definitely not what she imagined intimacy to be.

From outside, the sounds of Eirik's snow shoveling drifted into the kitchen. A drop in the ocean, Jonna thought. More snow was forecast for the night, and by morning, there would hardly be any sign of his efforts. But he loved winter, loved shoveling snow the way others loved their first cup of coffee in the morning. That was how she had met him. He was always in motion, always had a project up his sleeve, fixing something here, tinkering with something there. She should be grateful that he took care of these things, but sometimes, she wished he would take care of her a little more.

Just not tonight!

At the beginning of their relationship, he had spent more time with her in the house, although even then, he had spent almost every evening in his workshop. The difference was that back then, he usually returned to her after half an hour. Nowadays, it was common for her not to see him all evening—only when he slipped quietly into bed around midnight.

Sometimes she wondered what he was doing in there for hours. Did he just want to be alone? Away from her? Away from the kids?

Why did she love him, anyway?

Did she still love him at all?

When they had met eleven years ago, walking by the fjord, she had already been a widow for two years, had a one-and-a-half-year-old son, and feared that Eirik would struggle with his sudden father role. But he had taken on the responsibility and had handled it surprisingly well. Soon, her worries faded, and little Kristoffer grew up with a stepfather, got a baby sister two years later, and knew nothing about his biological father until he turned nine.

She had deliberately kept it from him. And for a good reason—or at least, that was what she had told herself for years. She feared the truth and how Kristoffer would react. She was afraid it might tear the family apart, that Kristoffer might have a problem with Eirik, and that was something she wanted to avoid at all costs.

Family harmony was important to her—something she had never known in her own childhood.

Yet, doubts kept creeping in, and she often found herself wondering whether Kristoffer deserved to know the truth.

If she had been in his place, she would have wanted to know who her real father was. But how and when should she tell Kristoffer? And what would happen afterward with Eirik? Would Kristoffer's good relationship with him suffer?

It was entirely possible.

One evening, about a year ago, it happened anyway. The whole family was flipping through old photo albums together. In many pictures, they were captured as a family—sometimes with both parents, sometimes alone, sometimes with grandparents.

Kristoffer had looked at these photos many times before, but until that night, he had never noticed a small but significant detail.

Eirik wasn't in any of his baby pictures.

"Why isn't Dad in any of these photos?" he suddenly asked.

At that moment, something inside Jonna crumbled—a wall she had built around herself for years.

All the doubts and questions, the sleepless nights, the headaches—none of it mattered anymore. Kristoffer had made the decision for her.

She remembered Eirik's pleading look, a look she had never seen from him before.

At the same time, she saw her son's eyes, demanding an answer—eyes that would no longer accept a lie.

No mother in the world could resist those eyes.

It was the most powerful weapon children had against their parents.

Without paying attention to Eirik's vehement head shaking, she told her son about Linus. How she had met him as a child, how they had grown up together, and eventually married. She told him that Linus had died in a boating accident, just like his brother Arne and a family friend.

Even now, she could still see Eirik's expression at that moment—a mixture of deep disappointment and blind rage. He had left the kitchen and disappeared into his workshop, where he spent the entire evening and half the night. It took nearly a week before he spoke more than a few words to her again.

But Jonna had noticed a change in him. He had become quieter, more withdrawn, and colder. She had hurt him deeply, and he had never forgiven her for it.

Jonna felt the weight of melancholy settling over her. Sadness welled up inside her, as it often did when she drifted into the past. She placed her cup in the sink and went into the study.

From a drawer, she pulled out a few letters and unfolded the first one. It was a love letter, written by Linus when he was sixteen. His handwriting was beautiful—so tender and soft, so devoted and open.

She couldn't remember how many times she had read these letters; she knew them by heart. And yet, every time she read them, it felt as if she were absorbing Linus' words for the first time.

She saw herself again as a young woman, hiding his letters under her pillow, keeping them away from prying eyes. At night, when she couldn't sleep, she would take them out, reading them over and over, feeling Linus beside her.

What would have become of her if not for him?

He had been her voice in the darkness.

Tears welled up in her eyes, blurring her vision. She placed the letters back in the drawer, locked it, and went upstairs to bed.

Chapter 13

After a late dinner, Harald sat down on his sofa and flipped through the day's newspaper, which he had only half-read during breakfast. There wasn't much of interest to note, so he set it aside after a short while and checked the time. It was half-past nine in the evening.

Runi wasn't home. He picked up his phone and texted her, saying that he would love to have a coffee with her right now. He had been wanting that all day.

He glanced over at the coffee machine and wondered if he should make one anyway. After a brief moment of consideration, he decided against it, sat down at his computer instead, and opened the saved newspaper articles about the boating accident.

He wasn't sure why he did it—maybe out of boredom or in the hope that rereading them might spark an idea. But by the time he finished, he was no wiser than before.

He rubbed his eyes and leaned back in his chair.

He thought about Neja Lundberg and wondered how she coped with the fact that her husband's body was never found. What kind of scars had that left on her? Had she ever truly found closure? Or did she comb the shoreline with every walk along the shore, hoping to discover some scrap of her husband's clothing?

A horrifying thought. A funeral without a body.

The uncertainty must have been unbearable. To know that the person you loved more than anything was lost forever, yet to have no real proof.

In two days, he would meet Neja again.

The thought gave him an uneasy feeling. He couldn't quite explain why. That never happened to him. After all, he had been in this job long enough.

But Neja Lundberg was different.

He was nervous about her reaction, especially since she hadn't been particularly enthusiastic about the interview. He was surprised she had agreed to it at all.

The conversation would surely be interesting — whether it would also be helpful remained to be seen.

Sighing, he shut down his laptop, packed his tobacco pipe, and stepped onto the terrace, where he enjoyed the sweet scent of tobacco beneath a thin band of green northern lights.

Chapter 14

Halvik, 1999

Peder Sørensen sat at his desk in the sacristy of his church and watched as the door to his office slowly closed, leaving him alone in the oppressive silence of his small refuge.

Normally, he enjoyed the stillness of his domain. Here, he could retreat when he needed peace or time to think. To him, this was more than just an office or a place to prepare for mass. He spent almost more time here than in his own home.

But today, the meditative silence of his sanctuary was unbearable. It was heavy, suffocating, and dizzying. He could hear the blood rushing in his ears, and his heart was pounding as if he had just run across the entire village. His eyes burned, and he had to close them. When he opened them again, tears rolled down his cheeks, and he wished he hadn't come to the church today—or at least that he had left an hour earlier.

Then he wouldn't have had to open the door when the knock came an hour ago.

Then he wouldn't have had to hear a confession.

Of course, listening to the sins of his parishioners was part of his duty, and he loved offering the spiritual guidance they needed. But with the last penitent, Peder wasn't sure if he had truly provided the comfort that person needed.

He feared that he hadn't responded enough, that he had been too overwhelmed by the weight of the confession to find the right words in their prayer together.

His gaze wandered to the only cabinet in the room. He stared at its wooden door for a while, torn between opening it or not. Finally, he got up from his chair, opened the door, and reached far into the back, where things lay that he hadn't seen in a long time.

For a moment, he rummaged through the shelf until his fingers touched something cold—glass.

He grabbed it and pulled out a transparent bottle containing a brown liquid. Holding it in his hand, he sat back down and suddenly realized how exhausted he was. His legs felt like jelly, he was sweating, and a dull ache pulled at his stomach.

He took a water glass from the drawer, removed the bottle's cap, and poured two fingers' worth of the brown liquid into the glass.

Before taking a sip, he stared at the contents for a long, uncertain moment, trying to steady his trembling hand. But he couldn't.

So, he closed his eyes and poured the burning liquid into his mouth.

He repeated the ritual a second time, grimacing as the warmth spread through his body and heat rose to his head. Then, he set the glass down and leaned back in his chair, eyes still closed.

A wave of shame washed over him, and he tried to push it down. But he couldn't.

He opened his eyes, looked at the bottle, and felt an urge to smash it against the wall. At the same time, he had to fight against another urge—the temptation to pour himself another glass.

For half a minute, he clenched his fists so tightly that his nails dug into his palms. He tore his gaze away from the bottle, looked toward the door—and buried his face in his hands.

The words spoken in this room just moments ago still echoed in his ears.

They crashed down on him like an unrelenting tide, coming and going, refusing to leave him in peace.

And just like the shame over the bottle, the words had burned themselves into his mind—etched there, permanent and inescapable.

He couldn't undo it.

Neither the act nor the knowledge of it.

A strange feeling rose within him, and at first, he didn't know what it was.

He tried to name what he was feeling.

Was it fear? Was it anger? Or was it grief?

But none of those emotions quite fit.

No. It was something entirely different. Something he hadn't expected at all.

It was: surprise.

But it was not a pleasant surprise—on the contrary, it left him speechless and powerless. It paralyzed him, draining every ounce of energy from his body.

He stood up, dragged himself to the window, and gazed out at the fjord.

What was he supposed to do now?

What was he supposed to do with the knowledge that had been entrusted to him?

Could he simply ignore it and move on without dwelling on it?

But the answer was as simple as the *Amen* in his church: there was nothing he could do as a confessor.

The seal of confession, *Sigillum confessionis*!

Until now, this duty of absolute secrecy had never troubled him. On the contrary, he had considered it a privilege—to receive people's confessions, grant them absolution, and hopefully, help them live a better life.

But at this moment, he no longer felt it was a privilege. Instead, it was an unbearable burden.

He could not—no, he *must not*—speak to anyone about it.

He could not seek advice. He could not ask for help.

All he could do was—pray. Pray for this lost soul.

But how would he react next Sunday, when he stood elevated behind the altar, looking down at them in the pews? Would the congregation sense his unease, catch his glances, and feel that something was wrong with him? That their usually eloquent pastor was distracted and absent-minded?

Peder looked at the Bible lying on his desk, knowing that God's word would give him the strength to carry this burden as expected of him.

It was not the first time he had heard a harrowing confession. He had experience in this, and he needed to rely on that experience now.

He was, after all, the strong link in the chain. He could not show weakness—not now.

With newfound resolve, he left the sacristy, lit a tall candle near the first row of pews, and knelt down. After crossing himself, he closed his eyes and spoke in a soft but clear voice:

"Heaven and earth are yours. You have created man as the crown of your creation. You have entrusted him with responsibility and granted him free will. But not all men wield this gift wisely. In their choices and actions, they are torn between good and evil. He is aware of his guilt and has asked for forgiveness. Your mercy knows no bounds, so accept his confession, forgive him his misdeeds, and grant him the divine strength to rise above himself and learn. Let this confession be the first step in his repentance. Do not leave him alone in his actions—may your divine power lead him back to the path of virtue and heal all that is wounded. In you, even the impossible is possible, and so I humbly ask for this miracle. Praise and glory be to you forever and ever. Amen."

Slowly, Peder opened his eyes, crossed himself once more, and rose from the pew.

At that very moment, he noticed movement at the edge of his vision. Startled, he turned around and found himself looking into the face of a woman.

She stood there, simply staring at him with a sorrowful expression—and in that instant, he understood.

He wanted to offer her a smile, but before he could, she turned around and left the church through the door.

The silence that followed was even more oppressive than the one he had experienced earlier in the sacristy.

Chapter 15

Halvik, 2018

It was February 22nd when Harald got into his car at nine in the morning and drove toward Halvik. He had slept poorly. The upcoming conversation with Neja Lundberg had occupied his thoughts for half the night.

The sky was clear, the sun hung low on the horizon, casting the surroundings in yellow-orange light. The long shadows of the mountain peaks alternated with the shimmering surface of the fjord, and a layer of mist hovered above the water, glistening in the sunlight like gold dust.

His thoughts wandered to the conversation ahead. He had no idea what to expect. When he had visited her home to request a meeting, she hadn't seemed particularly enthusiastic.

Situations like this were nothing new to him. Throughout his career, he had interviewed all kinds of people and learned a great deal about different personalities. Over time, he had developed an instinct for which questions would get him somewhere and which ones would hit a wall. Of course, it didn't always work, but in most cases, he could rely on his experience and intuition.

Whether that would also be the case today remained to be seen.

An hour later, he parked in front of Café Kystenshuset and stepped inside. The air smelled of fresh coffee and fried bacon. He had eaten a bowl of muesli for breakfast, but now, as the scent of coffee and bacon reached him, he felt as though his stomach were empty.

There were four people in the café, one of them being Neja Lundberg. She sat by the window, her hands folded under her chin. She gave him a brief nod, and Harald joined her.

She greeted him with a shy smile without changing her posture. She looked even more tired than she had two days ago. But perhaps she simply wasn't a morning person.

Today, Neja was wearing glasses that seemed more suited for a twelve-year-old. The eyes behind the lenses moved nervously, giving him the impression that she was either excited or unsure. He guessed the latter.

"You've already ordered, I see," Harald said, gesturing toward the steaming cup of tea.

She only nodded, saying nothing.

The waitress arrived, and Harald ordered a double espresso. He briefly considered getting bacon and eggs but decided against it. It wouldn't look good—asking her about her dead husband while tucking into breakfast.

Instead, he said, "Thank you very much for agreeing to this conversation. I can imagine this isn't an easy thing for you."

She pressed her lips together and nodded again.

The waitress returned with his coffee, and Harald took a sip.

Lukewarm. Great.

He set the cup back down, reached into his jacket pocket, and pulled out his small notebook, flipping to a fresh page and writing *Neja* at the top.

"I hope you don't mind if I take a few notes?"

She shook her head.

"Alright. As I mentioned before, I'd like to learn more about the events from back then. But above all, I'd like to know more about your late husband and the Pettersen brothers. Fishermen in our region have always impressed me—the winter temperatures out on the water, the high waves, the wind. My father used to go fishing often in his free time, and on many occasions, he dragged me along, I have to say. I had no choice."

Neja took a sip of her tea, which was probably still hot, and studied him closely.

"One time, we got caught in a storm and barely made it back," Harald continued. "So, I know what rough seas can be like. And that experience is one of the reasons I'd like to learn more."

"What do you expect to hear from me? The press covered everything the investigation revealed—no more, no less."

Harald smirked slightly. "I see it differently. If I had written about it, the reports would have been more personal. In my opinion, the words of the journalist back then didn't pay the victims enough respect. The readers would have wanted to know more about the incident, about the three fishermen, about their lives."

Harald cleared his throat.

"And that's what I'd like to do now."

Neja looked at him thoughtfully. She tapped nervously on her teacup with her fingernails while simultaneously biting her lower lip.

Harald couldn't read her expression. She seemed hesitant, as if she were reconsidering her decision.

On the other hand, he also sensed a certain curiosity in her eyes.

The constant tapping on the teacup was starting to get on his nerves. She did it relentlessly and rapidly. Harald wondered if the other guests could hear it too.

Time stretched, and Harald felt sweat gathering under his sweater. He shifted in his seat, feeling as if his legs were going numb.

After several more seconds, Neja suddenly nodded and said, "Alright. I'm willing to answer a few questions. But if they get too personal or if they're too much for me, I'll end the conversation."

"Of course," Harald replied, sitting up straight, notebook and pen at the ready. His T-shirt was already sticking to his back.

"How did you meet your husband?" he asked.

"We met while taking a walk—down by the fjord."

"When was that?"

"1987."

He noted down the year.

"Was Steinar already working as a fisherman back then?"

"Yes."

"Were you both raised in Halvik?"

"He was. I wasn't."

Harald waited to see if she would mention her birthplace on her own, but she didn't. "Where were you born?"

"Finnsnes."

"What brought you to Halvik?"

"Mainly work."

Harald was already getting irritated by Neja's short answers.

"You found work in this small village?"

"No, in Tromsø."

"I see. What kind of work, if I may ask?"

"I was—and still am—a legal secretary"

"Halvik isn't exactly well located for commuting to the city every day."

"No, it's not. But I couldn't afford a house in the city, and I didn't want to live in a rented apartment. So, I moved here. It's much quieter than in the city. I prefer the quiet."

"I can understand that," Harald agreed. "May I ask if you and Steinar had children?"

Neja's gaze dropped to her hands, which were wrapped around her teacup.

"No. God had other plans for us."

"I'm sorry."

She shrugged. "We still enjoyed life without children."

"I know what you mean."

She studied him for a moment. Then she opened her mouth slightly, as if about to say something, but closed it again.

Harald changed the subject. "Besides fishing, what else did Steinar do? Did he have any hobbies?"

Neja shook her head. "No. Fishing was his life. If he wasn't out on the water, he was simply too exhausted to pursue any leisure activities."

"Did he have his own boat? Or did he work for another fisherman?"

"Both. He had his own boat, but he also worked for others. His boat was just a dinghy compared to the Pettersen boat."

"So, he worked for the Pettersen family?" She nodded.

"Did he work for them often?"

She shrugged. "I don't know exactly. I rarely knew whether he was out on his own boat or with the Pettersens."

"If I understand correctly, it wasn't unusual for him to go out with the Pettersens?"

Neja Lundberg furrowed her brow at him.

"No, of course not. I already told you he worked for other fishermen."

Harald nodded, flipping through his notebook as if searching for something. In reality, he was thinking about his next question—or more precisely, whether he should ask it.

Neja stared absentmindedly at her teacup.

Harald couldn't tell if she was avoiding his gaze or trying to suppress images of her late husband.

Maybe she had already had enough of his questions.

Her expression gave nothing away.

Her eyes were not windows offering a glimpse into her soul. They were more like an impenetrable wall of mist.

"May I ask a few more questions?"

Neja Lundberg nodded.

"What kind of person was Steinar?"

She took a deep breath and looked out at the nearly empty parking lot.

Two cars passed by on the road, and in the house next door, an elderly man started up a snowblower.

"What kind of person he was…" she repeated, almost whispering, a hint of sadness in her voice.

Harald nodded, even though she wasn't looking at him. And he wasn't sure if she was repeating his question or simply thinking out loud.

"He was a good man."

A brief smile crossed her face.

"What do you mean by a good man?"

Now she looked directly at Harald. He lifted his shoulders uncertainly.

"I suppose everyone sees that a little differently."

Neja gave a slight nod, then turned her gaze back outside.

"When I moved to Halvik back then, I was very lonely. Or rather, I *felt* lonely. I missed my family, my home, my old surroundings. My mother died young, so I only had my father and my sister. My father was always very strict with us.

"As a teenager, I couldn't wait to leave home and take control of my own life.

"But when I finally managed to separate myself from my hometown, I hadn't expected to miss it so much.

"As a young person, all you want is to leave—to move to a bigger city with more life. Clubs, bars, shopping centers. But later, when you're older and wiser, you realize that life isn't just about having fun."

She sighed, shook her head slightly, and took a sip of tea.

"After spending a few weeks in this sleepy little village, I realized that a young woman didn't have to be lonely here. The people in the village were so friendly, so open and interested.

"I went to church, to village festivals and meetings, and I met a lot of people I became friends with.

"It made the homesickness less painful, but I could never completely push it away.

"It was during that time that I met Steinar.

"He quickly realized that, despite all my new friends, I missed my hometown.

"He was understanding, compassionate.

"He wanted to create a home for me here.

"I fell in love with him, and not long after, I moved in with him.

"It was the house I still live in today.

"It had belonged to Steinar's parents.

"They died in a car accident down in Nordkjosbotn.

"Steinar inherited the house—but no money.

"We were happy, and early on, he promised me that he would show me the world.

"All the countries—America, Asia, maybe even New Zealand. He always read travel magazines, and every time he found something he liked, he would say, *Darling, we'll go there together one day*." She paused and took a deep breath.

Harald let Neja's words sink in. It sounded like a classic love story. A tall, strong man protecting a delicate, lonely woman, promising her the world.

"He always wanted children, right from the start," Neja continued. "But—well, that never happened. I struggled a lot to come to terms with it. I cried often, almost daily. Steinar didn't notice much of it. He worked more than ever. I was alone most of the time. And that didn't change much until the day he died."

She emptied her cup in one gulp, leaned back in her chair, and raised her eyebrows at Harald. It seemed as if she had finished her story and wanted to make that clear to him.

Harald, however, was undeterred and asked the next question.

"Did Steinar ever have conflicts with the Pettersen family?"

Neja Lundberg shook her head. "Not that I know of. But I was never there. At least, he never mentioned anything."

"Was there any rivalry among the fishermen in the village?"

"I wouldn't know. But I don't think so. I never heard anything like that."

"The evening Steinar went out with the Pettersen brothers—was he, how should I say... different?"

Neja furrowed her brow. "Different...?"

"I mean, did he behave differently than usual? Was he quiet, angry, thoughtful? Did he break his routine in any way?"

Neja let out a short laugh. "Quiet? He was always quiet. No difference there. And no, nothing unusual happened that evening. I only remember that Arne Pettersen called after dinner and asked Steinar to come to the harbour. An hour later, he was gone."

"Nobody could explain what had happened on that boat. Do you have any theories?"

She looked at him in surprise. "Me? No, no idea. Why would I?"

Harald shrugged. "It was just a thought."

"No, sorry. You're probably asking the wrong person. I don't know anything about boats—I avoid them. I get seasick easily."

"But surely people in the village talked a lot about the incident, didn't they? There must have been speculation, different theories."

"I didn't take part in village life much after the accident. I don't know anything about local gossip."

This woman is going to drive me insane, Harald thought.

He considered ending the interview.

It was hard to tell whether she was avoiding his questions or genuinely had no idea.

But he doubted that she knew so little about her late husband's work—after all, Steinar hadn't been working for a secret intelligence agency.

Then again, maybe she simply hadn't been interested.

Either way, he wasn't going to get much more out of her than what she had already said.

"I really appreciate you taking the time to speak with me. Thank you."

Neja nodded and forced a smile but said nothing.

"Are you staying here a while longer, or are you heading outside too?" Harald asked, standing up.

"I'll order another tea."

Out in the parking lot, Harald stood by his car and checked his watch.

It was just before eleven.

He wondered whether he should head to the Pettersens' house right away or wait until the afternoon.

A snowplough roared past, making an unbearable noise.

Out of the corner of his eye, Harald noticed that Neja was watching him from the window.

She wasn't smiling, didn't wave—she just stared at him.

Harald held her gaze for a moment, wondering what she was thinking.

She had seemed extremely melancholic and withdrawn. Of course, that could have been because they had been talking about her late husband.

Or maybe that was just how she was.

Not everyone goes through life with a smile—especially not those who have lost someone they loved.

Harald opened the driver's door, got behind the wheel, and drove away.

Chapter 16

Neja Lundberg watched as Harald Strøm stopped in front of his car and typed something into his phone. He stared at the display for a while before lowering it and gazing thoughtfully out at the fjord. She wished she could read his thoughts. From their conversation, she hadn't been able to discern his true motives for writing this story. He had given her a few reasons, but she doubted they were the truth. If there was one thing she knew, it was that journalists could not be trusted. You tell them one thing, and they write another.

The waitress brought a black tea, and Neja took a sip with pursed lips, burning her tongue. Cursing, she set the cup down again and watched as Harald got into his car and drove off. Even as she saw him leave, she knew this wouldn't be the last time she encountered that journalist. An inner voice whispered to her that this old story would catch up with her, forcing her to relive all the torment she had endured. It was her own fault. She should have turned the journalist away two days ago and sent him to hell. Now she wondered why she had gone through with it. She found no conclusive answer. The truth lay somewhere in her past—a past she did not want to revive. But that wasn't so easy. Some things never disappear, as if someone had locked the images of those memories in a drawer and thrown away the key.

Sometimes she wondered how her life would have turned out if she had stayed in Finnsnes. Would she have met a man there? Could she have worked as a legal secretary? Would she have been happier? Would her life have been simpler? Or would she have died there as an old spinster?

After a brief moment of thought, she concluded that she had done the right thing. She was happy with Steinar—she had loved him, and she still loved him. No journalist in the world would ever understand, let alone put into words, the love she felt for her husband. That love was unique—it always had been. It was all she had ever needed in her life.

She closed her eyes, took a deep breath, and returned her attention to her tea.

Chapter 17

Harald steered his car into a parking space near the church in Halvik and got out. An ancient, brown Volvo stood a little further back, and Harald wondered how such a wreck managed to move forward in winter in these latitudes.

He left his car where it was and strolled along a white garden fence that completely enclosed the church. Hundreds of icicles lined the church's roof edge; a brown chimney protruded from the roof, and just behind it, a small tower with a window rose into the sky. Below it was the entrance to the church.

The midday sun hung just above the mountains behind Halvik, casting its rays onto the fjord. Harald studied the cloud formations on the other side of the water. The peaks of the Lyngen Alps beneath them were partially shrouded, their rugged slopes resembled razor blades.

A few seagulls bobbed up and down on the waves, and far out, the distant ringing of a buoy echoed.

At the end of the fence, Harald stopped and let his gaze wander to the three gravestones of the fishermen who had perished. What would the three lads have to say if they could be brought back to life? Would they incriminate each other? Or had their deaths truly been the result of an unfortunate chain of events?

At the edge of his vision, Harald suddenly noticed a figure dressed in black, standing with arms crossed under the church's eaves, watching him. When their eyes met, the man moved and walked toward him. He wore no jacket, just a black shirt, black trousers, and brown leather boots. A white clerical collar peeked out at the base of his throat. His hair was a wild, tousled mess, as if he had just got out of bed. A round pair of glasses perched on his nose. He had a round, friendly-looking face, was impeccably shaved, and exuded the scent of aftershave.

As he stopped beside Harald, he put on a friendly smile. "Are you looking for something?" he asked in a hoarse voice.

"No, not really," Harald replied. "I just stopped for a moment to enjoy the view." He gestured out toward the fjord.

"Ah," the man said, following Harald's hand with his eyes. "You're not from around here."

Harald wondered whether that was a question or a statement. "Not directly from the village—no. I live in the city."

"I see. First time in Halvik?"

"No… not quite. But it's been a while."

The man nodded and extended his hand. "I'm the village pastor. Peder Sørensen."

"Nice to meet you. Harald Strøm."

"Are you here on a day trip, or do you plan to stay overnight, if you don't mind me asking?"

"I have the day off and wanted to enjoy the peace of nature."

"Peace…" The pastor twisted his mouth and nodded. "You'll find peace out here. That's what makes this place special."

"But it's quite remote."

The pastor shrugged. "You get used to it. I moved here from Trondheim a few decades ago, when I was still young. I wasn't made for city life. And out here, I hear God's words more clearly than in the noise of a city."

Harald briefly raised his eyebrows and nodded but didn't respond.

"Would you like to go inside the church?" the clergyman asked, making a welcoming gesture with his right hand.

"No, thank you. Churches aren't really my thing."

Peder looked at him with a mixture of amusement and mild incomprehension. "That's all right. You're still welcome inside."

"Thanks, but I'd rather stay out here."

"As you wish." The pastor gave him a broad smile.

Harald turned his gaze back toward the fjord, hoping that would put an end to the conversation. But the pastor showed no intention of leaving him alone.

A seagull swooped down near the shore and snatched something from the water's surface.

"Do you know the story of those three graves?" Harald asked, pointing toward the cemetery.

Peder Sørensen frowned. "Which graves?"

"Over there, the ones with the three dead fishermen."

The pastor nodded. "Oh, of course. Everyone here knows that story. Those are the graves of the Pettersen brothers and that of Steinar Lundberg."

"How well did you know them?"

"The Pettersen brothers or Steinar?"

"All three."

Peder's expression darkened. "I knew the Pettersen brothers when they were still little boys."

"And Steinar?"

"I knew him too."

Harald waited to see if the pastor would say more about the fishermen, but he just gazed out at the fjord in silence.

"Must have been tough... for the community, I mean."

Peder nodded thoughtfully, his eyes narrowing into slits. "Indeed," he said quietly, then slowly shook his head. "I remember the funeral well; I gave the sermon. Almost the entire village was there. Not everyone could fit inside the church—many had to endure the cold out here in the graveyard. I had never experienced anything like it before, and I haven't since. Thank God."

Harald looked up at the church and imagined the scene. A sorrowful image unfolded before his mind's eye: cloud-covered mountains, snowfall, freezing and grieving people. He hated funerals. Though he wasn't sure if "hate" was the right word for it.

Was one allowed to hate funerals?

Probably. After all, who actually enjoyed attending a funeral?

He turned back to the pastor. "Were you in the village when the storm hit the fjord back then?"

Peder raised his eyebrows. "Oh yes, I was. What a storm that was. It tore half the roof off my garage. There was quite a bit of storm damage in the village, if I remember correctly. I wasn't the only one affected."

"Strange, isn't it? That fishermen would head out in a storm like that?"

He shrugged. "I don't know. I have no experience with fishing. But I can't imagine the Pettersen brothers knowingly took a risk. They were holding fishing rods before they could even walk properly. They knew their trade, grew up here, and knew these waters and the weather like the back of their hands."

Harald nodded. "Which makes me wonder even more—how could three such experienced men go overboard in a storm? Something extraordinary must have happened."

"That's undisputed. But accidents do happen, even to experienced people."

"I'm aware of that. I just thought that maybe something other than the storm was responsible for their deaths."

Now the pastor looked at him with suspicion. "Why are you so interested in this accident?"

Harald thought for a moment before answering. "I'm a journalist with *iNord*," he said, handing him his card. "I'm revisiting the events of that time to write a more detailed story about them. One that sheds more light on the lives of the three fishermen. The coverage back then wasn't very detailed—or, to put it another way, it wasn't very compassionate. I think those men deserve to have their heroic work highlighted."

A long pause followed, during which Harald couldn't tell whether the pastor inwardly agreed with him or opposed the idea. His expression hadn't lost its skepticism. His eyes had narrowed into slits, his lips reduced to a thin line. He turned the business card over in his hand a few times before slipping it into his phone case. After half a minute, his facial features relaxed again, and he said flatly, "I don't think that's a good idea."

"And why not, if I may ask?"

"That would only reopen old wounds for the bereaved. Wounds that for some have never truly healed."

Harald considered whether now was the right time to mention his conversation with Neja Lundberg. He decided against it.

"I'm aware of that. But those affected are under no obligation to speak with me. They can decline without guilt."

Another long pause followed before Peder replied. "Even so, just the mere mention of the events could cause a relapse for some." He gazed out at the fjord again, his expression now thoughtful, his arms crossed over his chest. Nearly a minute passed before he began to speak.

"The weeks after the accident were difficult for our community. The grief was unbearable, creeping through the streets like a wild beast searching for prey. No one engaged in idle chatter at the village store, greetings on the pavement were brief, the café was barely frequented, the school was closed for three days. A tragedy of this magnitude affects nearly everyone in a village, whether they were close friends with the victims or not. I had to provide a lot of grief counselling during that time. For some, their faith was put to the test, but I was able to guide lost souls toward salvation, to illuminate the path they needed to follow to understand God's will. That took a long time, believe me." He took a deep breath before continuing.

"I accompanied the victims' families for a long time. I led them through dark valleys and kept them from falling into the abyss. Those were long and difficult conversations." He paused briefly before continuing. "I can't stop you from pursuing your story—we live in a free country. But I ask you to let it rest. The village has already suffered enough. The people here don't want to be reminded of the tragedy, least of all the victims' families. Your story won't bring anything good—it will only stir up unrest in this place."

He looked Harald directly in the eye, his gaze flashing. "And no one here wants that."

His last words had been spoken with emphasis, almost threateningly. Harald furrowed his brow and, for a moment, didn't know how to respond. He held the pastor's gaze, searching for words that wouldn't come. A strange feeling crept over him, a sort of premonition he couldn't quite decipher.

After a few seconds of silence, Harald finally said, "I have no intention of influencing anyone. Everyone is free to decide whether they want to speak with me or not."

Peder sighed. "Once again, I'm asking you—leave it alone. This won't end well."

"I'm sorry, Pastor Sørensen. But this is my job. This isn't my first time working on a story like this, and I can put myself in people's shoes. I understand their grief. But I've also found that, after a few years, some bereaved people actually want to talk about their loss. They've learned to cope with it."

"Pfff…" The pastor let out a dry laugh. "You don't even believe that yourself."

Harald shrugged. "Yes, I do."

Peder nodded briefly, then turned to leave. "Do whatever you want. But believe me, you won't be welcomed with open arms."

With that, he stomped off, crossed the front lawn, got into his car, and drove away.

Harald watched him until he disappeared around a bend in the road. He had met many extraordinary people and had experienced strange moments in his career, and most of the time, he handled them well. But the sudden turn in his conversation with Peder Sørensen had caught him off guard.

Was the pastor simply trying to protect the villagers from emotional distress? Or was there more to it?

Did he perhaps know something that was better left hidden?

As a pastor, he must have known more than a few secrets about his congregation.

Chapter 18

Peder Sørensen steered his car through Halvik, trying to get home as quickly as possible. His conversation with that journalist had unsettled him, and right now, he needed a drink.

His house, an ancient structure, lay just outside the village near the water. It was a dark brown – almost black – with red window frames and a grass roof. In the shed in front of the house, he grabbed a few logs and lit a fire in the fireplace. Then he snatched the whiskey bottle and a glass and sat down in a rocking-chair near the open hearth.

The living room was as sparsely furnished as the other two rooms. Only the essentials were there—a sofa, a table with two chairs, a cupboard, no television. Since childhood, Peder had learned to get by with little, and he had remained true to that lifestyle. His father had always told him: *Be content with what you have, and you will be happier.*

As a boy, he hadn't always understood his father's words. Especially not when his friends at school showed off their newest toys after Christmas, while all he had to present was a new sweater or a new pair of shoes. He had often been laughed at for it, and his circle of friends had remained small. His mother had died early, and his father had tried to support him and his two brothers with odd jobs — managing more poorly than well.

But what did it matter now? He had his church, he had God, he had his prayers. That was all that counted.

The first sip was always the best. He closed his eyes and relished the warm feeling in his stomach and the slight burn in his throat. Leaning his head back, he started rocking gently in his chair. After a minute, he allowed himself a second sip and thought about the conversation he had had with Harald Strøm. A queasy feeling settled in his stomach, and he knew it wasn't just the alcohol. He knew this feeling all too well. And he didn't like it.

He had made peace with the boating accident. And he wasn't the only one. If that journalist started going around the village asking uncomfortable questions, it could have serious consequences. Some truths were not meant to come to light. And he, of all people, knew that.

Again, he raised the glass to his lips, sipping the brown liquid as he stared into the fire. He saw the funeral before him, the desperate looks of the mourners. It had taken all his strength to meet their eyes. With one exception. With her, he had never struggled — not even now. But he could not judge her — that would have to be left to God. Just as it would with himself.

But that time had not yet come. First, he needed to speak with her, warn her, and keep her from making a mistake.

He paused in his thoughts, considering whether that journalist might even be part of God's plan. That the punishment for the past had now arrived, and the price had to be paid. For too long, everything had gone smoothly, for too long, secrets had been kept—secrets too terrible to ever be revealed. Now, it seemed, the time of peace and quiet had run out.

He had always dreaded this moment—like the devil dreads holy water.

Peder turned his head and searched for his phone. It lay on the dresser next to the front door. For a long moment, he stared at it, brooding, accompanied by dark thoughts.

After one last sip, he stood up, grabbed the phone, and searched his contacts for her name.

Chapter 19

After his conversation with the pastor, Harald had got into his car and turned the bullet points of his notes into full sentences. Just as he finished, his phone rang. It was his boss, Lars Kallestad, wanting to know what story he was working on.

In brief terms, Harald explained that he was in Halvik, investigating the boating accident. Along the way, he had come across some inconsistencies that now demanded his attention.

"What kind of inconsistencies?" Lars asked.

Damn it, Harald thought. What was he supposed to say now? He had nothing more than a gut feeling, but he couldn't tell that to this idiot—otherwise, he might as well bury his story right here and now.

"Well," Harald said after a moment's hesitation, "one of the villagers told me that there were rumours back then suggesting the accident might not have been an accident at all. I followed up on that and have since learned that one of the deceased fishermen, Steinar Lundberg, supposedly had conflicts with the other fishermen from time to time. Apparently, he was jealous of their money."

For a moment, there was silence on the line. Harald could only hear Lars breathing.

"Not much to go on, don't you think?" Lars commented in his usual smug tone.

"I've had even less to go on in past stories and still ended up hitting the jackpot."

Silence again. Then: "How long do you expect the investigation to take?"

What a stupid question, Harald thought. Who could possibly know that? He should know better.

"I can't assess that at this point," Harald answered, swallowing his rising irritation. "I estimate that within two weeks, I'll have gathered enough information to form a picture."

"I don't need a picture, I need a story."

No kidding, you moron he thought. "And you'll get one."

A sigh on the other end of the line. "Fine," Lars said. "But I need results soon."

Harald promised what his boss wanted to hear and hung up.

Annoyed, he put away his notebook and felt a gnawing hunger. He hadn't brought anything to eat, and the village only had one café. If he planned to visit the Pettersens later, he needed to eat something first. So, he headed back to the café, and an hour later, with a full stomach, he got back into his car, entered the Pettersens' address into the navigation system, and drove off.

There were significantly more people out and about now. Some were walking their dogs, others were skiing on cross-country trails, and children were sliding down piles of snow left by the plows. The weather was nice, the few clouds had cleared, and a pale sky allowed the last rays of sunlight to fall over the fjord. In Halvik, the already short days were even shorter. The mountain range behind the village blocked direct sunlight as early as the afternoon — another reason Harald could never live here. His house was on a west-facing slope, giving him a front-row seat for winter sunsets. In summer, however, he had nearly twenty hours of sunlight a day — weather permitting.

He turned onto Skifervegen and looked for house number 26. After a few meters, a blue house with white window frames appeared on the left. Next to the garage, perched on tall wooden beams, sat a covered boat. The postbox read *J. + A. Pettersen.*

He parked in front of the house and noticed that the garage door was open — and the garage was empty. Not a good sign. Lights were on in some of the windows, but that didn't mean anything. In Norway, lights in homes burned day and night during the winter.

The Pettersens' house was impressively large. It had three floors, each with multiple windows, and a veranda that stretched from the south to the east and north sides.

The fishing business must be lucrative for the Pettersens, Harald thought as he climbed the three steps to the veranda. The white front door had a porthole in the upper half, with a white curtain hanging behind it. Harald rang the doorbell. While he waited for a response, he examined the surrounding houses. Compared to the Pettersens' home, they looked like garden sheds.

A minute passed, and no one answered the door. He rang the bell a second time, but again, nothing happened. Sighing, he retreated, got back into his car, and considered his options. Calling wasn't an option—he didn't have their phone number. Waiting here and hoping they'd return soon wasn't much better; that could take hours.

That left only one choice—driving home and coming back tomorrow. Two long drives he wasn't particularly eager for.

Just then, he remembered the sign in front of the restaurant that read: *Rooms available.* Should he rent a room for the night?

Why not? If he stayed, he could check in on the Pettersens again after dinner. Besides, he always kept an emergency overnight kit in his boot for situations like this.

Throwing one last glance at the Pettersens' house, he started the engine and drove back to Café Kystenshuset. When he entered the restaurant, he wasn't sure at first whether it was even open. None of the tables were occupied, and there was no sign of the staff.

"Hello!" he called out as he walked up to the counter.

"I'll be right there," came the reply from the kitchen behind the bar.

A minute later, a woman with teased-up hair and square glasses appeared. "What can I get you?" she asked in a deep voice, one that suggested a long history of heavy smoking.

"I'd like a room."

She hesitated for a moment, studying Harald before reaching into a drawer and pulling out a key. "We only have two, but both are available. You can take the one on the left. Through that door, up the stairs. Breakfast is served from six o'clock."

After checking into his room and sending Runi a text message to let her know he'd be staying in Halvik for the night, he lay down on the bed and stared at the ceiling. After a while, he closed his eyes and tried to doze off. But after ten minutes, he gave up. His conversation with the pastor wouldn't leave him alone. Again and again, he saw the clergyman's reaction before him—the way he had resisted Harald's plans, trying, more or less, to dissuade him. It was odd, to say the least. Could the pastor know something that no one else was supposed to find out? Or was he really just trying to preserve peace in the village?

Both were possible. The former, perhaps, even more likely.

Harald glanced around the room. It wasn't very large. A double bed, a wardrobe, a small table with two chairs, and two windows facing the fjord and the Lyngen Alps. The green wallpaper was decorated with small white flowers. A thick rug lay in front of the bathroom door; the bathroom itself was small but perfectly sufficient.

His phone vibrated, making him jolt. It was his father.

For a moment, he considered ignoring the call. He wasn't in the mood for another argument. But the phone kept buzzing relentlessly, and in the end, Harald gave in and picked up.

"Why does it always take you so damn long to answer?" his father barked into the receiver.

"A good day to you too, Dad," Harald replied.

A grumpy grunt came in response. "When are you finally getting me out of this hellhole?"

"It's not a hellhole, Dad."

"What the hell do you know? Are you here or am I?"

"You are, Dad."

"There you go. I can't stand it here. I won't let them boss me around all day."

"They're only trying to help. You need assistance with daily tasks, and you need to accept that."

"The hell I do! Who do you think you are?"

Harald sighed. He should have ignored the call.

"Hello? Are you still there?"

"Yes, Dad, I'm still here."

"Well?"

"Well, what?"

"When are you picking me up?"

"I'm not picking you up, Dad."

"Then I'll just leave on my own."

"Go ahead."

Harald knew his father could barely make it to his room door, let alone out onto the street.

The dial tone buzzed in his ear. His father had hung up.

Annoyed, Harald tossed his phone aside and stared back at the ceiling.

This couldn't go on. But what choice did he have? He couldn't just leave his father to fend for himself. The old man would take out his frustration on the poor nurses and carers. Harald wanted to prevent that, even though he was sure the staff there had dealt with worse.

It was maddening. Thinking about how his father had treated him like dirt his entire life and now expected him to be there for him—it enraged Harald. Once again, he wished his mother were still alive. If only she were here, so much would have been different. She had deserved a longer life. He would have taken her in without hesitation.

He turned onto his side and gazed at the now nearly dark sky outside the window. His eyelids grew heavy, and slowly, the room and thoughts of his father faded away.

When he woke up three hours later, his mouth felt like a desert. He got up, stumbled into the bathroom, and drank greedily, directly from the tap. Then he returned to the room and checked the time. It was half past five. A slight hunger set in.

Yawning, he walked to the window and looked out into the darkness. The fjord's water shimmered under the moonlight at the foot of the Lyngen Alps. A few scattered lights on the other side of the fjord were the only signs of civilization. In that moment, Harald was glad he lived in the city. Out here, it was simply too quiet for him. He appreciated peace, but this was too much. The isolation, especially during the polar night, would be suffocating.

He turned away from the window, picked up his phone from the bedside table, and sent his wife a message, letting her know he was heading out for dinner.

Fifteen minutes later, he was seated by the window in the restaurant, eating cod with a tomato salad. Four other guests had found their way to the restaurant—a group of three chatty women and an old man noisily slurping soup. Every now and then, the man would glance up and peer at Harald over the rim of his bowl, his expression a mix of *Who are you, stranger?* and *Stop staring at me while I eat.*

Harald wondered if this old man ate here every night. Maybe he lived alone, had already buried his wife, and now had to manage the household by himself. Did he have children who suffered under his bad temper? Or was he grateful for their help?

Harald finished his dinner, paid, and stepped out into the carpark. The air was icy, and he had to button his jacket all the way up. A harsh wind blew in from the water, making the cold feel even more biting.

He left the carpark heading south, looking for a path down to the water. A car drove past, kicking up snow, and on the opposite pavement, a man walking his dog crossed his path. Other than that, the place seemed deserted. Above him, a sea of stars sparkled, and a faint shimmer of the northern lights stretched from east to west. Occasionally, the glow would intensify, dancing in shades of pink and violet around the stars, only to fade again.

Near a barn, he turned onto a narrow footpath that soon led him to the gently lapping water. A trail ran along the shore, disappearing into the darkness around a bend. Harald followed it, keeping an eye out for boats, but saw none.

After about thirty meters, the path ended abruptly next to a half-collapsed boathouse, where an equally old-looking boat swayed in the water. Just behind the boathouse stood an aging house, its front side perched on stilts over the water. A single window was lit; the rest of the house was shrouded in darkness.

Harald shone his flashlight on the weathered wooden stilts and wondered if the residents weren't afraid of one day plunging into the water along with their home.

At that moment, he heard footsteps crunching in the snow and flinched. Not far from where he stood, he noticed a man moving toward the small house in a hunched posture, taking a drag from a cigarette. In the glow of the streetlights, Harald recognized him—the older man who had been noisily slurping soup at the restaurant earlier.

Just before reaching the house, the man stopped and gazed out over the dark fjord. Every now and then, the ember of his cigarette flared up, followed by a small cloud of smoke. When he finished smoking, he flicked the cigarette to the ground, and as if he had been aware of Harald's presence the entire time, he suddenly turned around, locked eyes with him for a few seconds, then disappeared into the house.

Odd fellow, Harald thought. But he probably knew a few stories about the village. Then again, judging by his grumpy expression, he likely wouldn't be willing to share them.

Harald turned away from the house and trudged through the deep snow back to the road. It was getting colder by the minute. The north wind swept through the village, brushing against his face like tiny razor blades. The stars had vanished, the northern lights were gone, and instead, the first snowflakes began to fall. Within minutes, the entire area was engulfed in a full snowstorm.

Harald debated whether to continue walking or head back to his warm room. He decided to postpone the conversation with the Pettersens until tomorrow. Warmth won out.

As he neared the restaurant carpark, he noticed a man and a woman engaged in a heated conversation. The man appeared calm, while the woman gestured wildly as she spoke, as if swatting away invisible flies. Harald stepped behind a pine tree, watching the scene from cover.

Despite the overall silence, he couldn't quite make out what they were arguing about. The man spoke as quietly as possible, while the woman, though louder, spoke so rapidly that her words blurred together. The only phrase Harald could make out from her was: *Well, now you've got what you wanted.*

After another rapid-fire string of words from the woman, the man turned away, got into a car, and sped off.

As the vehicle passed Harald, he had no doubt—it was Peder Sørensen, the pastor.

The woman also got into a car and drove off in the opposite direction. Harald was certain that the agitated woman was Neja Lundberg.

Chapter 20

The next morning, Harald woke up with a headache. He had slept poorly, dreaming a lot and tossing and turning throughout the night. He didn't know why—after all, it was as quiet as a coffin here. He should have slept like a baby.

The argument between the pastor and Neja Lundberg from the night before came back to him.

What the hell had that been about? What could the two of them possibly have to argue about?

Sighing, he picked up his phone from the bedside table, sent a good morning message to Runi, and briefly thought about how nice it would be to wake up next to her. She could have massaged his temples, and afterward, they might have had coffee together—maybe on the balcony, like they always did in the summer.

Still drowsy, he shuffled to the window and looked outside. The fjord lay almost mirror-like between Halvik and the Lyngen Alps. The sky was cloudless, a blend of pale blue and salmon pink. Any painter would have immediately pulled out a canvas and started capturing the scene.

After getting dressed, Harald went downstairs to the restaurant and ordered a small breakfast: an omelet, two slices of toast, and coffee. However, the waitress didn't have any painkillers to offer.

Harald rubbed his temples and thought about the day ahead. If the Pettersens weren't home, he would have to leave empty-handed, which wouldn't be good for the development of his story. His boss wouldn't let up, constantly checking in for progress. If he didn't deliver something *sensational*, he'd be sidelined — of that, he was sure.

But he wasn't there yet. And if things got tricky, he could always feed his boss a little white lie to buy some time.

The coffee seemed to ease his headache a little, so he ordered a second cup. After finishing breakfast, he left the restaurant and paused outside the building. The sun hadn't yet risen above the mountain peaks behind the village, and Harald felt as though his nose was about to freeze . He got into his car and drove off.

A few minutes later, he parked in front of the Pettersens' house once again. The garage door was open, and a light was on inside.

As he stepped out, a man appeared from behind a car with its hood open inside the garage. He wore a blue thermal suit, a thick wool hat, but no gloves. He was tall, broad-shouldered, with a beard, and had a firm but friendly gaze. In his hands, he held an oil-stained rag, which he used to wipe his fingers.

"Good day," he said with a questioning expression.

"Good morning. Are you John Pettersen?"

"That's me."

"Excellent. My name is Harald Strøm. I'm a journalist with *iNord*." He extended his hand.

John Pettersen first glanced at his own dirty hands before shaking Harald's. "What can I do for you?" he asked.

"Well, here's the thing," Harald began. "As I mentioned, I'm a journalist, and I'm working on a story from 2005."

At the mention of the year, John Pettersen flinched slightly.

"As you can probably guess, it's about the accident involving your two sons. A few days ago, I came across their story when I happened to discover their graves down at the cemetery." Harald paused briefly, giving John a chance to respond, but the man only furrowed his brow and remained silent. So Harald continued, explaining his intentions.

The lines on John Pettersen's forehead deepened. Then he tossed the rag back into the garage and asked, "You want to retell the story?"

"Maybe I should put it differently," Harald replied. "I don't want to rewrite it—I want to tell it in more detail, with more depth and emotion. The newspaper reports back then were very matter-of-fact. They didn't pay proper tribute to the victims or the hard work they did. People don't realize the risks you all take every day in your line of work. With my story, I want to shed light on that ignorance."

John pressed his lips together and studied him for almost twenty seconds before finally gesturing toward the house. "Shall we continue inside?"

A minute later, Harald was sitting at the kitchen table, directly in front of a large window with a view of the fjord and the mountains. John disappeared down the hallway, and soon after, voices could be heard from the upper floor.

Harald took in his surroundings. The kitchen was spacious, with a central island, white cabinets, and a dining table as large as an SUV. On the back wall hung a framed photo of two young men posing in front of a fishing boat, grinning at the camera. They looked very similar. The older-looking one had a chiseled face, tousled hair, and stubble. His smile seemed forced. His younger brother, on the other hand, beamed with ease and joy. His bright eyes and equally tousled hair made him look like an *Adonis*.

The photo next to it showed a bride and groom in front of the village church. The younger of the two brothers— the Adonis—held a woman dressed in white in his arms. Her radiant smile expressed pure bliss. With her long, wavy hair, perfect white teeth, and stunning wedding dress, she looked like an elf straight out of *The Lord of the Rings*.

"Can I get you a coffee?"

Harald flinched as John reentered the kitchen and walked over to the coffee machine.

"That would be nice," Harald replied. "Are those your sons?" he asked, pointing at the framed photos.

John nodded as he fiddled with the coffee machine. "They *were*, yes."

"Strong-looking boys," Harald remarked.

"Yes, they were."

The coffee machine hummed to life, and Harald reached for his notebook. Suddenly, he heard footsteps descending the stairs, and moments later, a woman appeared. She was barely over one meter fifty, with short, grey-black hair, glasses, and a round face with deep lines on each cheek. She wore grey jeans and a thick wool sweater, despite the warmth in the house—too warm for Harald's taste.

In her features, he could see a resemblance to the older of the two brothers—the same facial structure, the same eyes. She studied him curiously but with a friendly smile.

"This is Harald Strøm," John said to her. "He's a reporter for *iNord* and wants to retell our sons' story. This is Anne, my wife."

The smile vanished from Anne's face in an instant, replaced by an expression of shock. Her gaze flickered between Harald and her husband. She opened her mouth briefly, as if she wanted to say something, but then closed it again. She swallowed awkwardly and sat down at the head of the table.

"The story of our sons?" she asked, directing the question at Harald.

Harald explained his intentions again, emphasizing that he wasn't writing a sensationalist piece but rather wanted to honour their sons' lives and pay respect to their untimely deaths. He spoke calmly and compassionately, fully aware that he was treading on thin ice.

Anne listened, glanced briefly at her husband, then raised her eyebrows when Harald finished speaking. "Well, I'm not sure that's a good idea," she said, folding her hands in her lap.

"I completely understand your skepticism," Harald replied. "I'd likely feel the same way. I have no intention of reopening the pain of the past—absolutely not. I would even let you review my article before publication so you could check for any inaccuracies or misrepresentations. Naturally, I would correct anything necessary."

Anne Pettersen looked at her husband with raised eyebrows. John shrugged and placed three cups of coffee on the table. Anne took a sip, closed her eyes for a brief moment, and after some thought, said, "Alright. We'll try to answer your questions."

Harald thanked them and opened his notebook. "John, if I'm correct, you're still working in the fishing industry?"

"Yes, I am."

"Have you been doing this since childhood?"

"Yes. My father was a fisherman, too. We own a processing facility down by the water. That's where we handle the fish before selling them. Well, not all the fish— some are sold unprocessed."

"I see. And you're the sole owner of the facility?"

"Yes."

"What about the other fishermen? Do they have their own stations where they process their catch?"

"No, not exactly. Some of them use my facility and pay a small fee for it. But there aren't many fishermen here—only five, including myself."

Harald nodded, jotting down notes. "How do the fishermen get along?"

"What do you mean?"

"Do conflicts ever arise?"

"Well, I wouldn't call them conflicts. Of course, there have been disagreements, but nothing serious. Anywhere people work, mistakes happen—it's the same everywhere."

"That's true."

Harald glanced briefly at Anne. She now had her hands folded on the table and was watching him with sad eyes. He had already noticed their colour before—they reminded him of the crystal-clear blue coves of Sommarøy.

"Can you tell me what happened on the day of the accident? How did the day start? What were your sons doing? Who did they meet?"

John took a sip of coffee and leaned back. "The boys weren't living at home with us anymore at that time. Arne had moved out three years earlier, Linus two years after that. I—or rather, *we*," he gestured toward his wife, "don't know exactly what they did during the day. But since it was a regular workday, we assume Linus was at his carpentry workshop or out on a job somewhere, and Arne was out fishing at sea. But like I said, we can't say for sure."

Harald noted down John's response before moving to his next question. "But they both lived in the village?"

"Yes."

"Did they each have their own house?"

"No." This time, Anne answered. "My father had to move into a nursing home, so he let Linus rent his house."

Harald furrowed his brow. "And Arne?"

John sighed. "Arne wasn't a workhorse like Linus. He worked when he wanted to—when money was running low. Of course, he didn't earn much from fishing... or rather, he didn't *want* to earn much. What he had was enough for him. He was different from Linus, as brothers often are. Arne would disappear for weeks at a time, travelling around the country, enjoying life, enjoying his freedom. And when he needed money, he'd come back and work again. He had no interest in renting or owning an entire house. He didn't care about possessions. But eventually, he moved into the basement apartment of Linus' house and paid Linus and Jonna a small share of the rent."

Harald perked up. "Jonna?"

"Jonna was Linus' wife," Anne explained.

"Ah." Harald jotted down the name, then glanced briefly at the beautiful woman in the wedding photo. "Was Arne married as well?"

John snorted briefly, smiling as he did. "Arne had girlfriends from time to time, but never anything serious. Not like Linus and Jonna."

"I see. Were Linus and Jonna together for a long time?"

Anne nodded. "Since school."

Harald raised his eyebrows in surprise.

"A remarkable love story," Anne added. "No one believed their high school romance would last. I mean, where does that happen? Maybe on TV. But in real life?" She smiled and shook her head wistfully. "They proved everyone wrong. They even got married." She gestured toward the framed photo.

"When was that?"

"2004."

"Did they have children?"

At this question, the couple exchanged glances, and Harald sensed hesitation in their expressions. An uneasy feeling crept over him.

After a brief pause, Anne leaned forward, resting her elbows on the table. "Jonna had a miscarriage."

Harald's eyes widened, and he looked awkwardly from Anne to John and back again. "I'm so sorry."

"For Linus, it was like his world collapsed," Anne continued. "They had been so excited, and then... that. After that, nothing was ever the same."

"But they stayed together?"

Anne nodded. "They did. They helped each other through that dark time. They were always there for each other—always. Even as children. I remember once when Linus caught pneumonia again. He had to go to the hospital. Jonna went with him and didn't leave his side for an entire week. She didn't even go to school." Anne smiled at the memory and took a deep breath. "After Jonna's miscarriage, though, John and I noticed that something between them had changed. We had the feeling that something had happened between them, something unrelated to the baby. But that was just our impression. They never mentioned anything, but as parents, you develop a sixth sense for these things. Jonna was—or is—like a daughter to us. You notice even the smallest change. Normally, she was cheerful, talkative, always ready to help. But suddenly, she became distant, didn't visit as often, and when she did, she was quiet. Linus, too, seemed lost in thought all the time, often in a bad mood. We couldn't explain it. We tried several times to talk to him about it, but he always brushed us off, insisted that everything was fine—that the miscarriage had changed him—and asked us to leave him alone. So, we did." Anne sighed. "Today, I wish I had been able to get him to talk."

"I'm sure you did everything you could to reach him. Sometimes, people just don't want to talk about their problems, no matter who tries to get through to them. You end up hitting a brick wall."

Anne shrugged. "Maybe you're right. But that feeling—that we didn't do enough—will probably never go away."

A long pause followed. Harald mulled over his next question, but he worried that he was approaching the couple's breaking point.

"What exactly do you intend to publish in this story?" John suddenly asked. "These are intimate details about our family's life."

Harald set his pen down, searching for the right answer. If he was being honest, he didn't know. He wasn't even sure yet what he wanted to write—or, more importantly, whether he *could* write anything at all.

"At this point, it's hard to say," he admitted. "As I mentioned, you'll be able to read the article before it's published. If there's anything in it that you're not comfortable with, I'll remove it, of course. I don't want my story to hurt anyone. And ultimately, the final decision lies with the editor-in-chief. If he doesn't like the piece, it won't get printed."

John and Anne exchanged a brief glance. John shrugged, and Anne turned back to Harald, giving him the faintest nod.

Harald exhaled inwardly and continued. "If I understood you correctly, Arne was a fisherman as well—like you, John."

John nodded.

"Did you always go out together?"

"No. Sometimes I went out alone, sometimes with Arne, sometimes with another fisherman. Arne didn't have his own boat. But since I wasn't out every single day, he would take my place when needed. I own three boats. When it was just a small catch, Arne usually took the smallest of the three."

"I see," Harald said. "And Linus—he never went out with you?"

"Oh, he did. But he was a carpenter—he had his own work. He only joined when we were short-handed. As kids, though, they were out with me all the time. You could say they grew up on the boat."

"On the day of the accident, did Arne go out to sea with Linus and Steinar alone?"

John nodded, while Anne inhaled sharply through her nose.

"Is it common to go out after dinner?"

"Common…? Well, yes, it's not unusual. You can fish at night, too. But that evening wasn't about fishing. A severe storm had been forecast, and they went out to secure the nets."

Harald made a note, realizing that this matched what he had already heard. "But you didn't go out with them that night."

Anne lowered her gaze, and John did the same. Harald felt his mouth go dry.

"No," John replied, clearing his throat uncomfortably. "I had already spent the entire day at sea, and I was exhausted. Plus, I had a cut on my right hand, so I could barely grip a rope. I wouldn't have been much help."

Anne Pettersen placed a hand on her husband's arm and gave it a gentle squeeze.

Harald could see that they were reliving the minutes and hours of that evening, and suddenly, he felt bad. "So Steinar Lundberg stepped in for you that night?"

John nodded silently.

"What kind of person was Steinar?"

John studied him for a moment before answering. "Steinar was, by and large, a good guy. A quiet fellow who did his job well and reliably. I couldn't say anything bad about him, except that he sometimes drank too much. Once, I had to send him home, but that only happened once. As for what Steinar did outside of fishing, I can't say. You'd have to ask Neja, his widow."

"I already have."

"Then why are you asking us what kind of person Steinar Lundberg was?"

"Because it's always better to have multiple perspectives on someone. Neja described Steinar to me, but those are the words of a grieving widow. An outsider might have seen him completely differently."

"I didn't like him much," Anne suddenly interjected, surprising Harald. John, however, didn't react to his wife's contrasting opinion.

"And why not, if I may ask?"

Anne shot her husband a scrutinizing look before answering. "I can't say exactly. I didn't know him very well. I only saw him occasionally at the village store, in church, or when he was near our boat. I didn't find him particularly friendly or approachable. He always greeted people just barely, mumbling his words so that you could hardly understand him. But what bothered me the most was his gaze. It was cold, piercing, as if he saw everyone as an enemy."

"Oh, come on, dear, it wasn't *that* bad," John chuckled, shaking his head.

"Well, *I* felt that way. Don't laugh at me." She gave him a light slap on the back of the head. "Maybe you just didn't notice. You men don't pick up on those kinds of things. We women have a more sensitive intuition."

John winked at Harald and rolled his eyes. Harald didn't dare wink back—he didn't want to offend Anne.

"Was he unpopular in the village?" Harald asked instead.

She shrugged. "There were certainly people who didn't like him. When he was in the store, not many talked to him, which is unusual for a small village like this."

"He was a man who liked to keep to himself," John added. "He didn't interfere in other people's business and lived his own life. There's nothing wrong with that. Sure, he was quiet and minded his own affairs, but on the boat, he was a great help, and that was all that mattered to me."

"So it wasn't unusual for your sons to go out to sea with Steinar?" Harald continued.

"No, not at all," John replied. "Steinar was always there when we needed help."

Next, Harald asked the couple if they had any theories about what might have gone wrong aboard the *Malini*.

Anne shrugged sadly and looked at her husband. John sighed softly, took a sip of coffee, then set his cup back on the table. He leaned back in his chair and crossed his arms over his chest. "It is—or was—difficult to speculate. I've been out at sea in bad weather often enough. You learn how to handle it. The three of them were experienced enough to stay calm in difficult situations. Steinar, in particular, was fearless—nothing rattled him easily. I can only imagine that a strong wave tilted the boat so violently that they were washed overboard and couldn't make it back. Or maybe one of them fell in, and the others drowned trying to save him. I really can't think of any other explanation."

"Don't you wear life jackets in storms like that?"

John raised his eyebrows. "That's up to each person. My boys usually wore one. But when you're constantly moving around on deck, carrying crates, hauling in nets, and handling a gaff, a life jacket can get in the way. I don't always wear one myself."

Harald nodded understandingly and jotted down a note. "Could it be that there were no life jackets on board at all?"

John shook his head firmly. "Absolutely not. Not on my boats."

A long silence followed. Harald flipped through his notebook, while John and Anne sat quietly at the table. The coffee machine switched off, breaking the uncomfortable stillness in the kitchen.

"But only Arne and Linus were found," Harald eventually said, resuming the conversation. "Steinar's body never turned up."

"Steinar's body was probably carried out into the open sea. All we can do is speculate."

"And the boat was found the next morning?" Harald already knew the answer to this question, but it was always good to have information confirmed by multiple sources.

"Yes," Anne replied. "Ronald Thoresen found it. It had washed ashore south of the village."

The couple's account matched everything he had heard or read so far. No inconsistencies, no obvious lies, no cover-ups. He felt a slight knot in his stomach, the kind that came from the realization that he might be overinterpreting things—making a mountain out of a molehill.

Most likely, he was chasing a ghost, and once again, he wouldn't be able to deliver a solid story to his boss. He could already picture Lars' bloated, puffy face as he skimmed through his report with a bored expression, raising his eyebrows now and then in a way that made it clear—*this story is going nowhere.*

"So, who else do you plan to talk to?" John asked, pulling Harald out of his dark thoughts.

Harald thought for a moment before answering. He wasn't sure how much of his strategy he wanted to share with the Pettersens. "I'm not entirely sure yet; definitely with the harbour-master. But I doubt he'll have much to tell me." Harald leaned back in his chair and crossed his arms over his chest. "Would it be possible for me to speak with Linus' widow, Jonna?"

John and Anne exchanged a brief glance. Anne pursed her lips but then nodded. "I think so."

"Does she still live here?"

"She does. At the northern end of the village. She lives there with her two children and her second husband. But I can't promise she'll be willing to talk. Linus' death was the end of the world for her, as you can probably imagine."

Anne took a deep breath and ran a hand over her face. "On the day we buried our boys, Jonna and I held each other for a long time. She didn't want to let me go. When we finally pulled away, we looked deep into each other's eyes, and in that moment, I knew I wouldn't see her again for a very long time. The pain was too deep, and everything here was a reminder of Linus. She needed to heal, and those memories wouldn't have helped her. And that's exactly what happened. Jonna may have visited once or twice after that, but only briefly, and then she stayed away. We understood. It wasn't easy for us either, seeing Jonna—everything reminded us of our boys."

She paused briefly to collect herself.

"Today, after all these years, we see each other again. The wounds will never fully heal, but at least we can look each other in the eye without breaking down in tears."

Harald nodded understandingly and looked out the window. Then he said, "I understand your concern. Of course, I won't pressure Jonna into speaking with me. If she doesn't want to talk, that's her right, and I'll respect that."

Anne smiled and wrote down Jonna's address for him. Afterward, Harald put away his notebook and thanked the couple for taking the time to speak to him.

As he stepped outside, he noticed someone hastily moving away from the Pettersens' house, disappearing in the direction of the main road. The person was dressed entirely in black, and he was certain he had seen a white collar at the base of their neck.

Chapter 21

With trembling hands, Jonna Olsen placed her phone on the dresser and stared out the window through a film of tears. The call had caught her off guard, and now she needed to calm herself down.

You don't have to do this, Anne had told her.

No, she really didn't have to. For years, she had spoken about Linus only with John and Anne. A stranger wouldn't understand her pain, let alone be able to grasp Linus' essence, no matter how well she described him. A person couldn't simply be described. Not just with words, anyway. So what could a journalist possibly achieve with such a report?

Nothing—for her, at least.

For the readers—yes, for the readers, it would be a story worth reading. Of that, she was certain. But this wasn't about the readers. It was about the end of a long, dark tunnel she had been following since 2005, with the light at its exit visible only as a tiny speck in the far distance.

What would such a conversation mean for her?

A setback? A summoning of painful memories?

How would she react if she suddenly saw her own story in the newspaper? The story of Linus and Jonna, whose love endured to this day—if only in the secret corners of her heart.

So much had happened back then—things she wanted to forget, but couldn't. The beautiful memories, on the other hand, lingered far too briefly in the images of her mind, mostly existing only as faded dreams.

She saw the thirteen-year-old girl standing by the fjord, searching the water for answers, for a signpost, for a swift end. For a helping hand to pull her out of the swamp, out of this endless odyssey and the shame. That was the worst of all—the shame. It paralyzed you, impaired your life, and prevented you from doing the right thing. That is, if you even knew what the right thing was. And honestly, who always did the right thing?

No one. And certainly not her.

As a young girl, you have no idea about life, about right or wrong. Adults tell you what is proper and what isn't. As a child, you have no choice but to trust and listen. But she had never had that trust. Not until she met Linus and his family. Only then did she understand what trust truly meant. Linus showed her, and he sensed early on that her life was not the same as his.

For a long time, she was able to shield him from the darkness, to protect him, letting him enjoy his childhood and teenage years—until the time came when they had no more secrets from each other, and he looked into the abyss with her.

She still wished, more than anything, that it hadn't come to that. But she hadn't been able to stop it, and that was the beginning of the end.

Looking back now, she realized that over the years, she had asked herself again and again what she could have done differently. And she always found the same inadequate answers.

In the end, none of it mattered anymore.

She couldn't undo anything.

The real challenge was accepting that crushing reality — without losing her mind.

"Mama?"

Jonna flinched. Kristoffer stood behind her, looking at her expectantly.

"Yes?" she answered, her voice hoarse.

"Don't we have to go?"

She glanced at the clock and froze; her shift at the hospital started in an hour and a half, and she still had to drop Kristoffer off at her mother's place.

"Oh my God. I completely lost track of time. Have you packed your bag?"

Kristoffer nodded.

"Good. Go on ahead. I'll be right there."

Kristoffer shuffled off, and Jonna gathered something in the kitchen for her dinner break.

When she stepped outside, Eirik came running toward her.

"You're running late," he said, checking his watch.

"I know, I need to hurry."

"Drive carefully, though."

"Of course."

"I'll pick up Karoline from school later, and then we'll have a nice movie night."

"She'll love that," Jonna said, pressing a kiss to Eirik's cheek. "See you in the morning. Sleep well."

Eirik followed her to the car and ruffled Kristoffer's hair through the open window.

"Be good for Grandma."

Kristoffer rolled his eyes. "I'm not five anymore."

"Are you sure?" Eirik teased, winking, and Kristoffer stuck out his tongue at him.

"Alright, window up and let's go," Jonna said, shifting into reverse and pulling onto the road. She waved at Eirik through the window and sped off. She had exactly one hour and five minutes until her shift began.

She turned onto the main road and left Halvik behind. In the rearview mirror, she watched her son staring out the window, lost in thought.

His features—a mirror image of Linus. He had the same long, dark blond hair, the same nose, and nearly identical deep, dark eyes. Every time she looked at him, she saw Linus. Countless times, she had caught herself just watching him as he slept, lost in memories of the past.

And Eirik had noticed. He had stood at the end of the hallway in their house, watching as she stood in Kristoffer's doorway, staring into the room for a long time. "You're thinking about Linus, aren't you?" he had said to her. His sad expression reinforced his suspicion. But she had lied to him, not wanting to hurt him. She knew he wouldn't believe her lie, but he said nothing, just smiled and went back into the living room.

That evening, she had crawled into bed with him, nestled against his warm back, and told him that she loved him and that he shouldn't worry. But he didn't respond.

Jonna suddenly had to slam on the brakes, jolting her out of her thoughts. A few reindeer stood by the side of the road, and she wasn't sure if one of them might suddenly wander onto the asphalt. She slowly drove past them at a walking pace before accelerating again.

Her thoughts returned to the journalist. She had little desire to share her story with a complete stranger. But she also knew that she liked talking about Linus, and that a tribute to this wonderful person wouldn't be a bad thing.

She decided to listen to the journalist—and if he communicated reasonably and openly, she would give him a chance.

Chapter 22

Harald had to drive home after his conversation with the Pettersens. His boss had summoned him to the editorial office via text message. His visit to Jonna would have to wait.

He left the village behind, drove up the mountain toward the lake, and from there continued into the Breivikeidet Valley. Clouds thickened in the west, and the sky grew increasingly darker. Snow was on its way.

He thought about his conversation with the Pettersens and felt relieved that they had answered his questions so willingly. However, he wasn't sure whether the conversation had actually brought him any closer to the truth. His hope that some inconsistency, a grave suspicion, or an accusation might emerge had, much to his frustration, not been fulfilled.

This discouraging fact wouldn't make his upcoming conversation with his boss any easier. He still had no concrete evidence that something was wrong with the case. And yet, he couldn't shake the strange feeling lingering in his gut—especially after Rasmus' statement.

Anne's remarks about Steinar Lundberg had also been interesting. She didn't seem to have liked him very much. John, on the other hand, hadn't made any negative comments, but it was clear that he hadn't considered Lundberg a close friend either. That didn't necessarily mean much—some people were simply more likable than others.

And yet, Steinar Lundberg didn't quite fit into the overall picture. The Pettersens, along with Jonna, seemed to form a unit, while Steinar was an outsider—perhaps envious of the family. Jealousy had caused many tragedies before. Why not this one?

Harald's thoughts drifted to Jonna. The way the Pettersens had described the relationship between their son and Jonna, it must have been an extraordinary young love. His own teenage romances had rarely lasted more than a year and had usually ended in drama worthy of any Latin American soap opera. If Jonna was willing to talk, she might be able to shed more light on the matter. After all, she had known Linus best at the time of his death.

An hour later, Harald entered the editorial building and walked to his office. On the way, he texted Runi to let her know he'd be home later than planned.

Sighing, he rummaged through his notes, searching for Jonna's phone number. When he found it, he dialled it on his phone and waited.

Jonna didn't pick up.

He placed his phone on the desk and leaned back in his chair. Outside his office window, the first snowflakes began to fall, and the mountains on the mainland disappeared behind a white curtain. The wind picked up, blowing the snow sideways. Harald turned on his desk lamp, and the office immediately felt a little cozier. He checked the time—just before half-past one. Time to report to his boss.

Five minutes later, as he sat in an uncomfortable chair across from Lars Kallestad, he studied the man's smug face and, in that moment, wished for a pie to throw right into it.

He had known Lars for many years; they had started at the newspaper together and had even got along back then, though there had always been an underlying sense of competition.

Who wrote the better story? Who got the front page? Who won the "Story of the Month" award?

Most of the time, Lars had come out on top. But that was mainly because he had been romantically involved with the editor-in-chief at the time.

How much he has changed, Harald thought as he observed the bulky figure behind the desk.

"So, how's it going?" Lars asked, his tone laced with boredom.

"You mean with the Halvik case?" Harald replied in the same disinterested tone.

Lars nodded, pressing his thick lips together.

"I'm making progress," Harald said.

Lars tilted his head and raised his eyebrows. "What does that mean?"

"It means exactly that—I'm making progress. I've spoken to a few people and plan to speak with more."

"Have you found anything yet?"

"I can't say much yet. I haven't reached the key person."

Lars nodded slowly, making an irritating smacking sound with his lips. "So you still think something's off about this case?"

"I'm pretty sure," Harald lied. "As you know, I'm just at the beginning of my investigation. A lot is still unknown. You and I both know that these kinds of inquiries rarely go according to plan."

Lars shrugged slightly. "What makes you so sure that something's wrong?"

"Journalistic instinct."

Lars raised his bushy eyebrows again and smiled smugly. "That instinct hasn't always worked in your favour."

Harald had to fight the urge to stand up and punch him in the face.

"Sometimes you get lucky, sometimes you don't. In this case, luck will be on my side—you'll see."

The moment the words left his mouth, he knew he had stuck his neck out so far that he might just lose his footing altogether.

"Is that all? I have things to do," Harald said, standing up.

Lars Kallestad exhaled through his teeth and replied, "For now, yes. I expect a progress report in the next few days."

Harald gave a brief nod and left Lars' office. Annoyed, he returned to his desk, switched on his computer, and leaned back in his chair. He glanced at his phone and noticed a missed call. It was Jonna's number. She had actually called him back.

Excited, he dialled her number again. After three rings, he heard a young, clear voice.

"Good afternoon, Jonna. This is Harald Strøm from *iNord*."

"I know," Jonna said, catching him off guard.

"Did the Pettersens tell you I would be calling?"

"Yes."

"So you know... what this is about?"

"Yes. Linus' accident."

"That's right. May I ask you a few questions about it?"

A pause followed, and Harald waited tensely.

"Only on one condition," Jonna said after a while.

"And that would be?"

"That your report sticks to the truth and doesn't spread lies."

"Lies? How... what do you mean by that?"

"You journalists often tell lies just to make a report more sensational and appealing to readers. I don't want to read some sensational story about my Linus."

"That's not my intention. You can even read the article before it's published."

Another pause followed. Harald could hear Jonna's heavy breathing on the other end of the line. If she turned him down now, it would be a major setback.

"Alright," Jonna finally said.

"I'm willing to answer your questions."

"Excellent. Thank you so much."

She didn't respond to that. Instead, she suggested meeting in two days, at nine in the morning, at her home.

Harald checked his calendar, found no conflicting appointments, and agreed.

"You know where I live?"

"Yes. Anne gave me your address."

"Alright then. See you in two days."

Jonna said goodbye, and Harald hung up. Then, for nearly five minutes, he stared at the black screen of his computer, thinking about what questions he should ask Jonna. He needed to focus on Linus' life. He couldn't just barge in and start interrogating her about the accident.

He grabbed his notebook and scribbled down a few questions.

Chapter 23

On February 25, two days after Harald had spoken with Jonna on the phone, he stepped out of his car in front of her house and took in his surroundings. The red wooden house looked as though it had recently been given a fresh coat of paint. Everything appeared so pristine, so untouched. The exterior lights were on, and beside the entrance hung a bronze plaque that read *Velkommen.*

The house had two stories, with a bay window on the right side topped by a conical roof. The entrance was covered by a balcony, similar to houses in Sweden. It stood slightly apart from the others, offering a magnificent view of the fjord, the mountains, and the entire village. A white garden fence surrounded the property, though it was barely visible against the snow. In the yard stood a swing set that had seen better days. A small tool shed stood not far from the house; its wooden walls were also painted red, but in some places, the paint was peeling.

Harald stepped up to the front door and pressed the doorbell. Footsteps sounded, and a moment later, a woman with dark brown, wavy hair and a shy smile appeared in the doorway, extending her hand to him.

"You must be Harald?" she said, her voice soft.

"That's right."

"I'm Jonna. Come in."

Harald shook her hand and noticed how delicate and feminine it felt—almost as if he were shaking hands with a child.

"We can sit in the living room," Jonna said. "My husband and children aren't at home."

She led him through a long hallway, decorated on both sides with family photos. Two small chests of drawers stood against the wall, both looking as though they had come from an antique shop. The curved carvings on the drawers and the round handles hinted at their age. The air smelled of freshly brewed coffee and baking, making Harald's mouth water.

A staircase covered with a thick carpet led to the upper floor. To the left was a room with an open door, through which Harald could make out office furniture and an antique-looking piano.

He liked the decor. His own home was also filled with old furniture. Modern designs didn't appeal to him. Designers these days had no sense of beauty. Straight lines, plastic, glass, metal—there wasn't much left of true craftsmanship or good taste.

They entered the living room, and Jonna gestured toward an armchair near the window for him. She herself sat down on the sofa. On the table sat a steaming coffee pot, along with two empty cups.

"May I offer you some coffee?" she asked.

Harald thanked her and, at the same time, noted how melodic Jonna's voice sounded. He had already noticed it on the phone. She sounded young—younger than she probably was.

His eyes had immediately been drawn to hers: a mixture of blue and light green, reminding him of the midday sky during the polar night. Her complexion was flawless, without a single wrinkle.

After filling both cups, Jonna leaned back on the sofa and looked at Harald expectantly.

"Thank you for meeting with me," he began. "I don't take that for granted."

Jonna nodded and managed a hesitant smile.

Harald explained, in the same words he had used with Neja Lundberg and the Pettersens, what his article was about. Again, guilt tugged at him, but he pushed it aside and focused on Jonna's reaction.

"I understand," she said, taking a sip of coffee.

Harald caught the scent of baking again, and his stomach let out a quiet growl.

"May I ask how you and Linus met?"

Jonna gave a wistful smile.

"Linus and I met in primary school. But only when I was twelve. Until then, I had spent my childhood in Alta. My father took a job in Tromsø in 1993."

"May I ask why he wanted to work in Tromsø?"

"The pay is better here."

"Is he still working?"

"No. He passed away three years ago."

"I'm sorry to hear that."

She nodded slightly.

"Was the move difficult for you?"

"Not really. Of course, I lost some friends because of it. But Halvik wasn't unfamiliar to me. My uncle lived here with his wife—at least until the accident. I often visited them during summer vacations and spent several weeks here each time."

"So you met Linus at school, not during your vacations?"

"That's right."

"And did you become a couple right away?"

Jonna laughed. "I don't know if 'couple' is the right word. We were just kids, on the threshold of adolescence. But yes, we liked each other from the start."

"What fascinated you about him?"

She looked down and remained silent for a moment. A faint smile flitted across her delicate, almost fairy-like face. Harald could see that she was slipping into the past—into a time he didn't yet know whether it was painful or joyful for her.

He recognized that state—the moment when one tries to recall past memories, to relive the same emotions, whether they were good or bad.

Sometimes, accepting that state was difficult, because the emotions it stirred often carried grief, longing, or regret.

And afterwards, one always wondered: *Was it worth it?*

Or had there simply never been another choice?

"So many things," Jonna replied after what felt like an eternity. "So many things fascinated me about him. Starting with his chestnut-brown eyes, his messy mop of hair, the way he looked at me on the first day of school, his patient way of listening to me. He was so shy when we first met. He followed me after school, wanting to know where I lived. From that day on, we did almost everything together. Linus became the most important person in my life. That might sound cheesy or exaggerated now, considering we were only twelve or thirteen at the time. But my life hadn't been easy up to that point. My parents didn't pay much attention to me; their careers were more important to them. So Linus became my anchor, my best friend, my love. It's extremely difficult for me to describe our relationship. Precisely because we were so young, we grew up together, often faced the same problems, and could understand each other so much better because of it. I was not a happy child, and I was always afraid that Linus wouldn't be able to handle that and would leave me. But he didn't. He was always there for me, no matter what happened."

Jonna lowered her gaze and seemed lost in thought. Harald gave her time and tried to imagine how such a young love could endure through the years. What obstacles and challenges had been thrown at their relationship? And how was it possible that two inexperienced teenagers had navigated adolescence together as a couple?

Suddenly, Jonna smiled. "Linus sometimes struggled in school. Especially in maths and geometry. I often helped him with his homework. We always went to an abandoned house on the hill above his parents' home and sat down at a table there. He hated maths. He cursed it. He just couldn't make sense of it and often felt frustrated. Most of the time, I was able to help him out. In return, Linus taught me how to fish or how to survive in the wilderness. Those were his subjects; that was where he felt confident. They were the things he had learned from his father." She sighed and raised her eyebrows. "Back then, I was jealous of the relationship he had with his father. I would have wanted that for myself too."

She shrugged sadly and looked down again.

Harald wasn't sure if she wanted to continue speaking or if she was waiting for the next question.

"How did your lives develop after school here in Halvik?" he finally asked.

Jonna lifted her head. "After school, I went to university to study medicine, and Linus took over Gunnar's carpentry business. During my studies, we didn't see each other often. I was constantly studying, and Linus had a full schedule of projects. He loved his work, and his clients were more than satisfied. His creativity was in high demand everywhere. And he had always been creative.

When we first met, he carved wooden figurines for me. Sometimes an angel, sometimes a whale, reindeer, or Christmas elves. I kept all of them."

Harald glanced around the living room but didn't see them displayed anywhere.

"They're in my office at the hospital," Jonna said when she noticed his searching look.

At that moment, Harald wondered how much Jonna's current husband knew about her past. Did he know the full story of his wife and Linus? Everything they had been through together? He didn't dare ask her.

"And alongside all these carpentry jobs, he continued working for his father?" Harald asked.

"Yes."

"Voluntarily? Or out of obligation?"

"Well… I think a little of both. He always enjoyed helping his father. After all, he loved fishing just as much as the rest of his family. But it wasn't easy for him to balance both. His main job was demanding, and most of the time, he came home exhausted, only to—well, should—help his family as well. But he never complained. For him, it was natural."

She shrugged lightly. "It was a tough time—for both of us. But it never affected us negatively. On the contrary, we cherished the time we got to spend together even more. And in the end, we got married."

"Sounds like a fairy tale," Harald commented.

Jonna nodded. "That's exactly what it was. At least for us. Many people had written us off early on, never believing that our childhood love would last."

She reached for her cup, stared into the brown liquid for a moment, and then said, "And it could have lasted much longer…"

Harald didn't respond to Jonna's remark right away. Just like with Neja Lundberg and the Pettersens, he could feel the grief that still clung to those left behind, like a shadow.

How long does it take for such a deep wound to heal?

Does it ever heal?

Or does one carry it along until they themselves stare death in the face?

"Time heals all wounds"—but that doesn't necessarily hold true for everyone.

For some, time might do the exact opposite. When someone loses a loved one, they might lose their sense of purpose as well. They become melancholic, sluggish, and depressed. And pulling oneself out of that hole was a struggle—not one that everyone was strong enough to endure.

"Did you get along well with Linus' family?"

"Oh yes. His family was—or is—the kind of family anyone would wish for. I remember the first few times I went to his house. I thought it was such a wonderful place. His mother was almost always home, cooking, baking, taking care of the children. At the dinner table, they talked and discussed things together. I wasn't used to that; it was all new to me. But I loved every second of it. The Pettersen house became my second home."

"If I may ask—where is your mother?"

"She remarried and moved back to Alta. I don't see her often, and that's fine with me."

Harald nodded and thought about his own mother.

If she were still alive, he would still have regular contact with her today.

He always felt guilty when he thought about how he would have rather seen his father in the grave instead of his mother.

But that was just the way it was.

"Do you have any siblings?" Harald continued.

"No, I'm an only child."

Harald thought of a question he had meant to ask the Pettersens, but had forgotten. "Did John Pettersen make enough money from fishing?"

Jonna shrugged off the question. "I think so. As far as I could tell, they never lacked anything."

"Couldn't he have hired a few employees instead of asking Linus and Arne for help?"

"He had employees. Not all the time, though, which is why the boys helped out. John owned three boats, and most of the time, his employees took two of them out while John took the third, the *Malini.* Linus and Arne often went out with him."

Harald continued taking notes. Jonna took a sip of coffee, staring into her cup again. Harald noticed the dimples in her cheeks, which gave her a youthful look. The skin above them was slightly flushed—a natural color.

"May I ask how you experienced the day of the accident?" Harald asked, biting his lip.

Jonna set her cup down and leaned back, tucking her hands under her thighs. "The day started normally. I had just finished a night shift at the hospital, and when I got home, Linus was already gone. At the time, he was working on a big job for a farmer who needed his barn renovated. The roof had taken a lot of damage from the heavy, wet snow in winter. So I went to bed and slept all day. I woke up around three in the afternoon and made myself something to eat. Linus came home just before five. We talked for a while, he had dinner, and as soon as he was finished, his father called. He said a heavy storm was coming in and that he needed Linus and Arne's help. He had blisters all over his hands, was exhausted, and would be grateful if the boys could take care of the nets. Linus called Arne, and an hour later, Arne picked him up. That was the last time I saw them both."

Harald nodded and set his pen down. A ghostly silence settled in. He could hear the hum of a washing machine, the cries of seagulls down by the sea—but otherwise, it was quiet. He swallowed uncomfortably and cleared his throat.

"But Linus and Arne didn't go out alone. They took Steinar Lundberg with them."

Jonna nodded.

"Was that common?"

She shrugged. "Pretty much. Steinar often helped out. He was my uncle."

Harald froze. "Your uncle?"

Jonna nodded again.

That was a detail the Pettersens had failed to mention, Harald thought. Whether it was significant, he wasn't sure.

"So you spent your summer holidays with Steinar and Neja Lundberg?"

"Yes."

"What were they like?"

A slight twitch ran through her right eye, and for a moment, she avoided his gaze.

"What they were like?" she finally repeated.

Harald nodded.

Jonna glanced briefly outside before turning back to him. "They were... okay, I suppose. Steinar wasn't much of a talker. He always did his own thing, without much regard for Neja. But she never seemed to mind. She adored him, would do anything for him. And he took advantage of that. If my husband had treated me that way, I would have sent him packing long ago. As a child, I didn't understand it. It was only later, when I got older, that I started remembering their conversations. It's hard to understand how a woman can put up with that. But then again, that was her choice, and she's not the only one who has lived that way."

"Did they argue often?"

"Not that I know of. Of course, there were disagreements now and then, but where don't you find those?"

"Do you think Neja was happy?"

At this question, Jonna hesitated. She stirred her coffee absentmindedly. "I don't think so," she finally said.

"What makes you say that?"

"She loved him. No doubt. But in my eyes, it was an unhappy love. At least, that's how I see it now, looking back. I often saw her standing by the window, staring into the distance. It always happened when Steinar wasn't home. Sometimes, I even heard her crying. As a child, I didn't know what to make of it."

"You can't expect a child to understand something like that."

She sighed. "I don't think so."

Harald glanced at his notes.

"How did you find out about the accident?"

"John called me in the early morning hours, and that's when I realized that Linus wasn't in bed next to me. At first, I thought he had already left for work. But then John told me that the *Malini* had been found drifting, unmanned. We met at the harbour. Anne was there, too."

She lowered her gaze and took a deep breath in and out.

"And that was the beginning of the worst nightmare of my life."

A single tear rolled down her cheek, and she wiped it away. Harald took a sip of coffee and let a few seconds pass.

"Ronald Thoresen told me he couldn't find John and Anne at home that morning, so he called the police right away. Do you have any idea why they weren't at home so early?"

"As far as I know, they left early to help the Larsens repair storm damage to their house."

Harald nodded. "Do you have a theory about what happened on the boat?"

Jonna blew her nose into a tissue and tucked it into the sleeve of her sweater.

"No. I... no—not really. I mean, in a storm, so many things can go wrong. Anything is possible."

Perhaps all three of them were swept overboard by a giant wave, or maybe only one fell into the sea, and the others died trying to save him." She shrugged. "But these are all just speculation, and I probably don't need to mention that in the weeks and months following the accident, I went over every possible scenario in my mind, again and again. Even when I tried to suppress it, I simply couldn't. Today, I have come to terms with the fact that the death of the three will remain a mystery. And when you think about it, you realize that it's not such a terrible thing. Even if we had certainty about the cause of the accident, it wouldn't bring the dead back to life. Maybe it would even be harder to accept. It could have led to unjustified blame being placed."

"Do you still have contact with Neja?"

"No. I've barely seen her since the accident."

Harald frowned. "But she still lives here, doesn't she? You must run into each other."

Jonna let out a brief laugh. "One would think so, yes. But she lives up in the village, doesn't go out much, I work in the city and do most of my shopping there. So, we don't cross paths often."

"But…" Harald probed further, "as a child, you spent your holidays with Neja and Steinar. You must have had a close relationship."

Jonna's gaze drifted past Harald. Where to, he didn't know. The question was clearly uncomfortable for her, and he wondered if he had overstepped.

"I wanted to put the past behind me back then," she said after a long pause. "Seeing Neja always reminded me of the accident and of Linus. Besides, Neja withdrew from me too and never reached out. I don't miss her, and I suppose she doesn't miss me either."

Harald nodded hesitantly, jotted down a note, and considered what to ask next. He noticed a family photo on a small side table next to the sofa. Jonna, her husband Eirik, and the children—Kristoffer and his sister, whose name he didn't know.

For a moment, he studied the children and felt something about the picture was bothering him.

"My family," Jonna said, nodding toward the photo. "They went into the city. Kristoffer needs new shoes, Karoline needs schoolbooks."

Harald nodded without looking at Jonna and continued to study the family photo. His eyes lingered on Kristoffer.

He looked very much like Jonna. The same hair color, the same dimples, the same eye color. But from Eirik, he seemed to have inherited nothing at all. He bore no resemblance to him—not unusual, but still unsettling.

Was that what was bothering him about the picture?

Harald felt Jonna's gaze on him and turned away from the photo. And at that very moment, he realized what had been unsettling him: Kristoffer didn't just resemble his mother—no, he also resembled his father. Only his father's name wasn't Eirik—it was Linus.

Harald shifted uncomfortably in his seat, debating whether he should ask Jonna about it. It was a deeply personal question, one that might go too far.

But he asked it anyway. "Kristoffer… he looks like you. But I don't see anything of Eirik in him. Of Linus, though, I see a great deal."

Jonna swallowed hard and wrung her hands as if she were cold. She gazed out the window, her eyes filling with tears.

Harald's guilty conscience flared up again. He tried to ignore it, but he couldn't.

"Linus is his father," Jonna suddenly said, still looking outside. For a moment, she closed her eyes, and a tear rolled down her cheek.

Harald took a deep breath, waited, gave Jonna time to gather her thoughts and words. He could hardly imagine what it must be like for her, constantly seeing the face of her deceased husband before her.

"I was pregnant with Kristoffer when the accident happened," she said, turning back to Harald. "Kristoffer never got to meet his real father. That was an additional burden almost too much to bear. There I was, barely twenty-five years old, expecting a child, and the father would never get to hold his baby. The son would never hear his father's voice, never recognize his scent, never feel his rough carpenter's hands. It…"

Her voice broke, and she paused, dabbing her tears away with a tissue and taking a deep breath.

Harald swallowed a lump in his throat.

"About a year before Kristoffer was born," Jonna continued, "I lost a child in the fourth month of pregnancy. It was a heavy blow for us. That made our joy even greater when I got pregnant again. Linus couldn't think about anything else. He was so proud, so full of anticipation—and also full of fear. For him, after I told him about the pregnancy, nothing else mattered. He worked a little less, took such tender care of me, and fulfilled my every wish." She paused, smoothing her trousers with her hands. "We had so many plans for the future. We wanted to expand the house, renovate the interior, build a new garage. Linus could have done so much of it himself. He had already sketched and drawn everything out—even though, on the ultrasound images, the baby was barely recognizable as such." She closed her eyes for a moment. "And then came that fateful evening."

Harald let a few seconds pass before speaking. But all he managed to say was, "I am so very sorry."

He looked at this beautiful woman who had achieved so much in her life, yet the shadows of the past still reached out for her with their claws.

He wondered if she was as happy with Eirik as she had been with Linus.

Was there not one great love in life? And once it was gone, was there nothing left that could compare to that once-perfect time?

Or was that just a Hollywood cliché, a romanticized notion born from the scripts of sentimental movies?

Quite possibly. Maybe no one could truly answer that question. Who's to say that you can't find the right person twice in your life?

"Are you trying to find out what really happened back then?" Jonna suddenly asked, catching Harald off guard.

"I..." He swallowed. "Not really, no."

"I don't believe you," Jonna replied, now sitting up straight.

"Why not?" Harald asked, studying her with a faint smile on his lips.

"You journalists usually don't care about the well-being of the people behind the story. It's all about the sensation, about winning over the readers. Who gets the front page? Or am I wrong?"

Harald's smile widened slightly, and he cleared his throat. "I can't argue with you. That certainly happens a lot. But not all journalists are like that."

They looked at each other in silence for a while, each waiting for the other to either continue the conversation — or end it.

Harald leaned back in his chair and crossed his arms over his chest. "I want to be honest with you," he said. *"The first time I heard about this story, I was down at the cemetery in Halvik. I saw the three graves and the memorial next to them with the inscription. I read the words three times in a row, and then I asked myself what could have gone wrong on that boat. As I stood there, an older man suddenly joined me, and we started talking. I asked him if he knew more about the accident, and he told me what had happened that night — or at least what people in the village believed had happened.

"When I got home, I started going through our newspaper archives, looking for reports — and I found them. They were typical fact-based articles, without emotion or depth — just dry, objective facts. That's one way to do it. But for me, this accident is about more than just cold facts. It's about people who loved fishing and lost their lives doing it.

"I also want to give the families left behind a chance to talk about their loved ones — to share their stories, maybe even their grief. Their voices will be heard. Maybe it will help them come to terms with what happened, even though it's been quite some time now."*

Jonna stared at him, her eyes glistening with moisture, her hands clenched tightly between her thighs. "Those are honorable intentions, ones that are hard to turn down." She smiled and finished her coffee. "I don't talk to many people about Linus. Not even with my husband. So you're quite an exception."

"I truly appreciate that, and I will do everything I can not to disappoint you. I promise."

Jonna smiled and stood up. Harald put away his notebook and let Jonna walk him to the door.

"Linus deserves to be remembered. I look forward to reading your article."

Outside, snow had begun to fall. Harald hurried to his car. Just as he was about to get in, he noticed a white object tucked under the left windscreen wiper.

A note, folded, slightly damp from the snow.

He took it, unfolded it, and read the handwritten words:

Leave the old story alone!!

Chapter 24

Jonna stood by the window, watching as Harald's car pulled away from the house, turned onto the main road, and eventually disappeared from sight. She remained at the window for a long time, seeing nothing outside, lost in thoughts that carried her far away—not to the present, but to years long past, when everything was different, and the future seemed so full of promise.

Everything from back then felt vivid, as if it had happened just last week. She remembered so many details from her childhood, from school, from her family, from her life with Linus. Especially from her life with Linus.

She recalled the look on his face the first time he saw her. She saw his smile when she kissed him for the first time, felt his pounding heartbeat when she told him she was pregnant, and tasted his tears when they realized they had lost a child.

Who would have thought, on that very first day of school, what life would demand of them? Linus' life had been so innocent then, so pure and carefree.

How many times had she wondered how his life might have turned out if she had ignored him back then? Would he still be alive? Would he have stayed in Halvik? Or would he have moved to the city and built an even more successful construction company there?

She closed her eyes and took a deep breath.

What was the point of asking such questions? Nothing could be undone; no one could be brought back from the dead.

Sometimes, she wished she were in the same place as Linus—wherever that might be.

For too long, she had harboured this dreadful—yes, terrifying—wish. She lived with this longing as a blind person lived with a cane. It was ever-present, had settled deep within her, and showed no intention of letting her go.

No one knew of her yearning. Not Eirik, not Anne, not John.

Only Linus had truly known.

And in the end, it had cost him his life.

Chapter 25

Harald sat in Café Kystenshuset, staring at the note in his hand. Who the hell had tucked it under his windscreen wiper?

The waitress brought him a coffee and a slice of apple pie. However, his appetite had waned somewhat.

Who even knew about his investigation?

Not many people. Neja Lundberg knew about it, as did the Pettersens, the pastor, and Jonna. It couldn't have been Jonna—she had never left the living room while he was there. John and Anne Pettersen were also unlikely suspects; they had never expressed any objections to his inquiries.

Neja Lundberg?

That wouldn't make much sense. Why would she talk to him about the accident, only to later leave him a threatening note?

Peder Sørensen. The village pastor hadn't exactly been thrilled about his intentions. But a pastor?

Highly unlikely. And besides, he had been polite. Wanting to protect his community was probably just part of his job.

Harald took a bite of the apple pie, washed it down with a sip of coffee, and gazed out the window. The words on the note refused to fade; they kept reappearing in his mind's eye, word for word, letter by letter.

Any doubts he had about there being something more to this story had vanished in an instant. Now, he was almost certain that a tragedy had unfolded that night thirteen years ago—one that was definitely not just an accident.

The only question was whether he would be able to uncover the truth. And if he did, how cornered would the person behind the note feel?

Would they go further than just scribbling a simple warning on a piece of paper?

It was possible.

Should that frighten him?

No, he wasn't afraid. But he was more determined than ever.

His appetite returned, and suddenly, the apple pie tasted much better.

Two hours later, Harald was at home, sitting at his desk, going over his notes. His conversation with Jonna had been somewhat satisfactory, even though he hadn't really made much progress.

Or had he?

Yes, he had.

At the very least, he now knew that his suspicions had been right.

For a brief moment, he considered telling Tobias Grønvoll about the note, but ultimately decided against it. Tobias would undoubtedly urge him to hand it over to the police, which could seriously jeopardize—if not completely halt—his investigation.

Jonna had provided the most intriguing details so far. He now had a clearer picture of Linus and Steinar Lundberg's lives. He also knew that Jonna had preferred the Pettersen family over her own.

Now, he needed to decide who to visit next.

He picked up Tobias Grønvoll's witness list and scanned the names. His attention fell on the harbour master, Øyvind Johansen. Maybe he had overheard some revealing radio transmissions that night. Then again, he would have reported anything significant to the police, and if there had been something noteworthy, the investigators would have acted on it.

Still, it was worth a shot.

Unfortunately, Harald didn't have Øyvind's phone number. So he called John Pettersen, who recited it from memory.

After hanging up, Harald noticed the note again—the one telling him to stay away from Halvik and the incident.

He studied the handwriting. It was jagged, with hardly any rounded letters, written in a disconnected style.

He didn't know any woman who wrote with such reckless disregard for penmanship. Then again, maybe that was intentional.

He set the note aside, picked up the phone again, and called Øyvind Johansen.

The harbour master answered after just one ring. Harald introduced himself, briefly explained his reason for calling, and asked if he could ask him a few questions about the boating accident in 2005. There was a pause on the other end of the line. Harald could hear Øyvind breathing heavily—he was clearly engaged in some physical work.

"I don't have much to say about that," Øyvind finally replied.

"I know it was a long time ago. But I'd still like to hear your perspective on the accident."

Silence again.

"I don't really have time for this," Øyvind eventually said.

"I'll keep it as brief as possible. I promise."

A long sigh. "Alright then, fine. When do you want to come by?"

"Would tomorrow suit you?"

"No, I'm busy all day. The day after tomorrow would be better. Do you have my address?"

After Øyvind provided his address, Harald thanked him and hung up.

He leaned back in his chair, laced his fingers behind his head, and gazed out the window.

The snowfall had eased, and the setting sun bathed the landscape in shades of red, violet, and orange. It looked almost surreal.

On Kvaløya, he could see a few skiers making their way down the slopes toward Sund. The cross-country trail at the foot of the mountain was brightly illuminated by floodlights, and a plane was just taking off from the airport, ascending into the evening sky.

It would be a beautiful night for a hike.

There was nothing better than climbing Storsteinen under freshly fallen snow and a starlit sky.

He glanced at his notes and concluded that a trek up the mountain was exactly what he needed to clear his mind.

Chapter 26

Øyvind Johansen had called Harald shortly before their meeting to let him know that they would be meeting on his boat at the harbour.

When Harald arrived at the small harbour of Halvik, he found two boats. One was a small, aging fishing boat with a tiny cabin and a rusted bow. The other was significantly larger, well-maintained, with a spacious cabin, a radio antenna, a satellite dish, and a radar system. It bore the name *Malini* - John's boat.

"Are you Harald?"

Startled, Harald spun around and found himself looking into the face of a stocky man with a beard, dark sunglasses, a cap, and yellow rain pants. Underneath his suspenders, a white knitted sweater was visible. The man stepped out of the wheelhouse and stopped at the boarding ladder.

"Yes, that's me," Harald called out to him and approached the boat.

"Come up the ladder. We can sit in the cabin."

A minute later, Harald was sitting on a narrow bench at a table, while Øyvind sat on a chair across from him. He had placed two cups of coffee on the table, and Harald wondered how many cups he had already had today. He really needed to cut down on his coffee consumption.

He glanced around the cabin. In addition to the steering wheel, there were several digital devices, but he couldn't tell what they were. The only thing he recognized was a GPS device. On the back wall of the cabin, two nautical charts were hanging, along with a framed photo in the center. Harald recognized Øyvind and a younger man who resembled him.

"So, you want to know about the stormy night?" Øyvind asked, leaning back in his chair with his arms crossed over his chest.

"That's right," Harald replied, noticing that the harbour master spoke with a slightly muffled voice. He also noticed that his lower lip was swollen as if he were pressing his tongue against it from the inside.

"As I told you on the phone, there's not much to say. I wasn't out that night and had no reason to be. My boat was in for repairs that week, so I had no nets in the water."

Harald took more notes.

What kind of way was that to talk?

Just as he finished the thought, Øyvind reached for a small bucket and spat a brown liquid into it. Now Harald understood why the man spoke so strangely—he was chewing tobacco.

"You're a fisherman by trade?" Harald asked.

"I was, yes. Now I'm retired. But I still go fishing often."

"But you're also the harbour master?"

Øyvind Johansen laughed. "Well, 'harbour master' might be an exaggeration for just a few boats. But yes, I take care of the docks, rent out the berths, and oversee the safety of our little harbour. That also includes the rescue crew."

Harald nodded. "Were you born and raised here?"

"Yes. I've lived here for sixty-eight years."

"So you must know everyone in Halvik."

"You could say that."

"How well did you know the victims?"

He shrugged. "Very well, of course. Especially the Pettersen brothers. John often took them out fishing. It was always fun with those boys. Linus, especially, was a great kid. Arne was a bit cheeky, but always friendly." He took a sip of coffee and shook his head sadly. "What a terrible waste of life…"

Harald nodded and sighed quietly. "So far, I've only heard good things about the brothers. They must have been well-liked here."

"Absolutely. People just liked them." Another wad of chewing tobacco landed in the bucket.

Harald checked his notes before moving on to the next question. "You mentioned earlier that you were part of the rescue crew. Did you have to go out that night?"

He shook his head. "No. The boat wasn't found until early morning. We only go out for distress calls when a boat is in trouble. That night, it was a recovery mission for bodies. That falls under the police and the coast guard."

"I see. Was there anything unusual about the night of the accident?"

Øyvind furrowed his brow. "Unusual? What do you mean?"

"Anything that struck you as odd, something that didn't fit the usual pattern. Maybe it was reckless of the fishermen to go out in such conditions."

Øyvind shook his head again. "No, it wasn't reckless. Dangerous, yes. But that's part of the job. Those three weren't out in a storm for the first time."

Next, Harald asked if the harbour master had any knowledge of conflicts between the brothers and Steinar, but Øyvind denied knowing of any. He wasn't aware of any disputes, though he couldn't say for certain.

"Did you receive any distress calls that night?"

"From the Pettersen brothers?"

"Yes."

"No, not from them…"

Harald hesitated. "From someone else?"

Øyvind pressed his lips together. "Well, it wasn't really a distress call. More like… a tip-off from a local drunk."

Harald's pulse quickened. "A drunk? Did he sound intoxicated?"

"Yes. But then again, he always sounded like that."

"Did you know the caller?"

Øyvind nodded. "Karl Godal."

"And what did he say?"

"Karl was out on his boat that night, at the same time as the Pettersen brothers. He called me in the middle of the night, slurring his words. He rambled about a scream he claimed to have heard."

"A scream?"

"A scream. And in the middle of a raging storm." He laughed and shook his head at the same time.

"You didn't believe him?"

"No. It wasn't the first time he had called me in the middle of the night. Once, he even claimed he had seen a sea monster with armour and glowing eyes."

Now Harald had to laugh as well. "I see. Can you remember Karl's exact words?"

Øyvind thought for a moment. "Not really. First of all, I was half-asleep, and second, Karl spoke so fast and slurred that I couldn't understand everything. If I remember correctly, he just said that he had heard a piercing scream. No, wait—he said: *the scream of a woman.* Yes, I think that's how he put it. But to be honest, I'm not a hundred percent sure."

Harald thought for a moment. *The scream of a woman!* That wasn't possible. There had been no woman on board. So, Karl must have been completely drunk.

"Did you mention Karl's call to the police at the time?"

Øyvind shook his head. "No."

"And why not, if I may ask?"

"Because even back then, I knew Karl was just talking nonsense. In his state, he could have seen or heard anything. Besides, he would have gotten into trouble with the authorities if they had found out he was out at sea while drunk. I didn't approve of it either, but that boat was all Karl had left in his life. Karl had always been alone — he never had a wife or children. He lived in a simple hut at the edge of the village, rarely went shopping. He got by on what he caught in the sea. I felt sorry for him. I didn't want them to take his boat away, too, because it was the only thing that made his life worth living."

Harald nodded and jotted down another note in his notebook. "Where can I find this Karl? Still in his hut?"

Øyvind shook his head. "Karl died five years ago. His hut was torn down — no one would have bought it."

Damn it! Harald thought. Perhaps the most important witness in this case was forever silent.

Nonetheless, Øyvind's statement added a new layer to the case. Whether Karl had been telling the truth or not, the fact remained that he had been out at sea that night and claimed to have heard something. That couldn't be a coincidence.

The only question was: why would someone have screamed?

In his mind's eye, Harald saw the scene unfold — three fishermen arguing, a scuffle breaking out, blows being exchanged, and screams of pain echoing over the raging sea. A large wave approached from the port side, the boat reared up, and the three lost their footing, falling into the stormy waters without life jackets.

That's exactly how it could have happened.

Unfortunately, no one was left alive to confirm it.

"Harald?"

He flinched. "Sorry, I was just thinking about something."

"About what?"

"That scream…"

Øyvind clicked his tongue. "Forget it. Karl talked so much nonsense, no one took him seriously anymore. Besides, that night, I could already smell the alcohol on his breath through the phone. He slurred his words, his tongue lagged behind. He was probably as drunk as a barrel in spring."

"Too bad," Harald said. "If his perception had been correct, it might have helped clarify the accident."

"Why? Just because he *thought* he heard a scream?" Øyvind clicked his tongue again. "Even if he did hear one, what would that have told the police? If one of the three had screamed as they were swept overboard by a wave, it wouldn't have changed anything in the investigation. Scream or no scream, all three went overboard and drowned. End of story."

"But he specifically said it was *a woman's scream*."

"That doesn't mean anything. In a storm like that, sounds get distorted. I can't imagine he heard anything clearly at all."

He paused, seeming to think. Then he added, "Ask Doctor Jensen. He had to patch Karl up more than once after he got drunk and fell on his head aboard his boat. Doc Jensen could tell you plenty about Karl."

Harald noted the name. "Where can I find him?"

"See that white house up there? On the hill?" He pointed to a house slightly above the village. "That's where he lives. He doesn't practice anymore. He's enjoying retirement, just like me."

"I'd like to speak with him. Do you think he'd be willing?"

Øyvind gave a small nod. "I think so. Theo's a good guy."

"Thanks. I'll get in touch with him. Is there anything else important you can tell me about the three fishermen?"

Øyvind shook his head.

As a final question, Harald asked the harbour master what he believed had caused the accident. His answer matched those of the Pettersen couple and Neja Lundberg. None of them seemed to believe it was anything other than an accident.

Harald thanked him and returned to his car.

Chapter 27

Theo Jensen's house was even larger than that of the Pettersen family. It had three floors and was at least thirty meters wide. Painted dark green, it featured ornate window frames and gables, giving the impression that it could accommodate four families. On the right side, a small turret with windows all around added to its grandeur.

His practice must have been very successful, Harald thought.

He walked up to the front door and rang the bell. It wasn't long before an older woman with short grey hair, oversized glasses, and a round face opened the door and smiled at him with her head tilted slightly to one side. She was unusually elegantly dressed. She wore a brown short-sleeved blouse buttoned all the way up, with a light blue pearl necklace draped over it. On both wrists, she wore bracelets adorned with stones. Her beige skirt, reaching just above her knees, matched her blouse, and she wore stockings of the same colour. Her feet were tucked into brown suede high heels. She looked as though she were about to address the royal family.

Harald introduced himself briefly and explained why he was there.

"You want to speak with Theo?" she asked, and Harald detected a slight English accent in her voice, which suited her British, aristocratic appearance.

"That's right."

"About the Pettersen brothers' boat accident?" She frowned.

Harald nodded.

"But that was a long time ago."

"I'm aware. But I'm trying to gather more information about it."

"You can try. Theo is in the living room. Come in. I'm Alice."

Alice closed the door and led him through a long hallway. They passed several rooms that, at first glance, appeared to be impeccably decorated. The hallway itself was paved with cream-colored ceramic tiles, interrupted here and there by Persian rugs.

Those probably cost more than my car, Harald thought.

The walls were adorned with paintings whose meaning was not immediately clear. Harald had never understood how people could appreciate such artwork. One painting featured a black background with two yellow and four red brushstrokes randomly applied by what he could only assume was an uninspired artist. That was it. A painting that could have been done by a six-year-old.

The living room was just as impressive. A massive fireplace stood against the far wall, above which hung a mounted moose head. To Harald's left stretched a long beige sofa, accompanied by two matching armchairs. In their center stood a small mosaic table holding a half-full fruit bowl.

Harald thought the entire living room looked like the perfect advertisement for a home design magazine.

At the window, which spanned the entire length of the living room, Theo Jensen sat in a rocking chair, reading a magazine.

"Theo, this is Harald Strøm from *iNord*. He'd like to speak with you about the incident with the Pettersen brothers."

Theo Jensen placed the magazine on a small side table and peered at Harald over his glasses. At first glance, he seemed extremely likable. His face bore a few wrinkles, giving him a grandfatherly appearance. His brown eyes were clear and hinted at a smile. He showed no signs of balding; on the contrary, his dark grey hair flowed over his ears.

He was just as elegantly dressed as his wife. He wore a light blue shirt, a brown vest over it, brown trousers, and black leather shoes.

Harald wondered if the two always dressed this perfectly or if they were about to attend a formal event.

"Am I intruding?" he asked, smiling at the doctor.

"Not at all."

"Good to hear."

"You want to talk about the Pettersen brothers' boat accident?"

"That's right."

Theo shot his wife a brief glance, raised his eyebrows momentarily, then said, "Why don't you take a seat?"

He gestured toward the sofa. Harald hesitated before following the invitation. The sofa looked so pristine that he feared leaving a mark on it—or even just a stray fiber from his sweater.

Meanwhile, Theo crossed his legs and looked at him expectantly. He had put his glasses back on and now looked like a psychiatrist waiting for his patient to pour out his troubles.

Harald took out his notebook and explained to Theo what he had uncovered so far, as well as the people he had spoken with. He told him about the old newspaper reports, his conversation with the investigator, and his intention to bring more depth to the story.

Theo listened with intently, nodding occasionally. When Harald finished, he said, "If I can, I'll gladly answer your questions."

"That's very kind of you, thank you."

Harald started by talking about Karl Godal. "During my investigation, I learned that a certain Karl Godal was also out at sea on the night of the accident and claimed to have heard a scream."

Theo smiled and raised his eyebrows knowingly but refrained from commenting.

"I was told," Harald continued, "that you treated Karl multiple times after he injured himself during his drinking binges."

Theo sighed quietly. "Unfortunately, I can't tell you much about that. You know, doctor-patient confidentiality…"

"I understand that. You don't have to tell me what kind of injuries Karl came to you with. I'm only interested in whether he was really as often incoherent as people claim."

Theo glanced briefly at his wife before answering Harald's question. "The first thing you need to know is that Karl was a kind soul. He wouldn't have hurt a fly. When he wasn't drunk, he was easy to talk to. Unfortunately, he was far too lonely in his lifetime. Whether by choice or simply because life never placed anyone by his side, I can't say. But I do think that loneliness drove him to drink. I always tried to help him stop, but I never succeeded."

"Did the village know about his drinking problem?"

"Oh yes. He often staggered along the sidewalk through the village. More than once, someone had to escort him home."

"Wasn't there any way to help him overcome his addiction?"

Theo shrugged. "He once went to rehab at my recommendation. When he returned, we had high hopes for him. I had long talks with him, and he understood that things couldn't continue the way they were. But unfortunately, his resolve lasted only five months. After that, he started drinking again."

"Did he ever talk nonsense when he was drunk?"

"Nonsense?"

"Obvious lies—things that were so absurd, they were laughable."

Theo pursed his lips. "Well, he spent a lot of time at the pub, and let's just say, he wasn't always the most insightful storyteller. The people in the village knew him and usually didn't take his ramblings seriously. Many felt sorry for him, though. He didn't like being helped. He drowned his dark thoughts in alcohol—and along with them, his credibility."

"What do you make of his claim that, on the night the Pettersen brothers and Steinar Lundberg died, he heard a scream while he was out at sea?"

"What do I make of it? Well—honestly, not much. Karl was drunk that night, too. At least, that's what the harbour master told me at the time. What he was doing out there in that condition, in a storm like that, I'll never understand. But one thing I do know: as much as he could drink, he could navigate his boat just as well. He knew the sea and its dangers as well as he knew his own hip flask—no one could teach him anything about that."

Theo Jensen leaned back in his rocking chair and continued. "But the fact is, he did mention that scream to me once. Months later, when he was in my care. I remember asking him if he was sure it was really a scream. He looked at me seriously and said: *'I know you all think I'm just a crazy, drunken old man. And maybe you're right. But one thing I can tell you for sure—I know the sea, the weather, my* boat. *I know every sound, whether it's a storm or a dead calm. What I heard was a scream!'"*

Harald listened with growing curiosity and even forgot to take notes. What Doctor Jensen was telling him was of utmost importance. Unfortunately, Karl Godal's statement could neither be verified nor proven.

"Did he ever mention whether the scream came from a man or a woman?"

Theo Jensen nodded. "He said it had to have been a woman. No doubt about it."

Harald frowned slightly and gave a nearly imperceptible nod. But Theo noticed his reaction.

"Sounds unbelievable, doesn't it?"

"I don't know. Based on the known facts, it seems impossible. There were only men on board that ship. The likelihood of another boat being out there with a woman on it seems quite low."

"Infinitesimally low. There were no female fishermen in the village back then."

"Would it be entirely out of the question that a woman was on the Pettersens' boat that night?"

Theo regarded him thoughtfully for a moment. "I wouldn't know who that could have been. And, more importantly—why? What reason would a woman have had to be on that boat? There were no women in the village who fished. None who occasionally helped out, either."

"So we have to assume that Karl must have misheard."

Theo shrugged. "It certainly looks that way." He leaned forward. "Either way, the whole matter is and will remain a mystery. Scream or no scream, no one will ever find out what really happened out there. Those three took their secret with them to their cold, watery graves. And that's where it will remain for eternity."

Harald considered whether to press the issue of the scream further or let it go. He decided to leave it alone. Instead, he asked the retired doctor if he had been involved in examining the bodies.

"I was the first to be notified by the police that morning, and I arrived at Arne's body quite some time before the officers. The brothers weren't found at the same time. Linus wasn't discovered until a day or two later—I don't remember exactly."

Theo Jensen's gaze drifted toward the window, and he was silent for a few seconds before continuing. "Arne looked better than his brother. Linus' body was already bloated, and he had a severe head wound above his right ear."

Harald noted this new detail. "And what caused that wound?"

"It was difficult to determine. Either he had been struck on the head by something, or he had hit his head somewhere. Maybe on the railing, or somewhere else on the boat. It was impossible to pinpoint an exact cause. It's also possible that the wind had thrown some object at his head."

"Could the head wound have been the result of a fight?" Harald asked, watching the doctor's reaction closely.

Theo furrowed his brow. "A fight?"

Harald nodded.

Theo exchanged another glance with Alice. She only raised her eyebrows but said nothing.

Harald couldn't quite interpret her expression. Either she knew something, or she had a suspicion she preferred to keep to herself.

Theo ran a hand over his face before addressing Harald's question. "I'm not exactly sure what you're getting at, but to answer your question—yes, the wound *could* have come from a fight. But not from a fist—more likely from a hard and heavy object." Deep wrinkles formed on his forehead. "But I still find the idea of a fight absurd."

"And why is that?"

"Because in a storm like that, they surely had more pressing concerns than bashing each other's heads in. Besides, I don't see what they would have been fighting about. And even if they *had*—no one would have killed the other two and then voluntarily jumped in after them."

"You're probably right," Harald admitted, glancing out the window. He was about to formulate another question when Theo spoke first.

"There is something…" The doctor hesitated and looked briefly at Alice. "There is something you should know about Steinar. He was deeply in debt. Even as a teenager, he was always borrowing money from others. His parents were as poor as church mice. Many people in the village felt sorry for him and would occasionally lend him a few kroner. That never changed. Even as he got older—and one might have thought, wiser—he still had to keep borrowing money. He even left some of his medical bills unpaid. His wife, Neja, came by my practice a few times to ask if there were any outstanding bills. She had money; *he* didn't. But he wouldn't take money from her—he was too proud for that."

"But…" Harald interrupted, "Steinar worked, didn't he? Surely, at the end of the month, there was something left."

Theo shrugged. "Yes, of course. But not much. And what he did earn, he often spent at the pub. That led to more than a few arguments with the local fishermen because he sometimes showed up to work drunk. Before long, no one wanted to work with him anymore, which made his life even more difficult."

"But John Pettersen kept giving him work," Harald pointed out.

"I believe so, yes," Theo confirmed. "John is a good man. He wouldn't leave anyone out in the cold, not even someone like Steinar."

"Did Linus and Arne have a problem with that?"

"I can't say. Maybe they did, maybe they didn't. If he had shown up drunk that night, they certainly wouldn't have been happy. On the other hand, I doubt they would have let him on board in that state."

"Maybe that's *exactly* what led to a fight on board."

"It's possible. But I have a hard time imagining it. Besides, Linus wouldn't have hurt a soul."

"What about Arne?"

"No, that's not what I meant. I just didn't know Arne as well as I knew Linus. That's all."

Harald nodded and envisioned the scene on the boat. Two brothers helping with the family business and a drunk man growing belligerent, verbally attacking them, calling them rich sons of whores. A man who had nothing, who had never achieved anything. He was envious of the Pettersen brothers and made it clear. A fight broke out — and it must have escalated terribly.

"Anne Pettersen couldn't stand Steinar."

Harald and Theo both turned to look at Alice, who had spoken for the first time since the conversation had begun.

"She told me once during a walk," Alice continued.

"Did she tell you why she didn't like him?" Harald asked.

"She only said that he was a bad person and that she was glad her family had nothing to do with him. She also said that his wife, Neja, was no friend of hers. She was completely submissive to him, like a servant to his master."

"People are different, my dear," Theo said, shifting in his seat. "There are good people, and there are bad ones. Steinar probably had a bit of both in him."

Alice gave a small shrug. "You're probably right."

"Did Steinar have any disputes with anyone in the village?" Harald asked.

"I can't answer that," Theo replied. "It's possible, but I never heard anything to that effect. What about you, dear?"

Alice shook her head. "No, sorry, I have no idea."

Harald closed his notebook. "Well, I think that's everything. Thank you both so much for taking the time to speak with me."

"No problem," Theo said, settling back into his chair. "What's your next move?"

"I'm not sure yet," Harald admitted. "I need to go through all my notes and get a clearer picture. Maybe then I'll see things more clearly."

"When will your article be published?" Alice asked.

Harald sighed. "That—I'd love to know myself. If my boss doesn't like the story, then not at all."

"That would be a shame," Alice replied.

"I'll let you know."

Alice shook Harald's hand and wished him luck as he left.

He stepped out of the doctor's house and walked toward his car. Abruptly, he stopped.

A note was tucked under his windshield wiper.

Alarmed, he looked in all directions, but there was no one in sight.

He reached for the note and unfolded it.

You're playing with fire!!

Chapter 28

Peder Sørensen stood at the living room window of his house in Halvik, pressing the telephone receiver to his ear. His hand trembled slightly. His eyes were closed, focusing only on the voice on the other end of the line.

He had thought long and hard about whether he should make this call or if it would be better to leave things as they were. The question had robbed him of sleep for nights, and now, it had resulted in a pounding headache.

Lying awake—he knew that feeling all too well. Many nights of his life had been spent that way. Pacing from bed to kitchen, from sofa to window. Always searching for the right prayers, for answers to questions that weighed on him—whether his own burdens or those of his congregation.

Bit by bit, he had come to realize his mistake. He had acted on impulse, out of fear. That was so unlike him. He, who was usually thoughtful, reserved. His prayers had not yet provided an answer. Perhaps God had not heard him.

He tried to remain calm, as he was accustomed to doing in church. But that was not so easy—not for *this* call. Too much was at stake. One wrong decision, and he could set off an avalanche. But it was not entirely up to him; other factors played a role as well. However, those were largely beyond his control.

"No, I didn't tell him anything, I swear!" he cried into the receiver. "I..."

Again, the other person interrupted him. He shook his head repeatedly, covering his face with one trembling hand. The voice on the other end kept talking, but he only half-listened, his thoughts already racing ahead. He was searching for a way out of this situation, for an emergency plan. But he couldn't think of one.

Then, finally, the barrage of words ceased, and he was able to speak again.

"I assure you, I DIDN'T TELL HIM ANYTHING!"

A brief pause followed, and Peder took a deep breath.

The other person was silent. Or—were they crying? He thought he could hear quiet sobbing.

"The truth must come to light one day," Peder said now, his voice calm. "You shouldn't take this secret to your grave. Before you die, you need to make peace with yourself and with God. Otherwise, heaven will be denied to you."

A mocking laugh came through the receiver, followed by angry words.

Peder listened, looking up toward the heavens, hoping the Lord would grant him strength. Once or twice, he attempted to interrupt, but the person on the line would not let him speak.

When they finally paused to take a breath, he quickly said, "I won't tell him anything. But the way he's sniffing around here, he might soon uncover our secret. So far, he's met with almost everyone who was involved in this matter. It's only a matter of time before he finds something he can use to his advantage. And I guarantee you this—if she is dragged into this any further, you will go down with her. That's a promise."

Silence.

"Do you understand me?"

Silence again.

"Did you hear m—"

The line went dead.

Frustrated, he threw the phone onto the sofa and stared out at the cloud-covered fjord. From the north, snow drifted across the water and had now reached the village. The opposite shore disappeared behind a white curtain, and within minutes, the wooden façades of the houses were dusted with a fine layer of snow, as if someone had sprinkled them with powdered sugar.

A thousand thoughts ran through Peder's mind at once. So many questions, and he had no answers. At least none that satisfied him.

How was he supposed to get out of this dead end?

That journalist would not stop until he uncovered the truth.

But he could not let it come to that.

Things had been quiet for too long. He wouldn't let some nosy city journalist come in and disrupt everything.

The peace had to be maintained, and those involved protected.

The question was, *could* he still manage that?

Peder watched his neighbour as he parked his car in the garage and pulled the door shut. He saw his wife moving around in the kitchen window, preparing something, while the children played in the snow behind the house.

A tightening sensation spread in his stomach—a gnawing feeling that crept through his entire body.

But it wasn't hunger—no, it was thirst.

Not the kind of thirst that water could quench, but a craving for something that would dull his senses.

Resolutely, he turned away from the window, walked over to the sideboard, and poured himself two fingers of cognac.

He downed it in one gulp, refilled the glass, and repeated the process two more times.

After four glasses, he was finally ready for the sermon ahead.

Chapter 29

Harald tossed the note onto the passenger seat, steered his car away from the Jensens' house, and drove down to the harbour. He parked in one of the few available spaces, leaned back in his seat, and stared out at the fjord.

As he gathered his thoughts, he reviewed the conversation he had just had, glancing at his notes repeatedly. One thing was clear: things were picking up speed. First, the revelation about Linus' head wound, then Steinar's financial troubles, and now another threatening note on his windshield.

What the hell was going on in this village? And who was writing him these messages?

Was he being followed?

How did the writer—whoever they were—know exactly where he was?

Harald glanced around discreetly. A car passed by, a woman walked along the pavement holding hands with two children, and a boat was approaching from the water.

On the other side of the harbour, he noticed a car with its headlights on. Unfortunately, from this distance, he couldn't tell if there was someone in the driver's seat. From where he stood, it appeared empty. Either someone had forgotten to turn off the lights, or the driver was nearby and would soon return.

Could this be his follower?

Harald got out, scanned his surroundings, and walked toward the car. As he approached, just a few meters away, he saw that it was indeed empty.

Where the hell was the driver?

Just as he was about to turn around, the sound of a door slamming reached his ears. He turned and saw a cabin light flicker on in one of the boats at the pier. A door opened, and a man wearing a cap and a thick sweater stepped out, switched off the light, and left the boat. As he passed by Harald, he greeted him with a brief nod before getting into the suspicious car and driving off.

Shaking his head, Harald returned to his own car, considering his next move.

At the Jensens', he had uncovered some interesting details. The Pettersens hadn't mentioned Steinar's money problems. Was there a reason for that?

Either they hadn't thought of it or they considered it irrelevant.

Harald debated whether he should bring it up with them. How often had money been the cause of major conflicts—or even murder? Why not in this case?

Five minutes later, Harald knocked on the Pettersens' front door.

John answered, slightly out of breath, and seemed surprised to see him back so soon.

"Sorry to drop by unannounced," Harald apologized, "but I wanted to ask you a few more questions about Steinar Lundberg."

John furrowed his brow but let him in.

He led Harald into the living room, which, though impressive, lacked the meticulous tidiness of the Jensens' home. A fire crackled in the fireplace, the television was on, and Anne sat on the sofa knitting.

When she saw Harald enter behind her husband, she looked surprised. "Well," she said, "back again already?"

"He has more questions about Steinar," John answered for Harald.

"About *Steinar*?" Her face twisted into a grimace.

"Yes… I… sorry to bother you again. But I'd appreciate your help."

Anne placed her knitting in a basket and switched off the television. "Have a seat."

Harald sat down next to John on the sofa and told the Pettersens that he had learned about Steinar's financial troubles during his investigation.

John and Anne exchanged a knowing look. They were clearly well aware of what he was talking about.

"I heard that Steinar had been borrowing money since his youth—from various people," Harald continued. "That made me wonder… could he have also borrowed money from your sons? Could that have led to a fight on the boat?"

John frowned. "I can't imagine that. My sons didn't concern themselves with Steinar's financial situation. And even less do I believe they would have lent him money."

"But they knew about his problems?"

"Of course. Anyone who knew Steinar knew that."

"Is it possible that Arne or Linus lent him money without telling you?"

John and Anne exchanged another glance before shaking their heads in unison.

"But you *can't* rule it out," Harald pressed.

"Well—no, I can't," John admitted. "But my sons would never have lent Steinar money. Certainly not Arne. He barely had enough for himself."

"I see."

"I, however, lent him money once," John said.

Harald's ears perked up. "Oh? Really?"

"Yes. But he paid it back."

"Why was he always having financial trouble?"

John sighed. "Steinar took out a loan when he was younger and got in over his head. He was in debt for years."

"Didn't he have parents who could have helped him out?"

Anne shook her head. "Steinar's father died young of cancer, and his mother was an alcoholic. She passed away about ten years after her husband. After his mother died, Steinar became religious. He was constantly in the church, whether there was a service or not. I often saw him going in or coming out. And of course, he *never* missed Sunday Mass. He was very close with our village pastor."

She paused, then added with a hint of bitterness, "A shame that the pastor couldn't teach him any morals."

Harald furrowed his brow. "What do you mean when you say he got along well with the village pastor? How did that show?"

Anne shrugged slightly. "Oh, they would always chat. Before or after mass, sitting on a bench in front of the church, or at village festivals. That pious demeanor didn't suit him at all. Not with how rough he was."

"He had simply found God," John interjected with a grin, winking at his wife. Anne rolled her eyes.

"Couldn't Neja have helped with his financial problems?" Harald asked.

"He didn't want that—he never did. He was too proud for that."

"And yet, she has plenty of money," Anne added. "She comes from a wealthy family. But, as my husband just mentioned, Steinar never accepted money from her."

"Did you know Neja better than Steinar?" Harald asked Anne.

"What does *better* mean? No, not necessarily. I saw her now and then when she passed by our house on her way to her cabin."

"To her cabin?"

"She owns a weekend cabin up in the mountains." Anne pointed out the window. "The road in front of our house ends two houses down. From there, a hiking trail leads up to her cabin."

"Does she come by here often?"

Anne shrugged. "When Steinar was still alive, they would go up there almost every weekend. Jonna would also go with them during her summer vacations. Linus was up there a few times too. But in winter, they avoided it because it's difficult and dangerous to get up there in the snow. However, this winter and last, I saw Neja passing by with her touring skis quite often." She shook her head slightly.

"Why are you shaking your head?" Harald asked.

"Because there's an acute avalanche risk up there in winter," John answered in Anne's place.

"I think she's escaping from her sister," Anne commented.

"From her *sister*?" Harald asked, surprised.

"Yes. She moved in with her two years ago. Apparently, she lost her job and couldn't afford her own place anymore. Or maybe she's just too lazy to work. That's what people in the village say, anyway. Neja took her in, and she's been living there ever since. It doesn't seem easy to live with her—at least, that's what Neja's neighbour once told me."

"I see," Harald said, wondering why Neja hadn't mentioned this to him. Or had she, and he simply didn't remember?

"Have you ever been to that cabin?" he asked John and Anne.

"We haven't," John replied. "But Linus has."

"Was he up there often?"

"No," Anne said. "Maybe two or three times, but certainly not more."

Suddenly, Anne sat up in her chair, folded her hands in her lap, and stared ahead, lost in thought. "I..." she said hesitantly, pausing to think.

"Yes?" Harald prompted.

Anne looked first at her husband, then at Harald. "I left something out during our first conversation. Well—not *left out* exactly. It only came to mind afterwards."

Harald noticed John's puzzled expression.

"The night of the accident," Anne continued, "Linus stopped by here to borrow some ropes from the garage. I went outside to him, and we talked briefly. I told him to be careful, that the fishing nets weren't worth risking his life over. He just smiled and told me not to worry, that he knew what he was doing. As a mother, you constantly fear for your children's well-being, whether they're two years old or fifty." A fleeting smile crossed her face.

"But I had the feeling that something was wrong with him," she went on. "He seemed stressed, quiet, distant. There was something sad in his eyes, something that didn't suit him at all. I asked him about it, but he just said everything was fine, that he was just a bit tense. So, I let it go." She paused, took a deep, slightly shaky breath. "When I think back on it now, when I see those sad eyes before me... then..."

Her voice broke, and she reached for John's hand. He stroked hers gently, almost mechanically, like a robot. It was clear that he had done this countless times over the years.

Harald thought about how this pain would stay with the couple for the rest of their lives. An unimaginable burden that no one should have to bear. Losing a child was painful enough, but losing two at once—*that* was pure torment.

"Did you ever mention this to Jonna?" Harald asked Anne.

Anne nodded. "I did, yes. But she hadn't noticed anything unusual about him."

"Did Jonna herself seem different in the days before the accident? Did anything about her seem off?"

The Pettersens exchanged a brief glance. Anne pursed her lips and hesitantly shook her head. "No, nothing stood out to me. What about you?"

"Nothing to me either," John said.

Harald checked his notes and saw that he had no more questions written down.

"Do you need to know anything else?" Anne asked.

"No, that's all. Thank you for your openness."

"Were you able to speak with Jonna?" John asked as he accompanied Harald to the door.

"I was, yes."

"How did she take it?"

"She was very open and kind. I could feel, throughout our conversation, just how much she loved Linus—or still loves him."

John sighed softly and looked at the ground. "Jonna and Linus were one heart and one soul. And they always will be."

Harald nodded slightly. "That must be a difficult situation for Eirik, I imagine."

John shrugged and pressed his lips together. "Eirik knows about Jonna's past. He's known from the beginning. I've got to know him quite well over time. One evening, we had a long talk out in the garage. He told me that he's aware he will never be the number one person in her life. But that's okay with him. Life doesn't always give you everything you wish for."

Harald raised his eyebrows. "That's a rather pessimistic outlook."

John gave a faint smile. "Not everyone has a perfect life. Eirik seems to have made peace with it."

A few minutes later, Harald was on his way home. His thoughts revolved around Steinar, his financial situation, his relationship with Neja, and what the village community thought of him. He pondered Steinar's religious transformation and the many conversations he had supposedly had with Peder. What had all those discussions been about? Steinar's past? His future? Or simply about God and the world?

Harald's thoughts drifted to Steinar's widow and her weekend cabin in the mountains. He found it interesting that Neja had apparently rarely made the trip up there in winter in the past, but for the past two years, she had done so regularly.

What did that mean? Why was she taking the risk of getting caught in an avalanche?

Either she knew a safe route or she was deliberately putting herself in danger. But in that case, she would need a very good reason.

Harald turned off Breivikeidettal onto the main road toward Tromsø. The end of the fjord in Nordbotn was frozen over. He could see the blue-tinged ice, crisscrossed with cracks and fissures. Further out, the water shimmered in the low-hanging sun, while dark clouds approached from the west.

What had the sky looked like on the night of the accident? What had the eyes of the three fishermen seen? Had Linus sensed that something was going to go wrong? Was that why he had been so quiet with his mother?

Three fishermen, three bodies…!

No, there were only two bodies. Only two…!

The thought formed slowly in Harald's mind, as gradually as the dawn in the polar night. Piece by piece, hesitantly—but the thought was there: *Steinar Lundberg's body had never been found.* That alone wasn't a mystery; perhaps his body had simply sunk during the accident.

But what if Steinar was still alive?

What if he had somehow escaped the disaster and made it to shore undetected?

What would he have done afterward? Would he have gone into hiding? And if so—why?

A possible answer to that question was relatively easy to find: he had escaped his creditors—if he had any. He wouldn't be the first person to use such means to get out of debt.

Admittedly, it was a rather far-fetched theory, Harald thought.

But he liked it.

He liked it *a lot*.

If he could prove it, the front page was as certain as *amen in church.*

But there was still a long way to go, and he had no evidence to support his wild speculation. The only person who might be able to provide him with something useful was Neja Lundberg.

However, she certainly wouldn't do so willingly. And besides, he couldn't confront her with such an accusation. She would either call him crazy or chase him out. Neither scenario would get him anywhere.

Harald turned off the main road into a residential street and parked in front of his garage. He got out, slammed the door shut, and looked out at the strait. The sun hung low above the southern mountains, casting an orange glow over the water.

What had Anne said again?

That for the past two years, she had often seen Neja Lundberg passing by her house on her way up to her cabin. Even in winter.

Two years.

Could it really be possible…?

No!

Impossible.

Or was it?

Two years ago, Neja's sister had moved in with her. That *couldn't* be a coincidence.

That would be *outrageous.* That would be—*a sensation!*

Okay, maybe not a sensation in the *true* sense of the word.

But certainly, a sensational *story.*

He *had* to get to that cabin.

The only question was—how?

If there really was an avalanche risk up there, he would be putting his life in danger. However, the weather service had reported low avalanche risk on the radio this morning, though that didn't eliminate the danger entirely. This wouldn't be a casual Sunday stroll.

And besides—he didn't even know exactly where the cabin was.

The mountain was vast, stretching for kilometers to the south. If there were no fresh tracks leading up, he would never find it. So, he had to ask someone.

Neja Lundberg was out of the question.

The Pettersens, too.

John and Anne would only try to talk him out of it.

That left only Jonna.

She knew the cabin. She had to know the way.

He turned away from the strait and looked thoughtfully at his house.

It was calling to him.

He wanted to sink into the sofa, maybe chat with Runi for a bit, have a glass of wine, listen to some music. A walk to clear his head would also do him good.

He glanced at the clouds gathering in the north and decided to stretch his legs before the snowfall set in.

One last look at the house—then he started walking, typing a quick message to Runi: *I'll be back soon.*

Chapter 30

At half past five, Harald picked up his phone and called Jonna. When no one answered and he was about to hang up, he suddenly heard Jonna's voice. She sounded slightly out of breath.

"Sorry if I'm disturbing you," Harald apologized.

"It's fine. I just got home from the hospital."

"Oh, I see. I'll keep it brief. I just had another question about Steinar and Neja Lundberg."

There was a brief silence. Then she answered hesitantly, "Y-yes...?"

"John and Anne told me that Neja owns a weekend cabin."

"That's true," Jonna confirmed.

"You used to go up there as a child?"

Jonna took a moment before answering, but then affirmed his question.

"Did you ever go up there in winter?"

"No."

"And why not?"

"Because I was only here during the summer holidays."

Right, he had forgotten that. "Can you see the cabin from the village?"

"No. It's on a high plateau."

"Could you describe to me where this plateau is?"

"Why do you want to know that?"

"I'm just curious."

Another short pause followed. Harald could hear Jonna's rapid breathing.

"I'll answer your question if you answer mine," she said.

Harald bit his lip. There was no way he could share his suspicion—or rather, his theory—with her. She would think he was crazy. So what should he tell her? A lie? Or a half-truth?

He opted for the half-truth. "I want to find out why Neja only used to visit the cabin in the summer, but has been going up there in winter for the past two years as well."

As expected, there was no immediate response. He pictured Jonna in his mind, standing by the window with the phone in her hand, contemplating his question.

He was about to say something else when Jonna answered in a quiet voice, "The plateau and the cabin are southeast of the village, about five hundred meters higher up. Behind the cabin, a rock face rises steeply. You can see that from the village."

Harald thanked her and jotted down her description. Then he said, "I have one more question if you don't mind?"

"Go ahead."

"Anne told me that Linus seemed different on the evening of the accident. As if something was weighing on his mind. Did you notice that back then?"

The response was slightly delayed. "No, I—I didn't notice anything unusual."

"Did Linus tell you when he left that he was going to stop by his parents' house?"

"Yes. He wanted to pick up some ropes or something like that."

Everything lined up, Harald thought. The puzzle pieces all fitted together. And yet, he was convinced that something was hidden somewhere—something that no one, or almost no one, knew about.

"Did you ever suspect after the accident that Steinar might have had something to do with your husband's and his brother's deaths?"

Silence.

Harald held his breath. He feared he had just crossed a line. When Jonna still didn't respond, he asked, "Are you still there?"

A slight clearing of the throat. "Yes, I'm here."

Then, more silence.

"Uh—sorry if I'm being a bit insensitive about this."

"Why would Steinar have had anything to do with the accident?" Jonna suddenly asked, her voice tinged with irritation.

"It was just a thought. In my conversations with people in the village, I got the impression that Steinar wasn't exactly well-liked. He supposedly had debts and a short temper. Maybe he even owed your husband money, and you didn't know about it." He bit his lip, waiting for Jonna's reaction.

"Debts?" she asked. "What debts?"

"Steinar apparently borrowed money from various people."

"Certainly not from Linus. He wouldn't have lent him a single cent. Besides, Linus and I had no secrets from each other. I would have known."

Many people have thought that, Harald mused, though he kept the thought to himself.

"And besides," Jonna continued, "Steinar died in the accident as well."

Harald cleared his throat awkwardly, started to say something, then swallowed the words. After several seconds had passed, he finally said, "I'm not a hundred percent sure about that."

"W-what… what do you mean?" Jonna stammered.

"His body was never found…"

"That's not unusual. His body probably sank or was carried out to sea."

"And what if he actually survived and has been hiding somewhere all this time?"

A few seconds of silence. "You don't seriously believe that." Jonna let out a short laugh, but it didn't last.

"I know—it sounds like something out of a crime novel. But things like this *do* happen. It wouldn't be the first time."

"That may be true. But in *this* case, you're wrong. And even if he had survived, where would he have been hiding all these years?"

"Maybe he fled abroad, maybe he's been living in Neja's basement, or maybe—he's been holed up in his mountain cabin all this time."

Jonna did not immediately respond to Harald's statement. He could hear her breathing heavily, a faint clearing of her throat, and then: "Well... I... I'm not sure what to think of that."

"You don't have to think anything of it. It was just a hypothesis on my part. I was only curious whether you considered such a scenario possible."

"Not really."

Harald had the feeling that he had pushed Jonna enough. It was obvious that she either didn't know more or didn't want to say more. "I'm sorry, Jonna. I didn't mean to drag you into all this. It's just my job to ask questions and formulate hypotheses. I'll leave you alone now." "I don't know what to say."

"That's all right. I wish you a pleasant evening, and I'll be in touch once I've written the article."

With those words, he hung up and stared out the window for a long time, sorting his thoughts. He watched a plane take off from Langnes Airport and disappear into the southern night sky. Grabbing his sweater, he stepped out onto the balcony. Darkness had settled over Tromsø, and the island's lights shone across the sound. The air was so cold and dry that it almost crackled. The sky was strewn with stars, and if one looked closely, a faint shimmer of the northern lights was visible. The half-moon cast a milky glow over the mountains in the west and south. Beyond them lay only the polar sea to the west and fjords and valleys to the south, sparsely inhabited.

Sometimes Harald felt as if he were alone up here, as if life unfolded far to the south—at least in winter when time seemed to stand still, only moving forward again with the melting of the snow. He had had this feeling even as a child when his father drank, his mother withdrew into the bedroom in sorrow, and eventually turned to the bottle herself. He remembered how he would sneak into her bed, how she would hold him in her arms, singing a song with tears in her eyes. He could still feel her damp cheeks against his forehead, her tears trickling onto his face, and he could still smell her—the perfume that smelled of fresh flowers.

Only once, since the last time he had seen her, had that scent reached his nose in a store in town. He had turned in all directions, hoping she would be standing there before him, but the scent came from the saleswoman.

How often had he wished as a child that his mother would take his hand and lead him away from home? That they would start over somewhere, leaving the past behind? But they had never done that. Not together, anyway. She left alone and never returned.

Back then, Harald was convinced that his mother had thrown herself into the sea. But a few days later, he received a letter from her in which she explained her departure. She had only written a few sentences. The most important thing was that she promised to come back for him soon, that she had rented an apartment and prepared a room for him.

But that had never happened. A month later, he received the news of her death. Cardiac arrest, as he later learned.

Chapter 31

Peder Sørensen stepped out of the door of his church in Halvik and personally bid farewell to each of his parishioners. Today, that took barely two minutes, as only six people had found their way to the service. Once he had shaken hands with the last visitor, he closed the church door behind him and began extinguishing all the candles, collecting the hymnbooks, and tidying up the altar. Then he switched off the lights in the main part of the church and disappeared into the sacristy, where he changed back into his civilian clothes.

As he dressed, his thoughts wandered to Fred, who had informed him before the service that he had been diagnosed with cancer and that the prognosis was not good. They had prayed together, and Peder had tried to give Fred courage. Finding the right words had not been easy, but it seemed to have helped Fred.

A noise from inside the church startled Peder. Confused, he stepped out of the sacristy and stopped behind the altar. A narrow beam of light from the sacristy illuminated the otherwise empty nave.

"Hello! Is someone there?" he called, his voice echoing off the bare walls.

No answer.

He listened intently, but aside from the howling wind, he could hear nothing. Puzzled, he returned to the sacristy. He stopped in front of his desk and looked at the note on his desk: Iversen Wedding, it read. He absolutely had to prepare for that wedding. He had not yet written a single word.

Sighing, he sat down at his desk and scribbled a few sentences onto a piece of paper. After a few minutes, he paused and thought about the next words when another noise from the church reached his ears. He held his breath and listened. It sounded like footsteps. Footsteps on a stone floor, made by rubber soles.

A rush of adrenaline surged through his veins, and he set his pen aside.

"Hello, who's there?"

No answer.

With trembling knees, he rose from his chair and stepped out of the sacristy. He fumbled for the light switch on the outer wall, but before he could find it, he suddenly noticed a figure rushing at him from the darkness. With the force of an oncoming train, the person knocked him to the ground.

Peder's head hit the floor hard, a flash of light flickered before his eyes, and a searing pain immediately exploded in his skull.

In the next moment, he felt someone pinning him down. He sensed the weight of his attacker pressing on his upper arms and tried to think of a way to shake him off. Before he could finish the thought, a searing burn tore through his abdomen. He gasped for air as a pain like molten lava spread through his entire body.

After the initial shock, he attempted to break free from his attacker but was immediately forced back down. Then, more blows struck his stomach—searing, like red-hot pokers branding his flesh.

Everything began to spin. He wanted to scream, but his throat was parched; no sound came out. He felt his strength slowly draining from his body. He could no longer move his arms or legs—it was as if they no longer belonged to him.

Suddenly, the attacker let go of him and ran down the aisle towards the exit.

Groaning, Peder rolled onto his side and saw the figure pause briefly before the entrance door, looking back at him before vanishing in a single leap from Peder's line of sight.

He had only seen the face for a few fleeting moments, but in that brief span, he had recognized despair and regret, determination and love. And that was exactly how he had known this person for many, many years.

The door fell shut, and then silence settled over the church.

A silence Peder had always loved and cherished in his church.

But now, it unsettled him.

It was hollow and terrifying, making him feel as if he were utterly alone in the world.

The pain in his abdomen intensified. He spat out a mouthful of blood and coughed until he collapsed, exhausted.

After a minute or two, he rolled onto his back and stared at the church ceiling. He caught sight of the cross behind the altar and, whimpering, whispered a prayer. He made the sign of the cross, then fished his phone from his pocket and considered who he should call.

Chapter 32

Harald had just passed the lake near Halvik when his phone rang. He pressed the green call button, and at first, all he heard were loud breathing sounds. He briefly pulled the phone away from his ear and looked at the unfamiliar number.

"Hello!" he called into the phone.

A choking croak came in response.

"Who is this?"

Now he heard a rustling sound, followed by a hoarse, almost inaudible voice.

"You need to speak louder, I can barely hear you," he said, annoyed.

"I... it's me, Peder."

"Peder?"

"Yes... the... the priest from Halvik."

"You sound a bit strange."

There was no response, just loud groaning.

"Are you alright?"

No answer.

"Hello! Peder!"

"I'm wounded. Badly. Where are you?"

Harald stared at his phone. "You're wounded?"

"Where are you?" Peder asked again, ignoring Harald's question.

"I'm just outside Halvik. What the hell is going on?"

"Come to the church immediately, I don't have much time left."

This couldn't be happening!

"Did you call for an ambulance?"

Harald heard a dull thud, followed by only groaning.

"Peder. Hey, Peder!"

Damn it!

He tossed the phone aside and slammed on the accelerator, the car fishtailing on the icy road. It was still ten minutes to Halvik. In summer, he could have made the trip in five, but not with these road conditions.

He grabbed his phone again and called emergency services. They hadn't received any reports of an injured person in Halvik but immediately dispatched the rescue helicopter. Meanwhile, he had passed the ridge by the lake and was now racing down the mountain road toward Halvik at breakneck speed.

Seven minutes later, he skidded to a stop in front of the church, jumped out of the car, vaulted over the garden fence, and burst through the church door.

"Peder!" he shouted into the nave and was startled by the acoustics. Inside, it was dark, the shutters were closed, and he could only make out faint details thanks to a weak beam of light coming from the sacristy. He ran down the central aisle and then saw the priest lying on the floor in a pool of blood. His hands were clasped over his stomach, and he stared at Harald with a face twisted in pain.

"Dammit, what happened?" Harald asked, out of breath.

Peder didn't respond immediately but coughed up a mouthful of blood onto the floor.

"Isn't there any light in here?" Harald looked around frantically.

Peder pointed toward the sacristy, and Harald noticed some switches on the wall near the door. He ran over, pressed all four, and the room flooded with light.

Only now did he see how bad Peder's condition truly was. His black sweater had multiple stab wounds, from which blood was still oozing.

"Who did this?"

Peder looked at him with bloodshot eyes. "T... that doesn't matter."

"What? Are you crazy? Of course, it matters!" Harald pulled off his jacket and pressed it against the wounds. But it wasn't much use. There were too many wounds to cover them all.

Peder coughed again, and his face reflected the full extent of his suffering.

"I called for a helicopter," Harald said, placing a seat cushion under Peder's head.

"They'll be too late."

"No, they won't. You just have to hold on a little longer. You've got plenty of support in here, after all."

Peder forced a pained smile. "I need to confess something to you..." he croaked and motioned for Harald to come closer.

"You'd better save your strength and not talk," Harald protested.

Peder shook his head. "This... this can't wait." A tear rolled down his right cheek. "About twenty years ago," he swallowed hard, "a member of the congregation came to me for confession. He said he had done something terrible and could no longer keep the secret to himself. It was eating him up inside."

Another coughing fit followed, and Harald checked his watch. How much longer would the helicopter take?

"I was torn back then," Peder continued. "I didn't know whether to share this confession with a trusted person or keep it to myself. But as a priest, I am bound to the seal of confession, no matter what is entrusted to me."

For a moment, he closed his eyes and gasped for air. A rattling sound came from his throat, and he spat out more blood. "Until that day, I had never heard anything so horrifying from a confessor. All these years, I've carried this burden with me, fought countless inner battles, prayed countless prayers, and spent many, many sleepless nights in the silence of my home. The weight of this terrible deed is a cruel torment. It never left me, with or without God's support. I... I kept silent all these years, remained faithful to my duty as a priest, and committed no wrongdoing."

A spasm made him convulse. His face contorted in agony, and Harald listened for any sound outside, hoping to hear the approaching helicopter. But there was only silence. Even the wind had died down.

"Until now, at least," the priest continued. "In my desperate situation, my conscience alone must guide my actions. God's mercy will forgive my breaking of the seal of confession."

He tried to lift his head, but couldn't and fell back onto the cushion.

"That sinner, the one I've prayed for all these years, had repeatedly abused a girl from the village."

He paused and looked at Harald intently. His eyelids opened and closed in slow motion.

"You can't imagine how much it tormented me to encounter this person on the street, in church, at the store." He shook his head, covering his face with his hands. "And even worse was seeing the girl. She must have endured unimaginable suffering. And to this day, I doubt she has ever spoken about it to anyone. I so badly wanted to reach out to her, to support her in her darkest times. But because of the seal of confession, I couldn't."

Harald sat down and took Peder's hand in his own. He marvelled that the priest still had the strength to speak.

Peder looked into Harald's eyes, closed his own briefly, then continued. "The seal of confession is a challenging and demanding matter. Most of the time, you manage well enough. But there are moments when you wish you could damn this vow to hell."

Harald leaned in closer to Peder. "I still don't know who you're talking about."

"Do you really not know?"

Harald shook his head.

Peder looked at him, his eyes bloodshot with tears. His lips trembled. "The girl... the girl who was abused used to come to Halvik every summer for her holidays until her parents finally moved here. Back then, I was so close to telling the police everything." He began to sob.

Harald swallowed, but his mouth was as dry as the Sahara.

What had Peder just said? The girl used to come here on vacation?

That couldn't be true!

"You're talking about—Jonna?"

Peder Sørensen nodded, thick tears rolling from his eyes.

"And... and the one who confessed?" Harald asked.

"Her uncle."

"Steinar Lundberg?"

Peder nodded.

Harald felt as if the ground had opened beneath him. A wave of dizziness swept over him, followed by nausea, and then he lost his balance. He landed on his right hip and clutched his head. Cold sweat broke out across his skin, and he wasn't sure whether he was dreaming or actually sitting here, next to the dying priest, listening to this horrifying story.

Peder, seized by another convulsion, writhed on the floor like a worm in its death throes. Harald didn't know what to say or think. A whirlwind of thoughts rushed through his mind all at once. He saw Jonna's face before him, heard her silky voice, thought about her life before Eirik. About the life with Linus, her lost baby. And through all this time, she had carried this terrible secret, this almost unbearable burden.

And Neja Lundberg? Had she known about her husband's crimes? Had she covered for him? Or had she been as unaware as everyone else in the village?

"Does Neja know what her late husband did to Jonna?" Harald asked.

Peder stared at him, hesitated, and after more than ten seconds, he gave a small nod. "Neja came to me because of it," he said, his voice now a gurgling whisper. "She... she felt just as guilty as Steinar. But she loved him more than anything. She was devoted to him like a queen to her king. That's why she never intervened. He could do whatever he wanted with her. Even his perverse desires—she accepted them as if they were normal. She would endure anything, just to keep him."

He coughed again, but this time, he could barely recover.

"I'll be right back," Harald said, sprinting outside to look for the helicopter. Only then did it occur to him that he could have called the village doctor. But the number was on his desk at home. Cursing, he hurried back to Peder and froze when he saw his eyes. They had rolled back so that only the whites were visible.

"Hey, Peder…!" He gave him a light slap on the cheek. "Stay with me, do you hear?" He grabbed his hand and squeezed it.

Peder looked at him again. "I'm sorry…" he whispered.

"What are you sorry for?"

"The notes on your car."

Harald frowned. "That was you?"

Peder gave a small nod. "I didn't—I didn't want Jonna to be reminded of her torment because of your story. She's been through enough." He turned his gaze away from Harald. "When we first met, you told me you wanted to write an honorable story about the three fishermen." He shook his head. "But Steinar doesn't deserve kind words."

"Peder…" Harald began, staring at the floor. "Could… could it be that Steinar is still alive and that you know about it?"

Peder's pain-stricken expression suddenly smoothed. His eyes opened and closed, then finally settled on Harald. "You're a clever fox, Harald. You ask the right questions. And sometimes, a question sounds like the answer itself. But I've already said too much." He coughed again. "Just one more thing: On the boat—you know, on John's boat—there were four people that night. Four—not just three."

He nodded slowly, turned his gaze away from Harald, and stared at Jesus on the cross. With a trembling hand, he made the sign of the cross, and the last thing Harald ever heard from Peder Sørensen, the long-time village priest of Halvik, was a long, drawn-out sigh. Then he fell silent forever.

"No, stay with me!" Harald shouted, shaking him. "Stay with me, do you hear?" He reached for his neck, searching for a pulse, but there was none.

"Damn it!"

He dropped to his knees and started chest compressions. He pumped and pumped until sweat dripped down his face and he heard the ribs crack. Again and again, he checked for a pulse—nothing. He kept going for a while longer, then collapsed beside him, gasping for air.

In his ears, he could hear the rush of blood, his breath coming in ragged gasps. And then, suddenly, he heard something else—the sound of an approaching helicopter.

Chapter 33

Four hours later, Harald checked into the guesthouse above Café Kystenshuset. He called Runi, listened briefly to her voice on the answering machine, and then sent her a message. After that, he called Tobias Grønvoll and told him what had happened in Halvik over the past few hours. Tobias could hardly believe what he was hearing.

Harald debated whether he should tell Tobias about his suspicion or keep it to himself. In the end, he decided to be open about it.

"Do you think something like that is possible?" Tobias asked.

"I don't know. It's hard to imagine. But it's not impossible. It wouldn't be the first time someone faked their own death."

"Where would he have been hiding all these years?"

"There are several possibilities. In his old house, abroad, or under a different identity here in Norway. All he would have to do is change his appearance a little, move away from here, and that would be it."

"I don't know. Sounds a bit far-fetched," Tobias said.

"I agree," Harald admitted. "And yet, something doesn't add up."

"What are you planning to do now?"

"There's a cabin in the mountains behind Halvik. It belongs to Steinar and Neja. I want to take a look at it."

"You really think he's been sitting in that cabin twiddling his thumbs for thirteen years?"

"No, not for thirteen years. For two."

A brief pause. "Why two?"

"Because Anne Pettersen told me that Neja never—or only rarely—used to go to the cabin. But for the past two years, she's been going there regularly."

"That doesn't have to mean anything."

"No, it doesn't. But two years ago, Neja's sister moved in with her. It's possible that Steinar left because of that."

Another pause. Tobias seemed to be thinking. "Hmm—interesting," he finally said. "And now you want to climb up to that cabin all by yourself?"

Harald nodded.

"No way," Tobias protested. "I'm coming with you."

Now it was Harald's turn to be silent for a moment. "You want to come along?"

"Yes, of course. When are you leaving?"

"Well—I'm thinking tomorrow morning."

"Alright. Let's meet at ten in front of the café."

Harald agreed and hung up. Thoughtfully, he wandered over to the window and looked outside. He thought about the events in the church and saw Peder Sørensen's pain-stricken face before him.

After the helicopter landed, everything had moved quickly. The emergency doctor and paramedics had tried for a while to bring Peder back to life, but after fifteen minutes, they had to admit that he had embarked on his final journey.

Half an hour later, the first police officers from Tromsø arrived, and Harald had to give his statement. The church grounds were cordoned off and illuminated with floodlights so the forensic team could photograph every footprint around the building.

The lead investigator, Frank Haugsbø, had taken Harald into the sacristy for questioning.

"What was your relationship with Peder Sørensen?" Frank wanted to know.

"I didn't know him until a few days ago."

Frank frowned.

"I met him here in the cemetery," Harald explained.

"Do you have family buried here?"

"No. I just happened to pass by."

"If you only met Peder a few days ago, then why did he have your number? And why did he call you, of all people? Especially in his final moments?"

Harald had prepared a suitable answer in the short time between the arrival of the paramedics and the police. "I gave him my business card when we first met. If I remember correctly, he put it in his phone case."

"Was there a particular reason you gave him your card?"

"I'm a journalist, currently working on a story about an accident that happened here in town. I asked Peder a few questions about it and told him to call me if he remembered anything later."

"What accident are you talking about?"

"A boating accident in 2005. Three fishermen lost their lives back then."

Frank seemed to be thinking, gave a brief nod, and took notes. "I do find it rather odd that instead of calling emergency services, he called you," Frank remarked, eyeing Harald closely.

Harald shrugged. "I can't explain it either," he lied, hoping Frank wouldn't notice. But the inspector seemed satisfied with his answer and asked him to come to the station in two days for an official statement. Harald promised to show up the day after tomorrow. Then, the inspector left, and Harald walked away from the crime scene.

Now, as he looked out the window and saw the bright lights in the direction of the church, he wondered who the hell had killed Peder.

It had to be someone who wanted to silence a witness. Without a doubt, it had to be connected to the Pettersen brothers' accident. Peder had known something about that night—something no one else did. Maybe he had learned it from a confession, had conducted his own investigations, or had stumbled upon it by chance.

But why was he killed now, after all this time?

The most plausible answer to that question tightened Harald's throat: it had to be connected to his own investigation.

For thirteen years, the case had been dormant. Now, a journalist had appeared, asking uncomfortable questions—and suddenly, there was a murder.

That couldn't be a coincidence.

He pushed the thought aside and instead focused on Peder's last words: There had been four people on the boat that night. Four, not just three.

Four people…

So who was this fourth person? And how did Peder know about them? Could this unknown individual also be the murderer?

In any case, it had to be someone the three fishermen trusted. They must have willingly taken them on board. Unless the person had forced their way in at gunpoint or had been hiding somewhere on the boat—but that seemed rather unlikely.

So who fit the pattern?

Neja? Or rather Jonna? Both had been familiar with the people on board.

That would match Karl Godal's statement—the scream of a woman.

But what reason would Neja or Jonna have had to be on that boat? Linus would never have allowed Jonna to put herself in such danger. And as far as Harald knew, Neja had never been one to go out on fishing boats. Why, then, would she have boarded on a stormy night? It made no sense.

Harald rubbed his temples. He had a headache. The events in the church and these speculations were taking their toll on him.

One by one, the bright lights around the church went out, and a short while later, several police cars drove toward the edge of the village. The town fell quiet.

But it was a deceptive quiet. Something was lurking in the darkness—a murderer, a murderess, and an old story that refused to rest.

Chapter 34

Half an hour later, Harald was sitting in the restaurant, studying the menu—though he already knew it almost by heart. He wasn't particularly hungry, but he needed to get something into his stomach. The restaurant was sparsely occupied. Two women were drinking coffee and chatting with the waitress about the murder of the priest.

After placing his order, Harald leaned back in his chair. Absentmindedly, he gazed out at the illuminated parking lot, and before he could stop himself, his thoughts drifted once again to the events surrounding his investigation.

Was it possible that either Neja or even Jonna had the priest's blood on their hands? Neja, because Peder knew too much? Jonna, because she had discovered that Peder had known about Steinar's atrocities and had done nothing to stop them?

His mind wandered to Steinar. What a wretched monster he must have been. Peder Sørensen must have fought an unbearable inner battle to keep such knowledge to himself, never allowing it to show. It was an almost superhuman feat. How could anyone stand before God and justify such inaction?

The food arrived, and he shoveled mouthful after mouthful into his mouth without enthusiasm. Mechanically, he chewed, barely registering what he was eating. Staring at his plate, he replayed Peder's final words, running through different scenarios in his mind—only to discard one theory after another. After a few minutes, he set his knife and fork down and leaned back with a sigh.

What if the fourth person had thrown the three fishermen overboard, steered the boat to shore, and vanished into the darkness of the storm? No fourth person had ever been reported missing, which meant they must have survived the incident—implying they were responsible for the deaths of the three fishermen. The question was: what motive could the murderer have had to kill all three?

Harald rubbed his eyes. This constant speculation was driving him mad. And yet, he felt a fire inside him, a tension that was almost unbearable. The threads were beginning to come together, even if there were still knots to unravel.

An hour later, Harald lay in bed and sent Runi a goodnight message. Then he tried to focus on the words of a Swedish crime novel, but it was no use. He kept having to reread the same sentence, so he finally set the book aside, turned off the light, and soon drifted off to sleep.

In the middle of the night, he woke up.

Something had disturbed him.

He sat up and listened into the silence.

Nothing.

Groggy with sleep, he lay back down. But just as he closed his eyes, he heard a sound — coming from the door.

It sounded as if someone was tampering with the lock.

The room wasn't entirely dark. The building's exterior lighting was reflected by the snow, casting a dim glow that allowed him to see the door.

A faint clicking noise made him bolt upright. He reached for the light switch, but couldn't find it. As he threw back the covers, the door creaked open slightly.

Frozen in place, he stared at the gap. The hallway beyond was pitch black.

He tried to get up, but his legs refused to obey. It was as if an invisible force was pinning him to the bed.

The door opened wider. A faint light shone in the background, and standing in its midst was a dark figure, cloaked in a long robe, their face hidden beneath a hood.

Harald's heart stopped for a beat, and he felt the searing rush of adrenaline in his veins. His legs still wouldn't move, as though something was holding him down.

Paralyzed, he watched as the figure slowly entered the room, closed the door behind them, and stepped toward his bed.

Then, suddenly, Harald regained control of his limbs. He grabbed the bedside lamp, switched it on, and held it up threateningly.

A deep, guttural laugh — otherworldly, inhuman — filled the room.

Every hair on Harald's body stood on end.

A thousand thoughts raced through his mind. He wanted to run. He wanted to smash the lamp over the figure's head, punch them in the face, scream.

But he did none of those things.

He just sat there, frozen like an ice sculpture.

Then the figure took a step forward, stepping into the lamplight.

Harald was so shocked that he dropped the lamp.

Panicked, he scrambled backward—hitting his head on the bed frame.

The face…!

He recognized it instantly.

It was none other than—Steinar Lundberg!

It was him—without a doubt.

He wore wet oilskins and heavy boots, his face as pale as a fish's underbelly, his eyes completely white, without pupils. He looked like a corpse.

A corpse that suddenly reached out and touched Harald's leg.

The moment they made contact, a searing pain spread from the point of touch, radiating through his entire body, paralyzing him. It felt as if he were engulfed in flames.

He couldn't breathe.

He looked down at himself and saw water running over his body—ice-cold water. His pajamas were soaked, the bed dripping wet.

And suddenly, everything began to sway.

The noise grew deafening—a storm raged around him.

He saw Steinar standing before him, dressed in yellow rain gear, holding a fishing hook in his hand, laughing like the devil himself.

With a jolt, Harald shot upright in bed.

For a brief moment, he had no idea where he was.

His heart pounded violently as he looked around, remembering the room above the café—and Steinar, reaching for his leg.

With trembling hands, he switched on the bedside lamp and scanned the room.

It was empty.

Silent. No Steinar. No water. No storm. He had only been dreaming.

My God, what a nightmare!

Only now did he realize that his pajamas were sticking to his body. The blanket and sheets were damp—as if someone had dumped a bucket of water over them.

Harald climbed out of bed, his legs shaky, and staggered into the bathroom. He took a sip of water and then walked over to the window.

Outside, it was dark. He had no idea what time it was.

The snow had stopped falling, and the clouds had parted. Over the Lyngen Alps, the northern lights painted their living artwork across the sky.

He opened the window for a moment, took two deep breaths, then closed it again.

The dream replayed in his mind, and he saw Steinar Lundberg's ashen face before him.

Why the hell was he dreaming about Steinar Lundberg?

The nightmare had felt so real—he could almost smell the fisherman.

Harald pressed two fingers to his pulse. It was finally starting to slow down.

A boat chugged into view on the fjord, moving leisurely past Halvik toward the open sea.

Was it John Pettersen?

Or perhaps… Steinar Lundberg, straight from his dream?

Harald shook his head.

It had been a long time since he'd had a nightmare like that.

But after yesterday's events, it wasn't all that surprising.

He stripped off his damp pajamas and crawled naked into the other, dry bed. Then he reached for his phone and sent Runi a message, telling her he had just had the worst nightmare of his life and was now trying to get back to sleep.

When he finished, he placed the phone beside his pillow, closed his eyes, and focused on his breathing.

He pictured his sanctuary, the place where he felt safest.

That always helped him fall asleep.

But tonight, his peaceful retreat was overshadowed by the image of Peder's dying face.

The blood.

The lifeless eyes.

The priest's gurgling voice, whispering softly but unmistakably: *There were four on the boat, not three.*

Chapter 35

When Harald opened his eyes a few hours later, the first thing he noticed was that it was no longer dark outside. That was unusual for this time of year, but it meant he had slept longer than intended. He had forgotten to set his alarm, and it was surely past eight o'clock by now. With one eye, he glanced at his phone. Sure enough, it was ten past nine.

What a night.

He had a pounding headache and let himself fall back onto the pillow. At that moment, his phone vibrated, and he saw a message from Tobias: *Harald, something's come up. I won't be able to make it to Halvik until the evening. Please don't do anything without me!! Tobias*

Harald set the phone aside and thought for a moment. What should he do now? Go anyway? Wait until evening?

The latter was probably the wiser choice. On the one hand, he could use the backup. On the other, he had planned to speak with Jonna again and confront her with Peder's last statement.

After breakfast, he left the café and walked toward Jonna's house.

It was a beautiful morning. Fresh snow covered the street, his shoes crunching in the powdery white. The air was icy, and the sky was a blend of blue and salmon pink with violet undertones. It was so quiet that he felt as if he were in the vastness of the Arctic tundra. From the fjord, he could hear the gentle lapping of waves against the shore, and occasionally, a seagull broke the silence. The scene had something almost meditative about it.

When he reached Jonna's house, he saw that both garage doors were open, and the garage was empty.

That's not a good sign.

With little hope, he walked to the door, rang the bell, waited a few seconds, rang again... nothing. Jonna was probably at work. It could be hours before she got home.

Disappointed, he turned and strolled back along the street toward the café. His headache was still there, now spreading to the back of his head. He paused for a moment and turned toward the fjord.

The sun had yet to rise over the mountain behind the village, but the water of the fjord was already shimmering in the morning light. He closed his eyes, took a deep breath, and felt the cold air freeze the tiny hairs in his nose. Slowly, he exhaled and repeated the breathing exercise several times.

After two minutes, he opened his eyes again. The headache was still there, though not as strong.

Leisurely, he continued walking, wondering what he should do next. Tobias wouldn't arrive until the evening, but that wasn't a problem. Luckily, the weather service had predicted an almost cloudless sky for the evening, and the moon was bright enough that they wouldn't have to stumble through the snow in complete darkness. Headlamps were only to be used in an emergency anyway.

What concerned him more was the avalanche risk. While the avalanche institute had reported no increased danger, if John was to be believed, it was *always* red alert up there.

A police car drove past, and he wondered if the officers were still at the church. He decided to check for himself. Leaving the café behind, he continued in the direction of the church.

From a distance, he could already make out two police cars and a white forensic van.

So they're still at the crime scene.

Had they discovered anything?

Sighing, he turned back toward his accommodation.

Halfway there, someone approached him. As they came closer, he recognized Jonna. She was carrying a bag and walking briskly. She must have recognized him as well because she stopped.

"Are you going shopping?" Harald asked.

"Yes," Jonna replied.

"I rang your doorbell earlier. I wanted to ask you something."

"I just got home from work."

Harald nodded briefly, then asked, "Have you heard about Peder Sørensen?"

Jonna pressed her lips together and nodded slowly.

"An unbelievable tragedy. Unfathomable. Poor Peder. Who would murder a priest? He never did anyone any harm. Not Peder."

Harald looked at the ground before responding.

"I was with him in his final moments."

Jonna stared at him in confusion. "What?"

"Peder called me shortly after the attack and asked me to meet him at the church. At that point, I had no idea what had happened. When I arrived, he was lying in a pool of blood in the nave. I tried to help him, but his injuries were too severe."

Jonna shook her head in disbelief. "That's awful."

"It really is."

For a moment, neither of them spoke.

Harald debated whether to mention Peder's last words. It would be interesting to see how Jonna reacted.

"Jonna," he said finally. "Before Peder took his last breath, he said something very strange."

Jonna frowned, but remained silent. So Harald continued.

"Peder said: *There were four people on the boat, not three.*"

Jonna's expression was unreadable—like a closed book. Harald couldn't tell if she had fully grasped what he had just told her.

"Jonna?"

She swallowed hard, her eyes frozen in place. The redness that had been in her cheeks a moment ago was now completely gone, leaving her face pale as snow.

Harald gave her a moment to process what she had heard.

Meanwhile, guilt knocked at the door of his conscience again. It was hard to imagine what this woman standing in front of him had endured in her younger years. What had Steinar's horrific actions done to this delicate soul? How had she survived day and night without showing any signs of what she had been through? It was an unimaginable feat of strength—one that no young person should ever have to bear.

"There were four on the boat?" Jonna asked suddenly. "What did he mean by that?"

"I assume he was talking about Linus' boat on the night of the accident."

Jonna's expression changed almost imperceptibly—but enough for Harald to suspect that she knew exactly what he was talking about.

Her eyes had suddenly turned fearful and cold, almost distant.

"Impossible," she said. "Who else would have been on the boat?"

"That's what I'm trying to find out."

"Only three people died in the accident, not four."

"I'm aware of that. But someone must have steered the boat to shore."

Jonna shrugged. "If the engine was running, it could have drifted there on its own."

Harald nodded and gazed out at the fjord.

He could hear Jonna inhale deeply, then exhale just as slowly.

He wished he could read her thoughts.

After a while, he turned back to her.

"I'm almost certain now," he said quietly, "that Steinar is still alive."

Chapter 36

Jonna Olsen set the grocery bags down on the kitchen table, collapsed onto a chair, and stared into the void.

She had barely made it home.

Her legs felt like rubber, and her breath was coming as fast as if she had just run up a mountain. Over and over again, she heard Harald's words echo in her head.

Steinar… alive… Steinar… alive.

If Harald's theory turned out to be true, it would open the gates of hell. It would unleash a flood of emotions with consequences beyond comprehension.

Steinar… alive.

No. That was simply not possible. It *could not* be possible.

She stared out the window, watching the neighbourhood children play in the snow, following a boat with her eyes as it slowly chugged along the fjord. At the same time, her mind drifted back to her childhood and teenage years in Halvik.

It felt as if all of that had happened in another lifetime, and yet, she could see so many moments from back then as if she had just dreamed them. All those images and emotions were resurfacing now.

She felt the shame, seared into her insides like red-hot iron. She felt the same pain, the same rage, the same sadness as twenty years ago. It was as if she were twelve years old again. Or maybe twenty-four. It didn't matter.

And all of it was the fault of just *one* person. He had ruined her life.

And not just hers—he had ruined *three* lives.

Her gaze wandered to the mountains behind Halvik. With her eyes, she searched for the plateau where Neja's cabin stood.

It was *life-threatening* to climb up there in winter.

So why would Neja take that risk?

She knew the dangers all too well. There had to be a compelling reason.

She thought about Harald's suspicion, and her stomach twisted.

Could it really be true? How would that even be possible?

No. That *could not* be true.

Jonna buried her face in her hands, rubbing her palms over her skin as if trying to scrub away a terrible nightmare.

But the thoughts and images wouldn't go away.

They had taken root.

What was she supposed to do with this knowledge?

She would never sleep again, knowing that Steinar Lundberg *might* still be alive.

It would consume her daily life. It would destroy her family.

It would destroy *her.*

There was only one thing left to do. She had to take matters into her own hands.

Chapter 37

Harald had spent most of the day in his guesthouse room, nursing his headache. Shortly after noon, his father had called him—once again to blame him for his current situation.

"I can't believe you're letting me rot in this godforsaken hole, your own flesh and blood!" he had bellowed into the receiver. "I raised you, gave you everything you ever wanted, and this is how you repay me? I have never met a more ungrateful child in my life. Your mother would be ashamed of you."

Harald put up with a lot from his father. Over time, he had learned to just let him rant. There was no point in arguing—he might as well have been talking to a walrus.

But when his father spoke about his mother—the woman who, because of her husband's drunken escapades, had chosen separation from her son and, ultimately, death—Harald's patience ran out.

"Let me make one thing clear, you bastard. Because of you, my mother—your wife—left me. You drove her to her death. She and I were happy together. She could have taught me so much in life. But you destroyed everything—with your ignorance, your selfishness, your drinking. If you want company so badly, then have them bring you a bottle of whisky, just like you always did. Do you really think that after everything you put us through, you can just waltz into my life, move in with me, and I'll wipe your ass every day? If that's what you thought, then you're even dumber than I already believed you to be."

After this outburst, Harald had hung up and spent some time wondering whether his tirade had been justified.

He couldn't come to a conclusion, so he sent Runi a message asking for her opinion. Then he read his Swedish crime novel and browsed the internet for a while.

By evening, his headache had finally subsided, and he felt hungry. He went down to the café and ate an apple pie with vanilla sauce.

After his meal, he stepped outside the restaurant and looked up at the sky.

The moon was rising in the south, illuminating the snow-covered mountain slopes while leaving the valleys and ravines in deep shadow. A few clouds drifted over the fjord from the north, but they did little to dim the brightness of the night.

It was perfect weather for a nighttime ski tour.

A car pulled up, and Tobias Grønvoll stepped out.

"Good evening," he said as he approached Harald. "Are you ready?"

Harald shrugged. "I hope so. It won't be an easy undertaking."

"That's for sure," Tobias replied with a grin as he walked to the boot and pulled out two sets of ski gear. "Shall we head out right away?"

"I think so. No point in waiting. The sooner, the better."

Half an hour later, Harald and Tobias trudged past the Pettersens' house.

Through the window, they saw the couple sitting on the sofa, watching TV. Anne was also knitting. John looked as though he was about to fall asleep.

Leaving the house behind, they passed two more, and then the road ended, merging into a narrow trail that disappeared somewhere in the darkness. Harald and Tobias stopped and tossed their skis onto the snow.

"Look," Tobias said, pointing at the trail. "Fresh ski tracks. They must be from today—it snowed yesterday."

Harald felt a jolt of adrenaline rush through him. "Then someone must be at the cabin," he speculated.

"Not necessarily. It could just be another skier. Plenty of people go out on nights like this. Myself included."

Harald shook his head. "Not on this mountain. It's supposed to be dangerous."

"We're climbing it, aren't we?"

"Yes, of course. But we have a reason to put ourselves in danger."

They fastened on their skis and began the ascent.

At first, the slope was relatively gentle, but after about two hundred meters, it became steeper, and the tracks switched into a zigzag pattern.

Harald started sweating and was glad he had brought water. He paused briefly, reached for the bottle in his backpack, and took a few eager gulps. Tobias did the same.

"Pretty steep, huh?" Tobias commented, spitting a mouthful of water into the snow. "Really burns the thighs."

Harald nodded. "The plateau is about five hundred meters above the village. Let's just hope an avalanche doesn't send us tumbling back down."

They pressed on, following the trail.

The moon illuminated the landscape like a giant spotlight. The surrounding peaks and valleys looked as though they had been painted onto the scenery, and the water of the fjord shimmered like a silver tongue.

Not a single boat was out on the water.

The wind was completely still, making the fjord's surface look as if it were frozen solid.

The tracks continued up the mountain, winding around a few leafless bushes before disappearing behind a bend.

"Who do you think was ahead of us?" Tobias asked, panting.

"Hard to say," Harald replied. "Neja Lundberg? Maybe she's bringing supplies to her husband."

"You really think that bastard is still alive?"

"Honestly? No. Or rather, I *hope* he isn't."

They continued in silence, their breaths heavy, their legs burning, sweat soaking through their base layers.

"Are you armed?" Harald asked.

"Yes," came the brief reply.

Chapter 38

Jonna leaned on her ski poles, gasping for breath.

She had conquered the incline in record time and now stood about two hundred meters from her destination. Before her lay a moonlit plateau, bordered by rocks to the west and a steep drop to the northeast. It was deathly silent—no wind, not even the faintest breeze.

In the middle of this white wasteland stood Neja's cabin.

Built of dark wood, it had white window frames, a small covered porch, and an adjoining shed. Nothing suggested there was life inside—the windows were dark. But smoke was curling from the chimney.

She unstrapped her skis, tossed the poles into the snow, and crouched as she crept toward the cabin. In the moonlight, she could make out several tracks circling the area within about fifty meters of the cabin.

It snowed yesterday, so someone must have been out here today, she thought.

She crept closer.

When she was just a few meters away, she noticed a snow shovel leaning against the door and an axe hanging by the shed. She stopped and listened.

A muffled murmur drifted from inside. Were those voices coming from a television? But a *TV*? Up here? The cabin had no electricity, and she couldn't hear the hum of a generator either.

Cautiously, she approached one of the windows, trying to make out anything inside. Thick curtains hung across it, making it impossible to see into the rooms. But at the edges, a faint glow of light seeped through.

Jonna moved to the left side of the cabin and found another window—but it, too, was covered by heavy curtains. She remembered those thick curtains from the time she had spent here with Steinar and Neja during their vacations. In summer, they had always drawn them shut at night to block out the golden light of the midnight sun— otherwise, it would have been far too bright in the cabin, making sleep impossible.

The back of the cabin nestled against a rocky outcrop, meaning there were no windows there.

Cursing under her breath, she returned to the north side and stopped at a distance from the cabin.

What now?

She was alone up here. No one to help her.

She looked down into the valley at the glittering fjord and thought of Linus. How she wished he were here with her now. He would know what to do. He was never without a plan—every detail meticulously thought through. It had always served him well in his carpentry work. People loved his precision, his eye for what mattered. With Linus, there were no half-measures.

She turned her gaze back to the cabin, considering her options. She didn't have many. Either she waited outside until someone came out, or she kicked the door in and waited to see what happened. Neither option was satisfying.

She needed another plan.

The simplest way would be to lure the occupant—or occupants—outside with a noise. The sound of an animal, for example.

For a moment, she looked around for something she could use to mimic an animal.

What do animals even do?

Up here, the only likely creatures were foxes.

Her eyes fell on the door.

No, they didn't *bark*, but a dog might *scratch* at the door.

With trembling hands, she reached for the old hunting rifle she had strapped to her back the entire time and positioned herself beside the door—just far enough that she wouldn't be visible from the window.

Lifting the rifle, she gently dragged the tip of the barrel across the wood.

A soft scratching noise filled the silence. She took a step back.

Less than ten seconds later, the curtains parted slightly, and a pale sliver of light spilled outside.

Jonna's heart pounded in her throat, the rifle quivering in her hands. She had to control her breathing—if she didn't, she might pass out.

The curtains fell shut again, and the light disappeared. Nothing else happened.

Jonna waited two minutes, then repeated her manoeuver, retreating once more. This time, she heard the metallic *clang* of a fire poker. Her pulse spiked. Her knees turned to jelly as she took a step back, raising the rifle to her shoulder, ready to fire. She aimed at the door.

Chapter 39

He felt the exhaustion in his body. It was a *heavy* fatigue, the kind that came from too little sleep. Last night had been exhausting—the journey to the village and back had drained him. He wasn't as young as he used to be, that much was clear. A few years ago, the walk would have been nothing more than an easy exercise. But as he aged, physical exertion was no longer something he could just brush off. His muscles ached, his back hurt, and his throat was sore.

Great. Now I've caught a cold on top of everything else.

He yawned loudly, blinking at the screen of his laptop.

Thankfully, he had four batteries; otherwise, he would have to trek down to the village even more often.

For the past two hours, he had been watching an American crime series—a show he had probably seen at least five times over the years. His eyelids grew heavier, and he toyed with the idea of going to bed. It couldn't hurt. His tired bones would thank him for it.

He closed the laptop, walked over to the sink, brushed his teeth, and washed his face with melted snow. As he did, he studied his reflection in the mirror.

Tomorrow, I really need to trim my beard, he thought.

It had lost all shape, and the tip nearly reached his chest. His hair could also use a trim. He grabbed a small pair of scissors and snipped away at a few coarse hairs protruding from his nose.

At that moment, he heard a scratching sound. Startled, he froze and looked toward the door. But the noise had stopped. Holding his breath, he listened.

Silence.

Shaking his head, he turned back to his nose hairs, and just as he clipped the first one, the sound returned. He set the scissors down and looked at the door again. It sounded like something scraping lightly against the wood.

With three quick steps, he reached the window, carefully pulled the curtain aside, and shielded the room's light with his hands. The moon illuminated the snow in front of the cabin. He could see his own footprints, the shed, and the axe hanging from a nail on the shed wall. Everything else looked normal.

Maybe it was a fox scavenging for the bones of my leftover chicken, he thought.

Shrugging, he let the curtain fall back into place, walked into the small kitchen, and filled a glass with water. He gulped it down in a few desperate swallows, set the glass back down—and at that very moment, the scratching sound returned.

His pulse quickened.

Something isn't right.

He hesitated, scanning the cabin. His eyes landed on the fire poker. He grabbed it from its holder. Then he threw on his parka and crept toward the door. A few inches away, he stopped, pressing his ear against the wood and listening.

Nothing.

On tiptoe, he moved into the bedroom and peeked outside through a gap in the curtains. Still, nothing unusual.

Heart pounding, he returned to the door, placed his hand on the handle, and slowly pressed it down. At first, he only opened the door a crack, peering out with one eye. All he saw was snow, a sky full of stars, and the fjord beyond. Holding the poker at the ready, he carefully stepped outside.

Chapter 40

Harald fought his way up the mountain. He was quite active in sports, often went jogging, undertook ski tours, or was out on cross-country skis. But the climb to the hut was tough. The mountain was extremely steep, and on top of that, he was nervous, which further increased his breathing rate.

Behind him, he could hear Tobias gasping. He, too, seemed to be reaching his limits, which was not surprising—after all, he had a few more years under his belt than Harald himself.

Breathing heavily, Harald stopped, wished for a cold beer, wiped the sweat from his forehead, and looked back down the path. They had already covered a good distance. Below them lay Halvik. From afar, the village lights looked like Christmas garlands. It was dead silent. It felt as if someone had stuffed cotton into his ears.

In the white surroundings, Harald searched for a dark spot that could be the hut but could see nothing of the sort. The ski tracks led further up the mountain, straight in most places, curving slightly in others.

He thought of John's words about the avalanche danger in the area and cast a worried glance upward. If masses of snow were to break loose above them now, they wouldn't stand a chance. There was no rock in sight where they could possibly take shelter.

Grumbling, he continued walking, while his thoughts drifted to Jonna, to Neja, to the dead pastor, and to Steinar. So far, he had deliberately kept Tobias in the dark about Steinar's confession. But was that the right decision? Should he tell him now?

He stopped, and Tobias almost ran into him. "Do you need a break?" Tobias asked, panting.

"Yes," Harald replied, pulled out his water bottle, took a few greedy gulps, and then looked at Tobias. "I have something to tell you. It's about Peder Sørensen, the pastor."

Tobias raised his eyebrows. "When he was lying on the ground, dying in front of me, he told me about a confession he had taken from Steinar Lundberg many years ago. And it was about something so outrageous that I still can hardly believe it."

Tobias's eyes widened. "It's about rape."

"What?" Tobias paused mid-drink.

"Steinar repeatedly abused Jonna Olsen—then Jonna Lundberg—his niece. As a child, she used to spend her summer holidays with Steinar and Neja. At twelve, her family finally moved to Halvik. Whether Steinar continued to assault her after that, I can't say. The pastor might have been able to tell us more, but he is now silent forever. What

I do know, however, is that Neja Lundberg was aware of the abuse and did nothing to stop it. Can you imagine that?"

Tobias shook his head slightly and silently stared down at the fjord.

Harald followed his gaze, and for a long moment, they just stood there in silence.

"What a monster," Tobias finally said. "And we didn't notice any of this during our investigation." "Well, I only found out because Peder wanted to make peace with himself in his final moments. As you know, the seal of confession is sacred to a pastor."

"I'm surprised he revealed it at all."

"I think it took him as much effort as it also tormented him. With tears in his eyes, he admitted that the forced silence had shaken him to his core and that he had suffered immense agony for a very long time."

Tobias shook his head again in disbelief.

"Can we draw any conclusions from this knowledge?" Harald asked.

Tobias shrugged. "For me, the real question is: who could have murdered Peder? And his confession might help us with that. Maybe he even named his killer."

Harald looked at him, perplexed.

"Didn't he say that Neja knew about the abuse?" Tobias asked.

"Yes, but..."

"Maybe she wanted to get rid of a witness."

Harald thought about Tobias's statement. He could be right. And yet, one thing bothered him. "Neja must have known that Peder would never reveal anything because of the seal of confession. So why would she take that risk?"

Tobias pursed his lips. "Let's assume Steinar Lundberg is still alive. As it seems, he confided his most intimate secrets to Peder Sørensen. Let's assume he was—or is—a devout Christian and continued to go to Peder for confession even after his disappearance."

Harald opened his mouth to say something but swallowed his words. He thought for a while, going through different scenarios. "If that's the case," he finally said, "then Neja would know about it and probably got scared. Especially now that I started asking people in the village all sorts of questions. She wanted to be absolutely sure and eliminate the only witness."

Tobias raised his eyebrows. "Sounds plausible. But to be sure, we'll have to ask Neja."

They continued walking, following the trail around a long rock formation. On the other side, the path climbed steeply up another slope before disappearing behind a ridge higher up.

Suddenly, a cracking sound rang out, like a wooden beam snapping. Harald stopped in shock, and at that very moment, he heard a scream behind him. He turned around, and then everything happened very fast.

He felt the ground disappear beneath his feet and plunged into the snow. A sharp jolt of pain shot through his body as he hit the hard surface below. Almost simultaneously with the pain, he realized that John's warnings had not been in vain. They had triggered an avalanche.

Instinctively, he turned his skis sideways to the slope, just as he had learned in skiing courses in his youth, and tried to dig the sharp edges into the ground. But the layer on which the snow had started sliding was icy, so at first, Harald's manoeuver failed, and he kept sliding downward. Snow whipped into his face, forcing its way into his nose, ears, and mouth. He felt the wet cold on his legs and upper body.

With all his strength, he rammed the handles of his ski poles into the snow, pressed them into the ice layer, and managed to slow his fall. After several meters, he came to a stop, panting and terrified.

At first, he couldn't see anything. His face was covered in snow, and he wiped it away with his hand. The first thing he checked was how secure his footing was. The skis had found a hold and prevented further slipping.

Groaning, he propped himself up on his elbows and looked around. The masses of snow had slowed further down and eventually came to a standstill.

A snow slab, not an avalanche—they had been lucky, Harald thought.

Where's Tobias…!

Panicked, he looked around and spotted his companion standing on his feet a little below his position. "Hey, Tobias, are you okay?"

Tobias shook the snow off his body like a dog and signaled to Harald with a raised thumb that everything was fine.

"Can you climb back up?" Harald asked. "I'll try," Tobias replied, adding a curse under his breath.

He planted his ski poles into the snow and began climbing back up to Harald step by step. The ground beneath him also seemed icy, and a few times he slipped, but he managed to catch himself each time. After a few minutes, he reached Harald, panting heavily. "Shit, that was close!" he swore.

"You can say that again. We were this close to biting the dust. Thank God it was just a snow slab. An avalanche would have swept us over those rocks down there, and that would have been the end of us."

Tobias let out another curse and asked Harald if he was hurt.
"No, I'm fine," Harald replied, adjusting his jacket. "What do we do now?"

"We have to get back on the path and hope nothing else breaks loose. Maybe it would be smarter to call it quits."

Tobias thought for a moment, then shook his head vehemently. "Not an option for me. I'm going on." Harald looked up, searching for the trail. "Alright then. Let's keep going. But we have to be damn careful."

With shaky knees, they climbed back onto the path, and once they had solid ground beneath their feet again, they leaned on their ski poles and took a moment to catch their breath.

Tobias spat into the snow. "Come on, let's keep moving."

Harald took another sip of water, put the bottle away, and followed the tracks further up the mountain. Neither of them spoke a word; each was focused on the path, and with every step, the fear crept in that this mountain could become their grave.

Harald didn't even want to think about the descent. At least they'd be able to let their skis do the work then, but that would bring additional dangers. They'd be lucky to make it out of this situation in one piece.

After twenty minutes, they had conquered the incline and came to a stop. Before them stretched a high plateau, extending about three hundred meters north before ending at a vertical rock face. Right in the middle stood Neja's mountain hut. Smoke was rising from the chimney.

Chapter 41

The door slowly swung inward, a creaking sound echoed, and a shadow was cast onto the snow in front of the hut. Jonna pressed the shotgun even tighter against her shoulder bone, her pulse quicker than ever before. She quietly gasped for air and waited.

First, a head appeared, then a torso wrapped in a thick parka, and finally, he stood in front of her, armed with a fire poker. He hadn't noticed her yet, as he was looking in the opposite direction, towards where they had come from. He gripped the fire poker tightly with both hands and seemed ready to strike. Slowly, he turned his head in her direction, and when he saw her, he recoiled in shock, stumbling back into the doorframe.

For a brief moment, he seemed petrified. His gaze flickered between the gun barrel and her, his eyes wide open. He flinched slightly, as if he were about to retreat back into the hut, but Jonna lunged forward and aimed the barrel directly at his head.

"One more step, and it will be your last!" she shouted, and he stopped in his tracks. She couldn't clearly see his face. It was too dark outside, and the light from the hut wasn't enough to illuminate his features.

"Go inside. Slowly," she ordered. She pressed the gun's muzzle against his side and shoved him over the threshold. He obeyed without making a sound. Jonna followed him through the door, and when he finally turned to face her, she had to swallow down a surge of panic.

Time seemed to stand still for a moment, and she feared she might lose consciousness at any moment. The image before her blurred for a few seconds, and she felt a slight dizziness.

All the years she had spent trying to forget Steinar's face, his body, ignoring his odour—they were erased in an instant. All the horrifying minutes when she hadn't known what was happening to her, what he was doing to her, the hours that followed, the days, the weeks—all of it was suddenly present again, as if it had happened just yesterday.

She felt like that helpless, insignificant girl once more. A girl with a terrible secret, one she had told no one, one she carried with her to bed every night, one she dreamed about and woke up with every morning. A secret that had stolen her innocence, her childhood, and her youth. Deep inside, she had always remained that girl.

Now, as she saw him standing before her, much thinner than she remembered, she was on the verge of losing all courage and collapsing in tears. It took every ounce of willpower she had to resist gravity and stand firm like a rock.

She examined his sunken face; his cheekbones jutted out like lumps, dark circles lay beneath his eyes, his beard was much longer than she was used to, his hair was disheveled and greasy. In short, he looked like a homeless man.

His once strong build, shaped by thick biceps and a solid neck, now appeared weak and vulnerable. If she had encountered him like this on the street, she might not have recognized him. At least not in winter, with a hat and a thick jacket.

"What do you want here?" he asked in a hoarse voice, staring at her with bloodshot eyes.

"You can probably figure that out for yourself, can't you?" she replied, her voice thick with emotion.

He fixed his gaze on the shotgun in her hands and hinted at a smile.

Jonna stared at him, thinking of all the questions she had prepared on her way here in case she actually came face to face with her uncle. She had imagined what she would say to him, what she would scream at him. She had envisioned ramming the gun's stock into his stomach and scratching his face with her nails.

But now, standing in front of him—this ghost from her past—her voice failed her. Her mouth was completely dry. She tried to swallow and gave herself a push.

"How...?" she began, swallowing down a lump in her throat. "How the hell are you still alive? What...?" She couldn't get out another word.

For a long moment, he looked at her indifferently, opened his mouth briefly, then closed it again. A faint smile flickered across his gaunt face. But he didn't answer her question.

Jonna took a step forward and pressed the muzzle of the shotgun directly against his heart. "Answer me!"

He hesitated, his mouth twitching. "With a lot of luck."

Jonna nearly laughed. "With a lot of luck? That's all you have to say?"

Steinar shrugged and replied, almost bored, "What do you want me to say?"

Jonna wanted nothing more than to slam the gun stock into his face. "I want to know why you're still alive."

He smirked smugly and glanced sideways at the floor. "Arne and Linus couldn't do anything to me. They were too weak."

Jonna's eyes burned with fury. Just hearing Linus' name from this monster's mouth made her blood boil. She took a deep breath and stepped back slightly. If she had learned one thing from movies, it was this—you never stood too close to an opponent with a gun. It would be too easy for Steinar to knock the barrel away and attack her.

"All these years…" she began again, her voice trembling, "all these years, I've wondered what really happened on board that boat."

"Does it matter?"

"Of course it matters." Jonna nodded slightly, fighting against the tears. "What do you think?"

For a while, he just stared at her, not blinking, not moving.

"May I sit down?" he finally asked, pointing at the couch.

Jonna nodded and watched as the man—her uncle, a part of her family—groaned as he sat down, crossed his legs, and made a face as if he were attending a book reading.

Chapter 42

Steinar Lundberg scratched his face and thought that it was about time he shaved again. He could feel the effects of the previous night. It was as if his muscles were frozen, and he felt drained and exhausted.

Or maybe it was because of his niece, who was standing in front of him, aiming a shotgun at his chest.

It was a mystery to him how she had managed to track him down up here. How did she know? No one besides Neja and Peder Sørensen knew where he was, and they surely hadn't told anyone.

Now he was sitting on the couch, trying to figure out a way to outsmart Jonna, but nothing came to him on the spot. He had dreaded this moment—the moment when everything would be exposed, when his life would spiral into a vortex from which he would never escape.

In the back of his mind, he had always known that this scenario could become a reality, even though he had tried not to think about it.

"Start talking," he heard Jonna snap.

He saw John's fishing boat before his eyes, Linus and Arne. He saw the storm, he heard the roar of the wind and the waves. It was all so vivid in his mind, as if it had only happened last week.

The past had caught up with him. He had never thought it possible. But here she was, standing in his cabin, looking at him expectantly—perhaps even fearfully, though he couldn't quite tell. He saw the tears in her eyes, sparkling like emeralds. She was still beautiful. As beautiful as a woodland fairy.

She was...

He didn't finish the thought. He couldn't.

"Alright then," he began. "I'll tell you. I was in the middle of hauling in one of the nets when I suddenly felt a sharp pain in the back of my knees. I went down instantly. It hurt like hell, but I managed to turn around, and that's when I saw Linus and Arne standing next to me. Linus was holding an iron rod.

At first, I thought it was an accident, that he had hit me by mistake. But their faces told a different story. Linus had struck me on purpose. Why he had done it only became clear to me later.

Anyway, I managed to lunge forward and take him down with me. His head hit the planks hard, and he stopped moving. At that moment, Arne threw himself at me and started pounding on me. We rolled across the deck, from one side to the other.

Arne landed a few punches in my face, nearly breaking my nose. At some point, I got hold of him, pulled him to his feet, locked him in a headlock, dragged him to the railing, and threw him overboard.

By then, Linus had come to again, saw what I had done to his brother, and charged at me with the iron rod. He swung at me, hit me in the upper arm, then in the ribs. I blocked the third strike and grabbed the rod.

I managed to wrest it from him and struck him on the side of the head. He went down. I picked him up and sent him after his brother."

A long silence followed.

He could hear Jonna breathing heavily. He saw tears running down her cheeks. The barrel of the gun trembled in her hands.

For a moment, he felt sorry for her—after all, she was family. He regretted what he had done to her, of course. But back then, he had been young and foolish. He had believed that God would forgive everything.

How many times had he prayed with Peder, begged for forgiveness? Now he was getting his punishment after all. Just like Peder had gotten his.

Why had he threatened Neja? If he hadn't, he would still be alive.

"That's it?" Jonna asked him.

He only shrugged slightly. "That's it. You know what happened after that."

A mocking grin spread across his face. "After all, you were there."

Chapter 43

Harald stopped and observed the hut from a distance. Judging by the smoke, someone had to be inside. "How should we proceed?" Harald asked, turning to Tobias. "You know more about this than I do." "We go a bit further, leave the skis behind, and approach on foot. Maybe we can see something through one of the windows. Though I don't see any light inside." "But there must be someone in there. Smoke is coming from the chimney."

"I see that too. But we can't exactly knock on the door and ask them to let us in."

"Alright, then let's get closer to the hut and decide what to do from there."

They moved forward again, following the trail and slowly approaching the hut. The surroundings alternated between bright and dark, depending on whether a cloud passed in front of the moon or not. Harald felt thirsty again, but left the bottle in his rucksack. He wanted to keep going—he wanted to know who or what was inside that hut.

And then he suddenly stopped, staring at the hut.

Two dark figures stood facing each other at the entrance, barely visible in the faint glow spilling from the hut's interior. He couldn't make out their faces from this distance, but one thing was unmistakable—the shotgun held at the ready, aimed directly at the other person.

Harald froze on the spot and crouched down.

"What is it?" Tobias asked, kneeling beside him. "Look at the hut. There are two figures. One of them is holding a gun."

Tobias peered ahead and gave Harald a quick nod. "Can you recognize them?"

"No," Harald replied. "They're too far away." "Let's get closer. We should crawl toward the east side of the hut—they won't be able to see us from there."

They took their skis off and sank to their knees in the snow. As low as possible, they pushed through the deep snow, hoping the two figures wouldn't turn in their direction. The moon was currently obscured by a cloud, but it was still bright enough to distinguish the dark silhouettes against the white surroundings.

After a few minutes, they had crept to within a few meters of the hut and stopped at its eastern side. They took a short breather, considering their next move. Tobias nodded toward the north side of the hut, a silent signal— *Go ahead, I'll follow you.*

They straightened up slightly and moved cautiously toward the corner of the building. Harald stopped and listened. All he could hear was muffled voices.

"I think they went inside," Harald whispered to Tobias. Tobias nodded. "Take a look around the corner."

Harald's heartbeat quickened. Hopefully, they wouldn't be spotted. Carefully, he peeked around the corner and confirmed his suspicion—the two figures had disappeared inside. The door was left slightly ajar, allowing a sliver of light to spill onto the snow.

Harald turned to Tobias. "Let's get closer. We won't be able to hear anything from here."

Tobias nodded and reached for something under his thick jacket.

A revolver.

Harald stared at him in shock. Tobias shrugged and said, "I'll go first."

Harald followed Tobias in a crouched position, and as they neared the open door, he finally recognized one of the voices.

It belonged to Jonna Olsen.

Chapter 44

"You know what happened after that. After all, you were there..." she heard Steinar say, and it sounded as if he were speaking to her from far away.

In her mind, she was far removed from what was happening here and now. Before her inner eye, she saw the helm of the *Malini*, the raging storm outside the windows, she heard the wind and the waves. She saw everything so clearly as if only a few days had passed since then.

She was trying to keep the swaying boat on course through the storm, which was no easy task. Below her, on deck, Linus, Arne, and Steinar were working. Suddenly, she heard screams, and at that moment, she knew there was no turning back. They had chosen this path, and now they had to see it through, no matter what.

A violent wave threw her to the side, and she had to grip the wheel tightly to avoid being thrown from her seat. Various objects rolled across the cabin floor, adding to the noise. She wanted to activate the autopilot but wasn't sure if it was a good idea in this weather.

Another scream rang out, and now she *did* switch on the autopilot. She jumped to her feet in a panic, opened the door to the helm, and froze in shock.

Of the three fishermen, she could now see only two— Linus and Steinar. Arne was gone. Linus lay motionless on the deck, and Steinar, who had just been standing by the railing, turned around and walked determinedly toward Linus. In that moment, Jonna understood what Steinar intended to do to her husband, and she ran, screaming, the short distance to the stairs. In her haste, she nearly tripped and fell, but at the last second, she managed to catch herself. By then, Steinar had already lifted Linus and dragged him to the railing. Jonna jumped down onto the deck, sprinting towards Steinar, but she was one second too late.

Before her very eyes, Linus disappeared into the foaming waves of the sea, accompanied by her piercing scream.

A massive wave crashed against the side of the boat, drenching her from head to toe. She screamed for Linus as loudly as she could, but of course, there was no response.

The bright floodlights illuminated the immediate area around the ship, but the air was thick with spray and snowflakes. Visibility was no more than five meters.

She turned around and gasped.

Steinar stood only two steps away from her, staring at her with an expression she couldn't quite decipher. It was a mixture of determination and fear.

Determination—to finish what he had to do, to silence a witness. Fear—because he didn't know what would happen afterward.

Jonna seized upon his brief moment of hesitation and bolted. She heard him chasing after her, and at that moment, she knew her life would end here.

All the dreams she had built with Linus, dreamed up in long nights at the boathouse, vanished in a fraction of a second. There would be no family, no medical practice of her own, no house redesigned to her wishes. This trip had been meant to be the end of years of nightmares. Now, she was living her final one.

She glanced back, rounded the helm, and reached the starboard side of the ship. Steinar had gained on her—he was only two arm's lengths away. Then suddenly, she heard a scream, followed by a dull thud, and she stopped. Steinar had slipped on the wet deck, slid across the planks, and slammed his head against the cabin wall.

For a moment, he lay dazed, then started to push himself back up.

But Jonna had already armed herself with a wooden club and was charging towards her uncle. Before he could raise his hand in defence, she struck him on the side of the head. Steinar collapsed instantly and remained motionless on the deck. Blood dripped from a wound above his left ear, mixing with the snow on the planks.

She remembered the blood between her thighs when he had finally let go of her for the first time, sweating and panting. She remembered the shame that had haunted her ever since, robbing her of sleep.

She remembered the long, scalding showers, which had never been enough to wash away the filth. It had felt as if the water never even touched her skin, as if she were wearing an invisible raincoat.

That night on the boat was the first time in her life she had looked down on Steinar. Even now, she could feel the raw, raging fury that had seized her then.

Fragments of all the horrific moments he had forced upon her flashed through her mind, and for every one, she had kicked him—between the legs, into his ribs. Her helplessness had transformed into determination, into endless wrath. That, in turn, had unleashed a strength within her that she had never known she possessed.

The sense of liberation she had felt when she had seen Steinar's body tumble through the stern hatch into the water had been so overwhelming that she had wept for minutes on end. The weight that had lifted from her was beyond measure.

Finally, after almost ten minutes, she had managed to return to the helm and had collapsed into the captain's chair.

Jonna snapped out of her thoughts as Steinar made a movement in her direction. Immediately, she was fully alert again. "Don't move!" she shouted.

He froze and raised his hands.

Jonna took a deep breath, forcing herself to focus on him again.

"How did you make it back to shore?" she asked.

"I'm not that easy to get rid of," he replied, and Jonna could have shot him on the spot.

"Cut the bullshit, you bastard."

"Alright, alright." He ran his hands over his face. "When I hit the water, I instantly came to. Maybe it was the shock of the cold, or maybe I just had pure luck—I don't know. But suddenly, I found myself in the water, coughing up seawater, convinced that my last hour had come.

But, against all odds, I didn't sink. That's when I realized—I was wearing a thermal survival suit. I always wore one in that kind of weather."

Jonna gritted her teeth. That bastard had been lucky, on top of everything else.

"Once I realized that, I swam back to the boat," he continued. "You were just a few meters away, sweeping the area with a flashlight, shouting for Linus. After a while, you went back inside the helm, and I climbed onto the short stern ladder and held on until you ran the boat aground."

Jonna tried to recall the final moments on the boat. She had been completely unaware of the stowaway. After the boat had crashed against the shore around 1:30 a.m., she had climbed down and run home, where she had spent the entire night crying. The crushing realization that Linus would never return had been too much for her to bear.

For a moment, she had considered telling John and Anne but had ultimately not done so. Why? She didn't know anymore. Was it fear that John and Anne would blame her?

Or was she too much in shock to react to the situation properly?

"I can't believe you're sitting here alive in front of me." She spat out the words. "You should have died that night. You, not Arne and Linus."

Steinar just stared at her, but he made no comment.

Jonna could hardly think clearly. So many thoughts were racing through her mind at once that she felt almost dizzy. What was she supposed to do with him now? Shoot him right here and leave him lying there?

Indecisively, she looked at her uncle. "Have you been living up here all these years?"

He shook his head. "No."

"Then where?"

"In the beginning, I hid in our house. In the basement. No one ever goes down there except Neja. But about two years ago, Neja's sister moved in. I couldn't stay there any longer. She didn't know I was still alive. So, I decided to move into our cabin, though at first, I hated the idea. But I got used to it. Besides, I have more freedom up here than in our house. I can do whatever I want, and—most importantly—I can move around outside without restrictions."

"Why didn't you report to the authorities after what happened at sea? Why did you go into hiding?"

"Only you could ask something like that," he replied mockingly. "What do you think? If I had turned myself in, you would have had me charged with murder and a whole lot more. I would have ended up in prison."

"That's exactly where you belong."

He smirked and shrugged.

"Why didn't you leave? This isn't a life."

He studied her for a moment before answering. "I was born here—and I will die here."

He said nothing more, and Jonna thought she would gladly grant him that wish.

"And how do you survive up here?"

"Neja brings me supplies now and then. Or I pick them up from her place at night when everyone is asleep."

"Does Neja know about our past?"

Steinar didn't answer immediately. He just stared at her, his face unreadable.

Jonna repeated her question.

He nodded.

Jonna closed her eyes for a moment and took a deep breath.

"What are you going to do with me now?" Steinar asked, his voice slightly less firm.

"I'm going to finish what I should have done thirteen years ago."

Chapter 45

Harald and Tobias stood frozen near the door, listening to the conversation between Jonna and Steinar. Every now and then, they exchanged glances or shook their heads in disbelief.

For a split second, Harald thought about his front-page story and the sensation it could cause. But almost immediately, he felt ashamed at the thought and pushed it aside.

"I'm going to finish what I should have done thirteen years ago," Jonna had just said.

Did she really intend to kill Steinar here and now? Was she even capable of it?

He had no desire to find out. The consequences for Jonna would be impossible to predict, and that was probably the last thing on her mind in this moment. She was blinded by years of suffering and psychological torment.

Here and now, she had the chance to put an end to all her nightmares, to avenge the love of her life, and finally make peace with herself.

No one would blame her for doing it—on the contrary, everyone would completely understand. But it couldn't come to this. She couldn't throw her life away like this. Not for a man like Steinar.

Harald considered what they could do. If they suddenly stormed around the corner, they ran the risk of being shot by Jonna—whether intentionally or not.

"Move it," they heard Jonna say.

Harald and Tobias flinched and hurried back to the east side of the hut. There, they pressed themselves against the wall and waited. After a moment, they heard Jonna and Steinar step outside.

If they come this way, we'll be discovered, Harald thought.

He glanced at Tobias, who stared back at him with wide eyes.

They stayed like that for a minute, frozen in place, as nothing happened. Harald edged past Tobias and cautiously peeked around the corner.

Jonna stood behind Steinar with the rifle raised, pushing him away from the hut toward the valley. "Move!" Jonna ordered.

"Where to?" Steinar asked.

"Straight ahead. Down there." Jonna pointed with the barrel of the gun to the north, where the plateau ended at a cliff.

"You're planning to push me over the edge?"

"Just do as I say. Or you'll take a bullet."

Harald watched as Steinar shook his head and turned toward the cliff, marching ahead.

"She's going to push him over the edge," he whispered to Tobias. "What do we do now?"

Tobias looked unsure. "We have to stop her, I guess."

"You guess?"

He shrugged. "We need to be careful. If she sees us and we try to talk her out of it, she might just shoot him on the spot."

"So what do you suggest?"

"We follow them. Maybe we can use the element of surprise to overpower her."

Harald watched them move away and wished more than anything that he were at home right now — that he had never started this investigation in the first place.

Chapter 46

Harald looked ahead and estimated the distance to Jonna at around one hundred and fifty meters. Clouds had gathered, partially obscuring the moon, providing Tobias and him with some cover.

Harald observed how Steinar kept turning back toward Jonna, and he began to fear that Steinar was plotting something, perhaps looking for an opportunity to attack her. But each time, Jonna raised the barrel of her shotgun, forcing him to turn forward again and keep walking.

"How far is it to the cliff?" Tobias whispered.

"No idea. I'd say about a hundred meters."

"Damn. We need to catch up, or we'll be too late."

They picked up the pace, gradually closing the distance. Moving without skis wasn't easy. The wind had carried the snow toward the cliff, where it lay over a meter deep. Fortunately, it was fine powder snow, but even so, Jonna and Steinar were now struggling to move forward as well.

A few minutes later, Steinar and Jonna suddenly stopped. Harald realized they had reached the edge of the cliff. Beyond that, the ground dropped off vertically.

From where he stood, Harald could see the waters of the fjord and the Lyngen Alps in the distance.

Tobias pulled Harald behind a large snowdrift. They crouched down, trying to decide their next move. Harald saw that Steinar stood about two meters from the precipice, looking down into the valley. If they didn't intervene now, Steinar would be lying at the foot of the cliff in a matter of seconds.

Did he deserve such an end? Absolutely.

If it were up to Harald, he would have ripped out every one of Steinar's fingernails first. But this wasn't the Wild West. Vigilante justice wasn't tolerated in Norway. The alternative, however, was just as troubling. Even if they managed to convince Jonna to let her rapist and her husband's murderer live, could Steinar still be prosecuted after all these years? Or had the statute of limitations expired?

If that was the case, Steinar could even accuse Jonna of attempted murder.

The boat incident wasn't as far in the past as the rape.

"What do we do now?" Harald asked.

Tobias pursed his lips. "We get as close as we can, then spring out from cover and use the element of surprise to take Jonna's gun away."

"And if she spots us first?"

Tobias didn't answer. Instead, he waved his revolver in front of Harald's face.

"This better work," Harald muttered.

Suddenly, loud voices echoed across the plateau.

Jonna and Steinar were yelling at each other, but Harald couldn't make out what they were saying.

"Now!" Tobias whispered and started crawling forward.

He didn't get far.

At that moment, Harald saw Steinar take a quick step forward and knock the shotgun out of Jonna's hands. A second later, he had thrown her to the ground and was on top of her.

For a brief moment, Harald and Tobias were paralysed.

They watched as the towering Steinar Lundberg pinned the petite Jonna into the snow, his massive hands tightening around her throat.

They both sprinted forward at the same time, Tobias with his gun raised.

"Let her go!" Tobias shouted, aiming at Steinar as he ran.

Steinar's head jerked up in shock, as if he couldn't believe what he was seeing.

His hesitation gave Tobias enough time to close the distance, and a moment later, Tobias crashed into Steinar. They tumbled sideways off Jonna and disappeared into a cloud of snow.

Tobias's revolver flew high into the air.

Jonna remained on her back, now propped up on her elbows, watching as Steinar and Tobias rolled through the snow, landing blows on each other's faces.

Harald knelt beside her. She stared at him in bewilderment.

"What… what are you doing here?" she asked.

"Stopping you from making a huge mistake," Harald replied.

"But… I don't understand. How did you know I was up here?"

"There's no time for explanations. I need to help Tobias. You go back to the hut."

"No way!" she snapped, trying to get to her feet.

Harald helped her up. The moment she was standing, she took off toward Steinar and Tobias.

"Jonna, stay here, damn it!" Harald shouted.

She didn't react. Instead, she stumbled, fell, got back up, and kept moving.

Harald caught up with her after a few meters and grabbed her arm. "Don't do this. You're going to get yourself hurt—or worse."

"Let me go!" Jonna screamed, yanking herself free from Harald's grip.

Steinar and Tobias had stopped rolling and were now grappling where they had landed. Harald searched for Tobias's gun but couldn't see it anywhere. Shouts echoed across the plateau, bouncing off the cliffs behind the hut.

Jonna had stopped again, seeming uncertain about whether to intervene.

Harald ran to her and grabbed her wrist. She didn't respond, only continued to stare at the fighting men.

"Where's your shotgun?" Harald asked.

"I don't know. I dropped it when Steinar knocked me down," she replied slowly.

"It can't be far. Help me find it."

Tobias cried out in pain.

Steinar had just punched him in the nose, and blood spattered into the snow.

Tobias collapsed, and Steinar threw himself on top of him, flipping him onto his stomach and pressing his face into the snow.

"Jonna, find your gun—now! We're out of time."

She didn't react.

"Jonna, your gun!" Harald shouted.

She turned to him, her eyes wide with fear.

"Jonna!" Harald shook her. "Come on, find your gun!"

She blinked, as if snapping out of a trance, and ran off.

Harald turned back to the fight and trudged toward them. He had no idea what was about to happen. Steinar was a formidable opponent. At least a head taller than him, and as a fisherman, he was undoubtedly much stronger— though age had probably taken some of that strength. But none of that mattered now. Now it was all or nothing. There was no time to think.

Chapter 47

Jonna followed the tracks back to the cliff's edge, where she believed she had lost her shotgun. When she reached the spot, she knelt down and dug frantically through the snow. Faster, more desperately, and with growing rage, she ploughed through the snow like a polar bear searching for food.

She started to sob. Her hands were ice-cold, burning with pain. Sweat formed on her back, and she felt the damp chill seep through her clothes. Again and again, a scream pierced the silence of the mountain, making her flinch every time. What if Steinar managed to throw both men over the edge? Without her shotgun, she wouldn't stand a chance against him.

She cursed loudly. What was she supposed to do now? She could smash Steinar's skull with a rock, but there were no rocks here—just like there was no sign of her shotgun. Running back to the hut to fetch the fire poker wasn't an option either. It w was too far, and she wouldn't get there fast enough in the deep snow.

Desperate, she stood up, looked toward the three struggling men, and trudged back toward them. From a distance, she could see Steinar fighting like a cornered animal. He screamed, punched, kicked. Harald and the other man—Tobias, as Harald had called him—took some hits, but they fought back just as fiercely.

And when Harald fell to the ground and Steinar tried to throw himself on top of him, Tobias swung his fist upward, landing a powerful blow to Steinar's chin. Steinar's head snapped back as if yanked by an invisible rope. He staggered and fell backwards into the snow. For a moment, he didn't move.

Jonna had got closer now. Tobias, still catching his breath, leaned on his knees and spat blood into the snow. He wiped his mouth with a handful of snow, groaned as he straightened up, and marched straight toward Steinar, who had begun stirring again.

Groaning, Steinar tried to get up, but before he knew what was happening, Tobias was already beside him, grabbing him by the throat and hauling him to his feet. Then he started dragging him toward the cliff's edge.

"Hey, Tobias, stop that," Harald called out. "He's not worth it."

Jonna hurried after them, catching up just before they reached the cliff. Tobias still had Steinar in a chokehold.

She stepped so close to her uncle that their noses nearly touched.

"Why couldn't you just die at sea, you bastard?" she screamed at him.

Steinar didn't answer. He just stared at her with tired eyes.

Jonna slapped him across the face, hard.

"I... I'm so terribly sorry," Steinar stammered, saliva dripping from his mouth.

"Sorry for what?" Her anger flared even more.

Steinar began to sob.

Jonna slapped him again, this time knocking him to the ground. For the first time in her life, she saw her uncle as a weak man. For the first time, she saw him cry and beg for forgiveness. A man who had done almost nothing but evil in his life. Did a man like that deserve forgiveness? Did he have the right to beg for mercy?

Tobias grabbed him by the collar and yanked him back to his feet. "Answer her!"

Steinar lowered his head. "I'm sorry for what I did to you back then. I should never have done it. I'm ashamed of myself. God knows how many times I've begged Him for forgiveness."

Jonna let out a bitter laugh. "You can shove your God wherever you like. He doesn't give a damn about what scum like you do to children." She punched him in the stomach.

Steinar doubled over, gasping for air.

Tobias pulled him upright again and said, "That's enough, Jonna. We're taking him down to the valley. Soon enough, he'll be mumbling his prayers in a prison chapel."

"Are you sure about that?" Jonna asked.

"I think so."

"I think so."

Tobias's words echoed in Jonna's mind. There was no guarantee that Steinar would end up in prison. And what if he didn't? How could she go on living with that knowledge?

"I'd rather push him over the cliff," she said, staring into the abyss.

Harald stepped beside her and shook his head. "He's not worth it. He's already done enough damage."

Jonna's gaze shifted between Harald and Steinar. There he stood. Her rapist. It would take so little to avenge Linus. Just a few steps, and he would be out of her life forever.

"It's important that Steinar is handed over to the police and receives the punishment he deserves," Harald said. "You don't want to end up in prison because of him, do you?"

Jonna swallowed the lump in her throat and looked down. Of course, Harald was right. But accepting it was almost harder than the realization, on that tragic night, that the father of her child would never set foot on land again. And the man responsible was standing right in front of her.

She lifted her head and looked Steinar directly in the eyes. His face was a mess—blood smeared everywhere, scratches on his chin and forehead. His eyes were bloodshot, his clothes torn. And yet, she had the feeling he was smiling. Even if it wasn't visible on the outside, she saw it in his eyes. That same inner smirk she had always recognized. She had seen it every time he had come to their house and looked at her. She could still feel his damp goodnight kiss when he had told her to go to bed. She could still feel his heavy, hairy body pressing down on her. She could still feel his movements, the searing pain inside her, the shame, the humiliation. Yes, she would never forget any of it for as long as she lived.

Tobias had let go of Steinar and was now fiddling with a loose tooth. Steinar took a step back and spat blood into the snow. He stood just a few paces from the cliff's edge, looking down at Halvik.

Jonna watched him from the side.

And in that moment, she knew there was no turning back. She shoved Tobias aside, ran straight at Steinar, and slammed into him with full force.

Steinar stumbled backward, tried to regain his balance—but, instead of falling, he vanished into the darkness of the abyss.

Chapter 48

A day later, Harald was sitting in John and Anne's living room, drinking coffee. Jonna was in the room as well, sitting at the dining table, her expression dark. Harald wished he could read her thoughts. Was she relieved? Was she sad or afraid?

The truth was that she had finished what she and Linus had set out to do thirteen years ago. Steinar was dead. They had found him two hours later, a hundred meters below, lifeless. Only one of his arms stuck out from the deep snow—the rest of his body was buried.

Snow was forecast for the coming night, meaning their tracks, along with Steinar's body, would soon disappear entirely. At some point in early summer, the melting snow would reveal his corpse. The chances of him ever being found were slim, John had assured them. Hardly anyone climbed this mountain, especially near the cliffs, since rockslides were frequent. And even if someone did, no one knew what had happened up there last night.

Harald thought back to the conversation he had with Tobias during their descent from the mountain:

"Tobias?"

"Yeah?"

"Can I ask you something?"

"Of course."

"You used to be a police officer. You just witnessed a murder and know the killer. What are you going to do with that knowledge?"

For a long moment, Tobias didn't answer. Harald could easily imagine how much this decision weighed on him. Having served the law all his life, a situation like this couldn't be easy to ignore.

Finally, Tobias responded: "Honestly? I have no idea. If I think like a civilian, I see Steinar's death as deserved. What he did to Jonna was inexcusable and utterly despicable. A man like that deserves nothing better, and as far as I'm concerned, he can rot at the foot of that cliff. As a police officer, I would see it as my duty to report what happened. After all, we have a legal system designed to ensure justice. Though, whether justice would truly be served in this case... I have my doubts."

He paused, and Harald turned to look at him. "And how will you make your decision?" Harald asked. "As a civilian or as a former police officer?"

Tobias stopped walking and gazed out at the fjord. Harald halted as well, studying the retired policeman from the side. Blood clung to Tobias's chin. He had pulled out his loose tooth and tucked it away.

After a while, Tobias turned away from the fjord and said, "I'm a civilian now, Harald. My days as a cop are over."

Harald was also not convinced, even a day later, that things would be as simple as everyone was telling themselves. If Steinar were ever found, he could be identified by his dental records. A fisherman presumed dead for thirteen years turning up as a corpse on a mountain? That would make headlines and certainly trigger an investigation. What that would lead to was impossible to predict.

On top of that, there was still the matter of Peder Sørensen. No one officially knew who had killed him. The police hadn't leaked any new information, so they were likely still in the dark. However, Harald was certain that Neja was the murderer. She knew what Steinar had done to Jonna. She knew he was still alive. And she knew that Peder might suddenly decide to talk.

If Neja really was the killer, it was yet another testament to how fiercely she still stood by her husband. Even after all his atrocities, she had risked her life for him. That had to be true love, Harald thought. Or rather, blind, unconditional love.

He doubted the police would ever think to question Neja Lundberg about the murder. Why would they? She had nothing to do with the pastor. What would happen if Harald reported his suspicions to the police? Neja would certainly be summoned and questioned. If she told the truth about Steinar and even led the officers to the cabin, there was a good chance they would find his body. Most of the footprints and bloodstains would be erased by the snowfall, but there was still a significant risk that the police would stumble upon something.

In short, the situation was confusing and exhausting. And when weighing all the possibilities, the conclusion was clear—silence was the best option. Even if the guilt would eat them alive.

"What are you going to write in your article?" Jonna suddenly asked, still staring down at her hands.

That was a good question, Harald thought. He had no idea. He leaned back on the couch, clasped his hands behind his head, and stared at the ceiling.

"I don't know. I really don't know. My boss will definitely want a story, that much is certain. So I'll have to give him something."

He noticed that John gave Jonna a glance, but she didn't return it. Instead, she slowly nodded, then got up from her chair and walked to the window. Almost a minute passed in silence. Only the quiet hum of the refrigerator in the kitchen could be heard.

"When I first came to Halvik for vacation with Steinar and Neja at the age of six," Jonna suddenly began, "everything was still perfect. I loved their house. It was smaller than ours, but it had so many hiding places that I enjoyed discovering as a child. I loved the attention from my aunt and uncle. They didn't work as much as my parents, so there was always someone to play with. And if not, there were the neighbour's kids. Back home in Alta, we lived far outside the city. There wasn't much around. But my father liked it that way—he enjoyed his peace. Steinar and Neja took me on trips to Tromsø, to Sommarøy, out on the boat. We went fishing, spent weekends at the cabin. It was wonderful."

She paused for a moment before continuing.

"At least for the first four years. Then something changed—my body. I got taller, wore my hair longer, started developing a chest. I didn't think much of these changes. But Steinar did. More and more, he tried to be alone with me. He came into the bathroom while I was showering, into my room when I was changing. In the mornings before I woke up, he would sit by my bed and stroke my neck. From then on, he touched me regularly. At first, it seemed harmless—so much so that I didn't think anything of it. But over time, it made me uncomfortable. I tried to avoid him, but he was always there. I didn't dare push him away—after all, he was my uncle, and I had known him since I was a baby. I kept telling myself it was normal, that he just liked being around me. But deep down, I knew it wasn't right."

She took a deep, shaky breath before continuing. "When I was eleven, I spent another summer vacation with Steinar and Neja. Neja had to travel to Bergen for business over the weekend, so I was alone with Steinar. On the night from Saturday to Sunday, I suddenly woke up. Someone had climbed into bed next to me. I was terrified and screamed. My uncle pressed his hand over my mouth and said, 'It's alright, little one, don't be afraid.'"

Harald glanced at John and Anne. Both were looking down; Anne sobbed quietly, tears dripping onto the carpet. Harald had to look away and swallowed a lump the size of an apple.

"Afraid!" Jonna called out bitterly. "From that moment on, I knew what fear was. I had nightmares that haunted me even at the breakfast table. I didn't know what to do—I was helpless. I never told my parents anything. They never noticed a thing. Whether that was due to my acting skills or because they were too busy to see any changes in their own child, I can't say. Maybe a little of both." She shrugged sadly. "When my parents finally told me we were moving to Halvik, my heart nearly stopped. At first, I thought they were joking. But they weren't—they had already found a house. After that, I couldn't sleep for nights. I was so tired I almost fell off my chair at school. It was horrible. And that was when I first seriously considered telling my parents about what Steinar had done. I really wanted to do it. I practiced the sentences at night in bed when I couldn't sleep. I imagined myself standing in front of them, crying, and after everything was said, they would take me in their arms and call the police." She let out a small, bitter laugh. "I was so close. And then, when I stopped outside the living room, all my courage left me, and I ran back to my room. I never tried again."

Jonna stood so close to the window that her breath fogged the glass.

"A few weeks later, we moved here, settled into the village, met the neighbours, I went to school. I played along, acted like everything was normal. But inside, I was crumbling, like a glacier melting in summer. My parents still worked a lot, though not as much as in Alta. Still, sometimes Steinar had to watch over me when they were working late. I hated those evenings—he loved them." She paused briefly before continuing.

"That's when I met Linus. Before long, we became a couple. Today, I can hardly put into words what it meant to me back then to have someone like him in my life. He was like a lifeline in a storm."

"Did he know?" Harald interrupted.

She shook her head. "No. Not at first. Not until much later. By then, we were already married. I had just suffered a miscarriage, and we were both devastated. Maybe it wasn't the best moment, looking back, but I couldn't hold onto my long-kept secret any longer. A wall inside me collapsed, and everything I had buried for years came rushing out. For Linus, it must have been the worst moment of his life. That night, he swore that Steinar would pay for what he had done."

Jonna turned, looking into Anne and John's eyes in turn, then sat down and wept quietly.

The atmosphere in the room couldn't have been heavier. Harald struggled with a tight throat, and John had closed his eyes. Anne sat down next to Jonna and wrapped her in a trembling embrace.

Harald felt it was time to leave the Pettersen house. The family needed time to themselves. He stood up, placed a hand on John's shoulder, gave it a gentle squeeze, and said,

"I'll leave you alone now. I'll be in touch when I know more about my story." Turning to Jonna, he added, "I'm so sorry for everything you've been through. I hope you can find some peace now."

She gave him a tired smile and nodded.

Harald said his goodbyes and walked to the door. Just as he opened it, John appeared behind him.

"What are you going to do now, Harald?"

Harald paused and looked into John's sorrowful expression. For a long, very long moment, they stood there in silence, just looking at each other. Time seemed to trickle by like slow, thick honey. Then Harald pulled on his jacket and let his gaze drift toward the fjord.

"On February 3, 2005, three fishermen from Halvik set out into the fjord and never returned. That's what it says on the memorial at the cemetery. And that's all anyone ever needs to know."

He shook John's hand, got into his car, and drove away.

Chapter 49

The next day, Harald stood in the cemetery—not in Halvik this time, but in Tromsø—brushing the snow off a gravestone. He felt exhausted and drained. He had barely slept, waking up three times to go to the bathroom, feeling hungry at two in the morning, then thirsty, and when he finally managed to sleep, nightmares had haunted him. At five o'clock, he had finally gotten up, made himself a coffee, and written the newspaper report. When he had finished, he leaned back, read the article twice more, and came to the sobering realization that the truth would never come to light. For Jonna and the Pettersen family, that was the only option—to be able to move on and live in peace.

Harald felt the familiar throb of a headache spreading beneath his skull, and he massaged his temples. Right now, he was so sick of his job that he was seriously considering quitting and letting John train him as a fisherman. Spending the entire day in the fresh air, doing physical work, without a boss constantly interfering with every word he wrote. Maybe that was the only solution to his dilemma.

He shook the thought away and looked at the gravestone in front of him. Lovingly, he ran his fingers over it and knelt down.

"I haven't been home much lately, as you've probably noticed. I've spent a lot of time in Halvik, following a story that couldn't be more tragic. So many dead, so many shattered lives and dreams—and so many, many tears. I wish I could go home right now and tell you everything. I want to tell you how the people there have suffered, how they've carried their secrets for years. I want to tell you how peaceful it is, how beautiful it is to wake up in that little village when the morning sun kisses the mountain peaks and the fishermen set out from the harbour in their boats, heading for the open sea. I wish so much that you could talk to me, that you could give me answers to my questions, that you could hold me, touch my face as I wake up—like you did every morning. I wish I could stand with you on the beach in Grøtfjord, watching your delicate face as it's bathed in the warm light of the midnight sun. I have so many wishes, like a child at the start of the Christmas season. And it breaks my heart that none of them will ever come true again."

He wiped away a tear, glanced briefly out toward the sound, then let his eyes return to the inscription on the gravestone.

"My dearest Runi. In Halvik, I met a woman who has suffered terribly in her life. And yet, despite everything, she had to let go in order to keep on living. The memories of you will always be a part of me, for as long as I live. And

I can't wait to see you again someday—wherever that may be." He kissed his fingertips, touched the gravestone, and stood up. Then he took out his phone and scrolled through his contacts. When he reached *Runi*, he hesitated, tapped on her name, and waited until her voice played on the answering machine. One last time, he listened to her.

Then he deleted her name from his phone.

Chapter 50

Halvik, four weeks later

Jonna Olsen sat at the end of a pier, letting her legs dangle. In her hand, she held printed pages of Harald's newspaper article. She hadn't read the story yet. She was taking her time. First, she wanted to savour the moment on the pier — her pier. This was where Linus had always been with her. It was the only place where she could still feel him beside her.

She let her gaze wander across the water and breathed in the salty air. A few seagulls bobbed up and down on the waves, a car drove along the road behind the dock toward the village's outskirts, and far to the north, dark clouds hung over the Lyngen Alps, with a curtain of snow beneath them. She was looking forward to the snow. It would cover the past with its white blanket, erasing all traces forever, leaving the landscape — and perhaps even the souls of some villagers — untouched and pure once more.

Four weeks had passed since the events at the mountain cabin. At first, she had slept poorly. Multiple times a night, she had woken up and then struggled to fall asleep again.

Eirik had repeatedly tried to talk to her about what had happened, but Jonna had refused. She wanted to be alone with her thoughts and feelings, which saddened Eirik. She knew it wasn't fair to him, but when it came to Linus, she didn't want to share her emotions with Eirik. It would only hurt him.

After about a week, a certain calmness settled within her—an inner peace she hadn't felt in a very long time. The anger toward Steinar diminished with each passing day. She wanted to stop being angry. The anger had controlled her life for too long. That had to end now. Linus would have wanted her to be happy. That was all he had ever wanted for her—happiness.

And now, she was finally ready to give him that. He deserved it.

She looked down at the words in her hand and began to read.

The graveyard by the sea – by Harald Strøm

Three gravestones, three fishermen, three stories. These are stories that life sometimes writes for us, without us ever giving it permission to do so. We are not always the directors of our own lives. Whether that is a good thing or not is something each person must decide for themselves. On February 3, 2005, three fishermen from Halvik had that decision taken from them by nature—without warning, without mercy. Today, thirteen years later, the events of that stormy night remain a mystery. No one knows what happened aboard the Malini. The tragedy made sorrowful headlines in our region at the time. But as is often the case with such stories, the memory of it was soon drowned out by the endless flood of news, becoming nothing more than a faint fragment lingering in the back of people's minds. However, the protagonists of this story did not deserve to be forgotten. That became clear to me very quickly as I researched this article. For the families left behind, that night remains a dark stain in their memories. As a journalist, I had the privilege of speaking with the families of the deceased and learning about the lives of these three fishermen. The sea, the mountains, the snow, and the northern lights — these are the lifelines of us - the people here in the north. The stormy sea is as much a part of a fisherman's life as wood shavings are to a carpenter. It was no different for Linus and Arne Pettersen, nor for their friend, Steinar Lundberg. For February 3, 2005, the meteorological service had forecast an immense storm over the Tromsø region. For the fishermen, that meant hauling in their nets, securing their boats against the storm, and preparing the harbour. On the evening of February 3, Linus, his brother Arne, and their friend Steinar set out into the fjord, hoping to return to shore before the storm arrived. What no one knew at the time was that the meteorologists had miscalculated — the storm arrived much earlier than expected. The three friends, however, were not fair-weather sailors. Oh no, they knew the rough seas just as well as they knew the glassy stillness of the ocean on a windless summer morning. Linus and Arne had fishing in their blood. Their father, a professional fisherman, had taught them the trade from an early age. Whenever they had no school, they went out to sea with their father, helping him and his crew with their work. As they grew *older and had to decide what to do with their lives, Arne chose to follow in his father's footsteps. He became a fisherman, and from then on, he and his father ran the fishing business together. Arne was a young man who loved working at sea but dreamed of spending part of his life elsewhere. In the winter months, he was usually in Halvik, docking his boat and unloading the day's catch. But in the summer, he left the northern latitudes and travelled south, soaking up the warmth in order to endure the long winter nights back home. He loved experiencing different cultures, sharing stories with locals on distant islands, and then bringing those stories back to the north, where he told them to his fellow fishermen during work. Arne was two years older than his brother Linus, and as was typical for brothers in their younger years, they often wrestled and got into mischief. Linus was the gentler of the two, often taking more of the blows in their childhood fights. Like his brother and father, Linus loved fishing. But he never considered it as a career. With his skilled hands, he was drawn to craftsmanship, and so he became a sought-after carpenter. Yet, he could never completely leave the family business in his brother's hands. Whenever they needed an extra set of hands, Linus was there to help. On the fateful night of February 3, 2005, it was no different. The approaching storm demanded every available hand. What the three friends didn't know as they left the harbour was that this would be their final journey onto the fjord. A few hours later, the storm unleashed its full force — almost three hours earlier than expected — catching the fishermen in the middle of their work. The waves must have towered meters high, crashing onto the deck of the boat, creating challenges they had never faced before. However, Linus, Arne,* and Steinar were not the only ones out on the water in these conditions. Karl Godal, another fisherman from Halvik, was on his boat not far from the Pettersen brothers. As the wind picked up and the waves grew higher, Karl decided to head back to shore. Later, he would testify that, in the midst of the storm, he had heard a scream. Had it come from one of the three men on the Pettersens' boat? That question could never be answered—and likely never will be. That night, only Karl Godal made it back to land.

The Pettersens' boat was found empty on the shores of Halvik the next morning. There was no trace of the three men. The hopes of their families and the rescue teams that they might still be found alive were crushed a week after the accident, when the bodies of Arne and Linus were discovered in quick succession. Steinar Lundberg's body was never recovered. What had happened aboard the Malini? How could a storm bring three such experienced fishermen to their knees? Two questions to which I had hoped to find answers in my research. The families of the fishermen told me about the final hours and minutes they had spent with their loved ones.

I met Jonna Olsen, the widow of Linus Pettersen, and I had the privilege of listening to the stories of her youth—the time when she met Linus and later married him. She still lives in Halvik today and regularly visits the grave of her first love. John Pettersen, the father of Arne and Linus, told me about his experiences at sea and about the weather in the fjords surrounding Halvik.

"The waters up here are treacherous. You have to respect the sea, or it will take you faster than you can imagine. Everyone who takes their boat out into the raging sea knows the risks. Why do they do it? Because it's simply a job that needs to be done."

"So, what do you think?" Harald asked, sitting beside Jonna and looking at her expectantly.

"I like your words," Jonna replied. "They are carefully chosen, yet precise."

Harald smiled and gazed out at the fjord. "The article will never be published."

Jonna's eyes lingered on Harald for a moment, then drifted over the water and settled on the horizon. "I sat here on this pier with Linus for the first time so many years ago," she said, running her fingers over the wooden planks. "My God, so much has happened since then. I asked myself so many times whether I should leave, start over somewhere else, leave everything behind. But it never felt right. I would have abandoned Linus—the memories of him might have stayed here, and I wanted to avoid that. I need those memories." She paused and sighed. "When we sat here together for the first time, we had only known each other for a few hours. He was so sweet, so attentive, so nervous." A faint smile crossed her face. "He had no idea what was going on inside me back then. I was a broken, sad, melancholic girl. But that never bothered him." She wiped a tear from her face and placed her hand over Harald's. "I'm glad that these events will remain an unsolved mystery. If you had written the truth, many lives

would be turned upside down right now. And Steinar
would have won again."

"One thing about all this still bothers me," Harald said.

"And that is?"

"Neja will get away with Peder's murder."

"Are you sure it was Neja?"

Harald shrugged. "I think so. She was the only one with
a motive."

"Maybe it was Steinar?"

"I can't imagine that. He wouldn't have dared come into
the village in broad daylight. Besides, I saw Peder and Neja
arguing in front of the Kystenshuset café."

Jonna raised an eyebrow and looked back out at the
water. "What a bitch."

"We can still go to the police."

Jonna shook her head. "No, leave it. Neja loved Steinar
more than anything. Without him, she was nothing. That's
how it had always been. His disappearance will be
punishment enough for her. She'll never be able to go to
the police, and for the rest of her life, she'll wonder why
her husband just vanished without her."

Harald saw a hint of satisfaction on Jonna's face. "Can I
ask you something?" he said. Jonna nodded. "When you
boarded the Malini on that stormy night, you were
pregnant, weren't you?"

"Three months along."

"Weren't you afraid of putting yourself and the baby in
danger?"

"Of course, I was. But Linus didn't know about my plans."

Harald looked at her in surprise. "He didn't? How did you get on the boat without him noticing?"

"When Linus left the house, I knew he would go to his father first. In the meantime, I snuck onto the boat and hid in the cabin behind a curtain. I only came out once we were already far out at sea. Linus wanted to turn back immediately, but I wouldn't let him. And with the storm raging the way it was, he didn't have much time to argue with me. We went through with our plan—despite the pregnancy, despite the risk of losing another child."

She paused and took a deep, trembling breath. "Not a day has passed since then that I haven't blamed myself. I put my child's life at risk just to put an end to my past. I will never forgive myself for that." She exhaled deeply. "So, you see, I couldn't just let Steinar get away with everything. He had to pay. Finally."

Harald looked into Jonna's eyes, deep and blue like the ocean. He wanted to say something, but no words came to him. Instead, he put his arm around her, and for a moment, they simply sat there in silence. After a while, Harald's gaze drifted toward Halvik's church, where not long ago he had discovered the graves of Linus, Arne, and Steinar.

He thought of the inscription on the memorial and of his first conversation with Peder Sørensen. Who would have thought that the poor man would meet such a brutal death just days later? When you really thought about it, Steinar hadn't just taken two lives—he had taken four. Linus and

Arne drowned at his hands, Peder died because of Neja's unconditional love, and Jonna—yes, Jonna had lost her life the day Steinar first touched her. Four lives destroyed. Surely, a man like that couldn't end up in heaven—at least if one believed in the Bible.

Jonna rested her head on Harald's shoulder and handed him the unpublished newspaper article. Harald's eyes fell on the first sentence of his piece: Three people, three graves, three stories...

Well—when it came to the graves, one could now say that Steinar's headstone had not been placed in vain after all.

THE END

Acknowlegments

The inspiration for this story is thanks to my good friend Anita, who has been living in Tromsø with her husband Michael for several years. About three years ago, Anita sent me a photo of three graves in a cemetery located near the water. The three gravestones had been erected for fishermen who lost their lives at sea in the 1930s.

The names and locations in my story are randomly chosen and do not reflect real-life circumstances.

The creation of a book always involves a number of people in one way or another.

Once again, I thank Anita and Michael from Tromsø for their hospitality during our vacation and, of course, for their insights regarding local customs. My sincere thanks to my good friend Ralph for designing the book cover. Parts of the original photo come from photographer Dominic Kurz. I thank Nadine, my dear wife, for her first critiques of my story. I am grateful to my editor, Lucilia Mendes von Däniken, for her valuable suggestions concerning logic and dramatic structure.

Heather Jordan and Peter Hobbs—I thank you warmly for proofreading.

Special thanks go to Major Niklaus Büttiker of the Solothurn Cantonal Police, who gave me valuable input on police investigation procedures. Any errors in police procedures are entirely the author's fault. I would also like to thank Sven Altermatt of the *Solothurner Newspaper* for answering my questions about how a newsroom operates and what a journalist's responsibilities are.

A pastor plays a significant role in my story. To better understand a pastor's mindset and the duties surrounding confession, I had the privilege of speaking with Deacon Max Herrmann. Thank you, Max, for answering my questions and offering insight into the practice of confession within the church.

A big thank you goes to the writer Christoph Gasser, who is always there with advice and support. And to you, dear Malini—thank you for the ship's name.

And of course, I want to thank all my readers. I hope you were able to spend a few meaningful hours with me in the far north.

The Author:

Reto Koller was born in 1980 in Solothurn. His first short novel, *Winter's Darkness*, was published in January 2019. All of his stories take place in the northern part of Norway, which he visits several times a year to take in the mysterious scenery and the lights of winter.

Published so far:
- Winter's Darkness
- Shadow Waters
- The North Bay